NEVER MARRY IN MOROCCO

NEVER MARRY
IN
MOROCCO

Virginia Dale

FITHIAN PRESS ❂ SANTA BARBARA ❂ 1996

Copyright © 1996 by Virginia Dale
All rights reserved
Printed in the United States of America

Published by Fithian Press
A division of Daniel and Daniel, Publishers, Inc.
Post Office Box 1525
Santa Barbara, CA 93102

Design by Eric Larson and Karim Marouf

Library of Congress Cataloging-in-Publication Data
    Dale, Virginia.
        Never marry in morocco : a novel / Virginia Dale.
        p.   cm.
        ISBN 1-56474-174-5 (pbk. : alk. paper)
        I. Title.   ·
    PS3554.A4159N48 1996
    813'.54—dc20   96-3500
                                     CIP

The chapter entitled
"The Dowry"
was first published in
The Weekly Synthesis

To Hansi and Jean Michel,
my dearest friends

CONTENTS

NEVER MARRY IN MOROCCO

☼ LA CRUZ

I THOUGHT EMILIA had died of old age. She was seventy-two. Encrypted in a Catholic cemetery in Nice, France, I assumed she rested in peace. Gentle Emilia. I remember her aristocratic profile and sparkling blue eyes the time she told me stories of old Santa Paula, the fishing village she knew and loved. She spoke of another world, another time, a time when the world turned in harmony with nature.

"It is not the same now," I can remember her saying. "I miss the old fishing boats that had sails instead of noisy motors, the old farms that the young people have abandoned for the cities. I miss Algiers." So did the rest of the multi-national family I had married into.

"Virginie." She leaned forward so I wouldn't miss a word. Her eyes lit up and her thin frame seemed suddenly young, her face radiant. "My parents immigrated to Algiers from La Cruz, our farm. It had already been divided into eleven portions. One of my uncles agreed to take care of our portion."

I put my hand on Emilia's, gently interrupting her flow of words. "Emilia, how did you get this farm?"

Her eyes beamed her approval. I had asked the key question that would unravel her story.

She took my hand and held it lightly as she talked, smiling and occasionally wrinkling her forehead in deep thought.

"In the 1800s all the land belonged to the king of Spain or his nobility. Ours belonged to a general who used to come here to hunt while his wife stayed at the farmhouse. His wife grew so attached to this land," she indicated the almond and pomegranate orchards with an outstretched hand, "that when she got old and sick, she asked if she could stay here at the farm. My great-grandparents naturally said 'yes.' When she

13

died, she left them the farm in her will."

I started to say something about *Fuente Ovenjunas,* a play written on an almost identical subject by Lope de Vega, the Spanish playwright most likened to Shakespeare, but she kept talking.

"My father was very hard-working, very ambitious. The French had opened up the colony in Algeria to everyone, so my parents immigrated to Algiers, the capital." Her face flushed with the excitement of remembrance. "It was an exquisite city full of sun and light and air. Everyone loved Algiers."

"And your father, Pierre's grandfather, made his fortune there?"

"A vast fortune," she clutched my hand tightly. "I miss Algiers."

Who wouldn't miss Algiers? A beautiful city with white, sun-drenched walls, perched on the Mediterranean, where Pierre's extensive family had amassed an enviable fortune and created an unparalleled lifestyle, it remained alive in the family's memories. Fortunately for us, Pierre's parents, Tilman and Françoise Moulet, had sold some of Françoise's inheritance to start an antique shop in Rabat, Morocco. Most of the family had investments in Spain and France as well as Algeria, so they had not lost everything. But Camelot was gone, forever.

I luxuriated in the torpor of the moment, letting the rich warmth of the sun seep into my pores and fill me with a sense of well-being. Completely relaxed on the terrace in front of my French in-laws' gardens, I surveyed the pomegranate groves directly in front of me, bursting with red, ripe fruit. About a mile beyond, I could make out the blue Mediterranean, where we had our beach house, or chalet, as Françoise, my mother-in-law, liked to call it. The heat of the August afternoon made me agreeably drowsy, as did the steady whir of locusts' wings, a lulling, lush sound which tranquilized the mind and toned the spirit.

Later in the day, when the air had cooled, I would meet with other members of Pierre's family for a light meal on the terrace of their two-hundred-year old family farmhouse, part of a farm that had been passed from generation to generation, each one cherishing its value as a place of complete repose. There one could tap one's roots and revitalize oneself from arduous winters spent in the various capitals of Europe. In these cities, as Sebastian put it, "The sun shines infrequently; for those of us who have been raised in Algiers, it is a sort of purgatory for the soul. We exist for the month of August, when we know we will find a benevolent climate full of pleasure and love."

I smiled fondly as I thought of Sebastian, for he was my closest companion other than my husband, and he certainly understood me better. But something was amiss at the farm this summer. Emilia had died quite young at seventy-two, quite young for this hardy family that prevailed into their nineties. Marie Claire, Pierre's oldest aunt, had lived to be 103.

One day as I entered our antique shop, Art et Style, in Rabat, Morocco, Françoise told me Emilia had died. I burst into tears. Françoise didn't seem upset, herself. She was very matter-of-fact, standing there in her elegant but slightly eccentric gold dress. She had had to spend a year in a Swiss sanitarium when she went officially crazy. Back to her normal self, she was still high-strung, but not regarding her older sister's sudden death.

I was so innocent. I still had unprotected feelings, and I readily registered my emotions. So I cried when Françoise told me gentle Emilia had died. Everyone talked about my outburst and then Françoise said, "You lost your grandfather this summer also, so you must be very sensitive to death right now." They wanted to understand me, which was so kind. I wasn't used to this gentle treatment, this consideration for one's feelings.

I shook my hair over my shoulders and sat up, trying to rid my mind of any morbid thoughts about Emilia. The large double doors to Tilman and Françoise's "castle in Spain" were to my right. They led directly to the double living room furnished with some of the most elegant French antiques I had ever seen. They planned to retire here when they pulled completely out of Morocco. Retired is not really the right word, because the French, or the *pied noir*, the black feet, the Europeans who had settled in North Africa when it was a protectorate or colony of France, were being slowly but surely kicked out of Morocco unless they took on a Moroccan partner, who would accuse them of embezzlement or worse, then take over their business. After watching our friend Mr. Leblanc being led away in handcuffs, I understood why Tilman and Françoise were leaving Rabat, the capital of Morocco.

The rest of the family sometimes resented the way Tilman and Françoise, especially Françoise, who was imperialistic in her gestures as well as thinking, always came out on top. Apparently no matter what world disaster occurred, my in-laws ended up living like pashas. They had always lived out their fantasies. With the help of my father-in-law's fertile imagination and ability to do almost anything well, from drawing up blueprints for houses to making delicious blackberry jam from scratch, and with the wise investments he and Françoise had made with her share of the inheritance, the elegance of their lifestyle remained less compromised than the rest of the family's.

In Algeria, they had lost everything in 1960. After the Battle of Algiers, the French fled with little but their lives. Françoise told me that Emilia had died of a broken heart. She still mourned the loss of their thirteen-bedroom home, where peacocks strolled the parklike grounds like royal birds. As an American, I tried not to take sides with the French or the Algerians. My country was founded by revolutionaries as well.

The sun milked my mind of all dark thoughts as it toasted my skin the color of a lightly cooked pancake, a beautiful almond beige. Its warmth penetrated my body like an invisible balm. I luxuriated in this precious moment, putting all thoughts out of my mind. This was easy to do, lying on a chaise lounge on the terrace in front of my in-laws' house. The ancestral family farmhouse loomed just around the bend.

Pierre was helping his parents make this move to Spain.

We, too, would soon leave Morocco to join them. The French were being forced to sell any farmland they owned to Moroccans, for next to nothing, or lose everything. Marc, one of Pierre's uncles, his Moroccan wife, Sifia, and their children, Lassan and Marguerite, could lose their vast farm in Ouezzane, near the Rif Mountains in Morocco, that Tilman and his brother Marc had built in the early twenties, when Morocco had become part of the French Protectorate and land was given away. They had thought that Marc's marriage to Sifia would make it all right for them to stay, because she was Moroccan, but they had been wrong. The *coup d'etat* at the king's palace in Skhirat changed that. Nothing, not even human life, was guaranteed in these strife-ridden countries that had once been under the French Protectorate.

It was so different from the predictable suburban dullness in which I had grown up in the 1950s. Surrounded by block after block of cement sidewalks and well-tended lawns, it never had occurred to me that fortunes could be made and then completely lost. I had never dreamed of anything but profit and increase.

When I was twenty-two I took my savings of $1,400 and flew to Madrid to learn a new language, perhaps even assume a new way of looking at life, at myself...and here I was now married to Pierre, adopted unanimously by the rest of his family as "*la petite Americaine*," the little American. It was love at first sight, especially after I mastered French with almost no trace of an accent.

After five years of marriage, Pierre and I still had no children, first because we wanted to keep traveling unimpeded by babies, and also because there was that rumor that if you had children in Morocco, they would belong only to your husband if you divorced. I knew that applied only to Muslims, but somehow I didn't want children with Pierre.

I had left the United States for various reasons, one being a desire to have a less cynical view of life, the defense I had learned in a riotously critical navy family in the United States. I was reborn, not exactly a Christian, but more a pagan, reveling in whatever revelry was available. I think I might have been somewhat the typical American brat, as the French called us. Learning a new language, immersing myself in a different culture, and acquiring a new family had slowly but surely transformed me. I had felt happy and fulfilled in the seven years I had known Pierre. Like me, he was high-spirited and would do almost anything for kicks. Things were different this year.

I had landed at the airport next to Madrid with little more than a hotel reservation and my nerve, which had not yet failed me. I was gutsy, an adventuress, as my mother-in-law put it.

I had left the United States in 1965 in search of so many things, not only adventure. People, especially men in my age group, judged me by my father's wealth and the size of my bust, neither of which was considered substantial in the United States in the early sixties. Tired of this narrow-minded attitude, I had responded in various ways, the ultimate being departure. *Au revoir, Etats Unis.*

Besides, Garcia Lorca's poetry had excited me with its striking images of beautiful young men, slender and supple, with alabaster skin and smooth, firm bodies. I wanted to meet men who were like those in Lorca's poetry—sensual, exciting men. Much to my disappointment, most of the men I met were short and stocky, nothing like those in Lorca's poetry. Then I fell in love with Sebastian.

This was not the way I had planned it, of course. How could this be, me in love with my husband's cousin? And he with me? He was just a baby, just nineteen years old, when we fell in love, unintentionally, innocently, passionately. And I was twenty-six. I tingled with acute pleasure when he looked at me, asked me for advice, or just stared at me like a helpless puppy. Our trust had become implicit two summers ago, while he was spending some time with us at our beach house near the farm.

I can still see our bronzed bodies next to each other, clad only in bikinis. He would step toward me and I would have to step backward for fear of reaching out and touching him, embracing him, kissing him. Not that I didn't want to. It was just that I was married to his cousin—well, second cousin. Honor was all important within the Moulet family. They still lived very moral lives based largely on the traditions of eighteenth-century Spain.

Immersing myself in a new culture and acquiring a new family had slowly but surely transformed me in the years I had known Pierre. I now stood up whenever an older person came into the room and shook his hand to acknowledge his presence. In France and Spain it was the custom to honor older people, and to at least shake everyone's hand and say *"bon jour"* the first time you saw them each day. What a change from the awkward "hi" or "hullo" in English-speaking countries. My confidence leaped as people respected me more for respecting them. I learned good manners at age twenty-three. And I loved these formalities that honored people rather than ignoring them and making them feel like they didn't exist. Not that Americans weren't generous and caring people; they just preferred to heap kindness on strangers, give money in foreign aid, anything rather than deal directly with their feelings. At least, that's how it had seemed in my family. But the world was changing, and I was changing with it.

"Virginie, Virginie, where are you?" called out the familiar voice of Sebastian's older sister, Marie Hélène. She stood next to her seven-year-old son and mother.

"Over here, in front of the house, soaking up the sun!" I laughed, making fun of my self-indulgent nature.

"Come with us!" she shouted back.

"Where are you going?" I took one last look at the sea glinting just beyond the pomegranate orchard and stood up.

"To the garden to pick tomatoes, near the almond orchard."

"Okay, I'm coming!" I shouted and headed in the direction of Marie Hélène's voice.

Ahead of me loomed the large, tile-trimmed farmhouse, rising solidly from the earth, its large doorframes and ancient stable blending agreeably with some morning glory vines, bougainvillea, and haphazard fig and carob trees that grew around it. No one really tended the farm anymore except for a couple of elderly servants. The ancient Bonmari family and their descendants had used it only for their summer vacations for many years now. My in-laws had built a beach house perched on a slope above the Mediterranean, where Pierre and our friends usually stayed.

When he and Sebastian went to Ibiza for a week to water-ski, I decided to stay at the farm with the other relatives since it was so peaceful there. I loved good company, and I needed a change of pace. Staying at the farm was perfect.

As I walked toward the farmhouse, I spotted Marie Hélène and her mother, Mia, waiting in the garden. Marie Hélène's seven-year-old little boy, Jean, was reading a book in the room where they stored the honeydew melons.

"Are you coming, Jean?" I asked.

He squinted his eyes in the direction of the almond orchard and nodded his head. He and his mother resembled each other, she with her face of a precocious child, and he with his preoccupied air of an adult.

"Mama, is Don Celin still indisposed?" Jean asked, referring to his seventy-eight-year-old uncle, a renowned Spanish philosopher and the owner of the largest book exporting enterprise in Spain.

"No, he'll be at the dinner table tonight, *cheri*. Aunt Aurelia fixed him some yogurt with his tea this morning and now he's feeling better. Don't worry. Come pick tomatoes with us."

"Good. I want to hear him talk about the Pope," Jean said petulantly as he slid off a wooden peasant's chair and laid his book aside. Then he smiled brightly, his reddish baby curls making his bright blue eyes sparkle all the more.

"The Pope?" I laughed, catching up with them.

"Yes," replied a very serious Jean, looking up at me. "I want to hear Don Celin talk about the Pope."

I smiled at him and took his hand. We started walking toward the tomato patch. I was entranced by this precocious child's interest in world affairs, and especially the rapport he had with his seventy-eight-year-old uncle. I remembered the serious conversation Jean had had with his uncle at the dinner table last night, worried about the health of the Pope. Their lively intellect and family cohesiveness intrigued me. No wonder the farm had an almost sacred feeling about it. So many enlightened spirits had lived in it! Marie Hélène and her mother walked ahead of us, chatting about the day's events. "How fascinating they all are," I thought. Marie Hélène had married a Spaniard who claimed to be the bastard son of a nobleman. He said that he had been born during the Spanish Civil War, when divorce was legitimized, and many "single mothers" had emerged during that chaotic period.

A bastard is what Marie Hélène's husband turned out to be, for all of his airs of having noble blood in his veins—he was above working for a living! When her father's generosity and patience ran out, so did her husband. Brokenhearted, she stayed on in Madrid and worked as a translator for a Parisian newspaper, as she was perfectly bilingual. Her parents quietly obtained an annulment of Marie Hélène's marriage and now she planned to marry another Spaniard. *His* parents objected furiously because she was a divorcée.

"How complicated they are," I mused to myself as I meandered toward the tomato patch, Jean's baby-smooth hand clasped firmly in mine.

Their Spanish blood came from Pierre's grandparents, who had left Spain to seek their fortune in Algeria in the late 1800s. And fortune had smiled on them, for they had amassed a vast amount of farmland, factories, and real estate.

Emilia had told me about the family house.

"All thirteen bedrooms," I remember her telling me, "were upstairs where the children were kept. My three sisters and I were only allowed downstairs for dinner and when or if we were invited by the adults. And the park in front was so beautiful. It was lined by orange groves, and peacocks wandered freely near the reflecting pool...." I looked at her that calm summer day, and her face was radiant. Then she frowned. "Leaving Algiers was the hardest thing I've ever done! De Gaulle should have warned us!"

Then I put my hand on her arm and tried to calm her. I knew she was referring to the fierce war the French colonialists had fought with the indigent Algerians, who wanted their independence at all costs. De Gaulle probably saw that it was a hopeless battle, but he gave up without warning the French who lived in the colony of Algeria, and those he abandoned felt betrayed. Everyone in Pierre's family had lost a great deal, millions in land and apartment buildings and factories.

Their hasty departure from Algeria was legendary, and they all still talked about it. "I've never packed a suitcase so tightly," Emilia had recalled. "We were only allowed to take two. We had thought de Gaulle would fight for us, but it was no use. There was no stopping the Algerians after Ben Bella won the Battle of Algiers, but de Gaulle should have warned us. To leave your home, a place as beautiful as Algiers, with only twenty-four hours' notice—it broke our hearts!"

"Not to mention our pocketbooks," Sebastian would insert sardonically. Then he would look ruefully at the ground and say, "I'm sorry, Emilia. It was terrible. I miss Algiers, too. Paris is the most depressing city I've ever lived in."

"And Algiers was exquisite," Emilia had continued. "So clean, so warm. The French had done so much there... planted orange groves, cultivated farms, built hospitals, schools...."

"I'm sorry you had to lose it all," I would tactfully insert before Emilia got too upset. Then I looked at Sebastian. His family had lost their share of the inheritance, too. My eyes caressed his smooth face, square jaw, and muscular shoulders. I wanted to reach out and console him, take him in my arms and caress him until he felt happy, but of course I couldn't. I was married to Pierre. Sebastian's face was serious, perturbed, beautiful. He empathized with Emilia.

His father was a physics professor at the Sorbonne, France's most renowned university. Still, they had lost everything they had in Algeria. He seemed so much older than his nineteen years, perhaps because of this loss.

"Come on, Virginie!" called Marie Hélène, bringing me back to the present, out of my reverie. "Are you on the moon, again?"

I laughed at this French reference to my tendency to daydream. "I'm coming!" I quickened my pace and headed in their direction.

Inhaling deeply, I filled my lungs with the sharpening coolness of the evening air. It exhilarated my senses. I could already smell the deep, pungent odor of fresh tomatoes. The familiar scent wafted into my nostrils, and suddenly I was in Falls Church, Virginia, picking tomatoes with my mother and grandmother.

I could remember myself at age four, laughing merrily with my grandmother. She told me, "Be careful of the dragonflies because they can stitch your clothes to your skin."

We were at my great-grandmother's house twenty years ago, and I, like Marcel Proust, was reliving my past through my olfactory senses.

A great sense of well-being flooded my senses and I smiled up at my companions.

"I just had a *déjà vu!* I remembered as if it were yesterday picking tomatoes with my grandmother at the old farm in Virginia. I was only four years old at the time!"

"Have you read Proust?" said Marie Hélène, impressed.

"Just *Swann's Way.* It's the best book I've ever read."

"Did you read it in French?" asked Marie Hélène.

"Yes, *bien sur!*" I laughed at her astonishment. "What do you take me for? An illiterate? An American?" We all laughed as I made fun of myself.

I knew they considered me better educated than Pierre, who had failed the baccalaureate and learned Spanish on the farm during summer vacations from the farmhands who lived there year-round. Mine was textbook Spanish. Although his accent was much better than mine, I knew my grammar cold.

After picking a basketful of tomatoes, we headed back to the farm and gave them to Joséfina, the eighty-year-old servant who came to help at the farm every summer when the family stayed there. She had started the ancient wood-burning stove. We would have a simple dinner of macaroni with tomato sauce, delicious because of the smoked flavor given off by the stove. "How much have our senses been deprived of by our modern conveniences," I wondered.

Jean and Don Celin talked about the Pope's health and we chatted amicably about the good food and a plan to spend the next day at the beach. Yet something was different at the farm this summer. Marie Hélène had confided that she had to take sleeping pills every night. It didn't seem possible in such a peaceful setting.

After dinner I sat next to Aurelia on the outdoor terrace that overlooked the almond orchards. The pungent fragrance of almond blossoms wafted up and titillated our nostrils.

"It's so serene at the farm," I remarked as I gazed at Aurelia's sharp features accentuated by a crisp bun drawing her hair up tightly on top of her head. Her skin was like fine porcelain, wrinkled but lovely. Yet I sensed something different about Aurelia, too, this year.

I remembered the bash my in-laws had thrown last summer in their new home. Françoise had neglected to invite her older sister, inviting only her younger nieces and nephews. But Aurelia had seen all of the cars pass by the farm on their way to the family get-together, and we had all repented for not having invited her. She finally came on her own just to say "hello." We entreated her to stay, but she felt in the way, as if she were imposing, so she left with a polite *"bon soir."* Emilia's daughter, Claudine, made fun of her because of Aurelia and Don Celin's vast fortune and their inability to spend it. They said she should have been a nun, she lived so ascetically. I liked Aurelia, so devoted, so dedicated to the farm and those around her.

Aurelia never spared herself. When her sister, Margarita, and her husband, Pedro Salinas, were dying of cancer in the United States, where they had fled after the Spanish Civil War, it was Aurelia who obtained a visa to care for them in the United States. She still spoke of Boston, where they lived, in glowing terms. Her sister had married Pedro, a renowned Spanish poet, a member of the Generation of 1927, and he had been the head of the Spanish department at Harvard until his untimely death.

"Yes, it is peaceful here," answered Aurelia. "Celin and I prefer it to Madrid. We spend four months here every year from the beginning of June."

She smiled brightly at me. Her eyes sparkled like those of a much younger person.

"Don't you ever get lonely?" I asked.

Aurelia hesitated for just a moment.

"Not really, although a few years ago it was livelier—before so many of my nephews and nieces bought apartments in Santa Paula and Benidorm to be closer to the sea. I don't understand why they did it. The farm has everything anyone could want, and it is not more than six kilometers from the beach." She turned her head away from me, and I admired her strong profile, the crisp bun accentuating her sharply angular features. Aurelia turned to face me again and added, "Fortunately, Juan and Bernarda still join us frequently."

Juan was her only child, the vice-president of the Bolsa, or the Spanish stock market. Bernarda was the self-professed communist he had married while studying in France. They were the richest members of the family, and Bernarda's childish insults of the family's exploitation of the Algerians did not sit well with anyone. She was the reason everyone had bought apartments away from the farm. No one could stand her. And I knew Aurelia shared some of her unpopularity. I looked for signs of self-pity in Aurelia's face, but found none.

"Proust said the only constant is change," I remarked, trying to placate whatever inquietude I might have created.

"Yes. But that doesn't mean we should ever abandon anyone or anything we love."

We exchanged somber looks. I knew she had saved the farm from destruction by Franco's troops during the Spanish Civil War. I knew she was a valiant woman. And she was giving me advice, indirectly.

I stood up and kissed her affectionately on the cheek. Pierre was her favorite nephew, so I tried to be especially nice to her. I would have liked to walk in the garden with her and talk about the Civil War, how she came here alone and kept the farm from being plundered by General Franco's soldiers, but it was getting late.

I went into the bedroom I shared with Marie Hélène and found her brushing her long, thick blond hair. She was such a beauty that she had been asked to model on television in Madrid. Her lovely skin glistened in the room lit by a single light bulb. "I love to stay up and talk at night, don't you, Virginie?" she said, swinging her diminutive form around to face me. She had inherited her mother's lustrous complexion.

"Oh, sure." I answered hesitantly because there was nothing I loved better than a good night's sleep. Sleep was my friend, my oblivion, the thing that sewed up the tattered sleeve of care, as Shakespeare put it. Besides, I had been brought up in the Yankee tradition, all practicality, productivity with some Ben Franklin homilies mixed in. I was American. I had been nurtured on Bird's Eye peas and bargain hunting. Which is probably what drove me to Europe. Boredom. Not bargain hunting.

"Why are you taking sleeping pills this summer, Marie Hélène?" I queried. If we were going to talk, I wanted to clear up a few things in my mind.

Marie Hélène looked up pensively, a sad look in her large, doe-like brown eyes, from the rustic vanity where she had been brushing her hair.

"I can't tell you, Virginie. I mean, it's too horrible. You wouldn't want to know why."

She got up and sat down on her bed, her cotton night dress making her look all the more feminine. Hers was a delicate beauty, a soulful beauty, with her stories of abandonment by her husband when her son was only three. She put her feet under the bed covers and looked over at me. I looked at her somberly for a few seconds. I didn't know what to say. I was so often at a loss for words when it came to intimate subjects.

"I don't know if I should tell you...it's too terrible." She hesitated, again.

"What...what do you mean?" I faltered. What could possibly be so bad? In this serene setting? But there was something different about the farm this year, something amiss, something no one talked about, but what? Marie Hélène looked at me. "Virginie, you are a member of the family. You are one of us. I think of you like a sister."

"Umm, thank you."

"Virginie, the other day while Aurelia was in town, an old friend of the family ran up to her and told her everything. We wanted to keep it a secret, especially from her, as she loved Emilia so much."

"What do you mean?" I began to feel alarmed. What could Emilia possibly have to do with this? She had died a few months ago—of old age, naturally.

"You have to promise to keep it a secret and not repeat it to a soul." She looked at the ceiling with its huge supporting beams. "I don't know if I can tell you, Virginie. It's too...."

"What? What happened to Emilia?" I was truly alarmed now. I steeled my nerves.

"Emilia committed suicide." Marie Hélène's face stared into mine. I winced. Not Emilia. My mind reeled. I felt a bit faint. Our eyes riveted together, Marie Hélène and I began to talk in earnest.

"No, no, I can't believe it. I don't want to believe it! That's too horrible! At her age...no!"

"She was visiting Claudine and André in Paris. They left her alone in the apartment one day, and...."

"No! Don't tell me how!" I cried out in anguish. I didn't want to visualize Emilia in a pool of blood on her daughter's Louis XVI bed. "My God, why would she do such a thing?"

"We think it was because of Algeria. She couldn't get over the loss. She and Jean Marc, her husband, had only a tiny pension to live on and she was miserable. She blamed herself for not listening to her children and selling when she could...she just couldn't forgive herself. She couldn't get over losing everything in Algiers.

"Having someone so close to you do such a thing changes you," Marie Hélène volunteered quietly. Our eyes were welded together, almost like in a trance. I was so shocked by the thought of Emilia, elegant, gentle Emilia, killing herself that all I could do was listen helplessly, aghast at what Marie Hélène had revealed to me.

"It makes you think that maybe you could do such a thing someday."

"But no, Marie Hélène, not you. Why would you think such a thing?"

She looked up at me from under her long lashes. Her eyes were limpid but not wet. She was very lucid.

"Would you ever think of suicide, Virginie? Under any circumstances?" The question was so direct. I had never thought of suicide in my entire life.

"No, I don't think so...."

The high ceilings of the room closed in on us, and the atmosphere took on an intensity, an intimacy.

I wanted to keep talking.

"I think that maybe I could...." Marie Hélène stared into my soul, or I felt like she did. I blanched, recoiled from the intensity of her midnight confession.

"Marie Hélène, Camus said there are only two choices in life, to commit suicide or not. Once you have decided to live, there are no more choices."

Marie Hélène looked at me and smiled. "Virginie, we tend to be depressive in our family. You'll have to forgive me. It's just that the thought of Emilia makes me think..."

"Too much! Besides you have your son, Jean, to live for!"

"It's true, I think only of myself sometimes."

"Good. Because the rest of us would miss you, too."

"But Emilia...how could she?" Marie Hélène looked at me plaintively.

"I don't know. She must have been very unhappy," I ventured. "There are some things you just have to accept."

Marie Hélène nodded in acquiescence.

I nodded back to reassure her. Then I turned out the feeble light and put my head on my pillow, pulling only a sheet over my body on this hot, August night. I heard Marie Hélène lie down in her bed. I turned over and listened to the crickets chirp. Thoughts of the letter Sebastian had received by now whirled through my mind. Marie Hélène slept soundly. I got up and walked onto the moonlit terrace to calm my racing mind.

It had all started in Madrid, I reflected.

☼ ¡ARRIBA LA FIESTA!

STUDENTS JOSTLED ONE ANOTHER as they passed in front of the food service counter at the University of Madrid's student cafeteria. A cheaply made paella cooked in lots of grease was the specialty of the day—namely, the only thing they were serving. I had a hard time digesting the food, but the eight *peseta*, or twelve cents, price was hard to beat. A jovial young woman with her dark hair pulled back in a French twist dished up a hearty portion of paella today, and I politely asked for *sal de fruta*, the Spanish version of Pepto-Bismol, to go along with it. Just in case. I had only been in Madrid for a month, and my tender American stomach had run into a collision course with the heavy olive oil in which almost everything except bread was cooked.

I took my tray and scanned the hundreds of students ingesting paella. I spotted Mike, another American. He waved at me, so I sat down next to him. The din created by students madly jabbering all at once in God knows how many languages was fairly daunting, but he had to tell me about his travel exploits anyway. I listened politely. Just as he got to his story about how he was going to spend a ton of money touring the Ivory Coast, a stranger walked up to me and smiled the biggest, toothiest, friendliest grin I had ever seen.

"*Hola, me llamo Pierre Moulet.*"

I looked up at a wiry man. He looked older than the rest of us. And he was. Twenty-seven years old, which seems like a lot when you are only twenty-three. His skin was already creased in places. The slight space between his two front teeth commanded my attention for some reason. Then he stuck out his hand and I had to put my fork down and stop wolfing down my ill-fated paella. I shook his hand and smiled into an interesting face. Two big brown eyes squinted merrily at me from under some curly brown hair. That smile…it was contagious. The impish sparkle in his eyes was full of mirth.…

I liked him!

"*Me llamo.…*" I faltered. Virginia was the hardest word in the Spanish language for me to pronounce, but I was determined to get it out. After all, it was my name! "*Me llamo.…me llamo Vir…Vir…heen-ya.*" I almost yelled the last part, peaking at the *heen.* Vir*heeny*a.

His grin never flinched. "You obviously can't speak Spanish, so as my English is better than your Spanish, we should speak English together." He spoke with authority.

"But I came to Madrid to learn Spanish!"

Pierre ignored my protest. My Spanish pronunciation was abominable, even though I had minored in Spanish at Berkeley. I just couldn't pronounce the Js and Gs. And his English was disgustingly good.

"I'm French. My English is very good, as I just studied it at Cambridge for four years." He stood there smiling his giant grin, and I grinned back, letting him take the lead.

"Hi, Mike," he smiled at Mike now.

"Oh, hello, Pierre. Why don't you sit down?"

All confidence and smile, Pierre sat down and made himself right at home.

"How long have you been in Madrid?" he asked me.

"About a month," I answered. "How do you know Mike?"

"He's the American in our group," laughed Pierre.

"Your group?"

"Yes, there are lots of us. We do things together like go to the theater, restaurants, the Rastro. We have a good time."

I assessed him. He was a small man, not much taller than me, but bursting with vitality, wired to the max. Unlike the rest of the students, who wore plain slacks and shirts, Pierre sported a tie and white collar with a heavy knit sweater over his shirt.

"Would you like to go for a drink, Virginia?"

"Why don't we all go…your friends can come, too," I

countered. "Please call me Ginny, if you're going to speak English."

"Fantastic, Geeny!" exhorted Pierre. "Hey, let's go to the Plaza del Sol for a cognac!" he shouted to a group of students seated nearby, who had been following his antics.

They turned and waved at us, all smiles.

"*Bueno! Vámanos!* Let's go!" they chorused.

And before I could take my *sal de fruta*, we bustled out of the student cafeteria and got into two tiny Fiats with sunroofs, each just big enough for four people. There were eight of us, so it was a tight fit. I was the only American. The others were Spanish, British, and French.

Off we tore through the streets of Madrid, two small cars full of spirited students. Pierre wove in and out of the busy traffic like a race car driver, and Manolo, the Spaniard with the other car, stuck to us like glue. Suddenly, Pierre stood up, his torso and upper body sticking out of the sun roof. We all started laughing and waving back and forth out the car windows, egging each other on. Pierre, guiding the steering wheel with apparent ease with his knees, waved to the astonished pedestrians like a conquering prince. Never one to be outdone, I stood up and poked my torso out of the sun roof and waved to the people on the street. Then I motioned for Manolo to do the same. Looking less like a conquering prince than someone about to lose control of his car, Manolo stood up and guided his car with his knees.

I laughed, huge hoots of mirth, and waved merrily to the people on the sidewalks. Some of them laughed and waved back. The wind whipped through my hair at forty miles per hour. Now I knew why I had come to Spain. To cavort madly through the streets of Madrid. It never once occurred to me that we might have an accident; after all, Pierre was driving. I already had total confidence in this maniac; I had always had a fondness for spirited men. They were never dull, and boredom was my only fear. Tedium meant death to the soul. I had learned that the year I worked at the Department of Employment in California. The rules and other employees were incredibly humorless and rigid. Rigor mortis had almost set in by the time they fired me.

"Never again," I had vowed to myself.

Screech! We squealed to a halt in front of a restaurant at the Plaza del Sol. Laughing and joking, everyone piled out of the cars. As we filed noisily into an expensive restaurant, heads turned with disapproving looks. Pierre spoke to the waiter in Spanish, and we were quickly seated at a long table for eight.

"What would you like to drink?" asked Pierre.

"A cognac. Isn't that what we came here for?"

Everyone quickly ordered, and Pierre just as quickly began to tell me about his family fortune. It was considerable and contributed to the free-swinging part of his identity.

It was as if he were saying, "Hello, my name is Pierre Moulet, and these are my family assets."

He grinned as he told me about his family's thousand-acre farms near Alicante in Spain and Ouezzane in Morocco, and an antique store in Rabat, the capital of Morocco, which Pierre planned to take over when he was through traveling and studying abroad. He obviously enjoyed talking about his family's fortune, yet he seemed to have very little pretention while talking about considerable wealth. Clearly, he was a character. His sense of humor and disarming grin told you he was a down-to-earth guy. When he got to the part about the unoccupied apartments in Alicante and Benidorm on the Mediterranean coast, I stopped him.

"If no one is living in them, why don't we go there this weekend?" I hated to see those apartments going to waste. The concept went against my Protestant ethic, instilled so arduously by my well-meaning mother.

"Ter-rif-ic!"! exclaimed Pierre, a seemingly endless fountain of enthusiasm. "It's a national holiday and we'll have three days!"

"Let's all go," I waved my hand to include everyone sitting at the table. "I'm sick of this rainy weather we've been having in Madrid, and it must be sunny on the Costa del Sol—the sunny coast."

It had been raining for a solid week in Madrid when

Pierre and I took off for his beach house near Alicante. During that week all of us had gone to nightclubs and restaurants together, and we were fast friends by the weekend. Pierre and I were always together, an evolving couple. Everyone who had been at the table went with us. Jean Paul was a French friend from Cambridge University, and Veronique, a French woman, was another great friend of Pierre's from Cambridge. She had moved into his apartment in Madrid— just as a friend, he explained.

"Veronique and I are great friends! We can sleep in the same bed and not even touch one another."

"Admirable!" I enthused, sick of being pawed by just about every American man I had ever gone out with, and they were legion. After losing my virginity in my sophomore year at Berkeley, I dove into sexual adventures with an enthusiasm that my partners did not really reciprocate. They thought I was cheap. Some thought I was crazy. Unaffectionate creatures, they wanted a pseudo-mommy, not a woman, which I had become. The Europeans had been ready for me for at least a century.

Veronique rode in the car with us, and two British girls, Geraldine and Caroline, rode with Manolo and the other Spaniard named Manolo, in Manolo's car. We called Manolo the driver Manolito to distinguish him from the taller Manolo. He took everything with his unshakable good humor. Besides, he was quite the "pistol" with women and ended up living with Veronique in Pierre's apartment. *And* he had an American girlfriend to boot, but she was back in Boston, so she didn't count.

It was almost midnight when we arrived at the dirt road that led to the beach house a mile from the two-lane highway. The road had been washed out by the unusually strong rains. Pierre immediately set out to find a peasant in the nearby village to lead us there with a lantern.

"It's a wild goose chase!" I chided mirthfully as we followed the poor man, wearing a typical peasant's beret, over muddy, rutted paths. He trudged obligingly along. We followed at a snail's pace in our tiny Fiats. "There's no such thing as a beach house! He was just trying to impress us!"

Manolito gamely trailed behind in his car, but he joined in my spirit of poking fun at Pierre and soon we were all chanting, "There is no beach house! You've led us on a wild goose chase!" Our tiny cars bumped along a mile or so of muddy, badly rutted peasant's paths until something did, indeed, loom ahead of us on a hilltop in the distance. As we got closer I made out the contours of the beach house. We all cheered, and Pierre jumped out and got out a huge key to let us in. Pierre lit antique kerosene lamps, which cast an eerie light in the rooms. There was no electricity, nothing to suggest the modern world. Several large earthen urns decorated the living room along with a few beach chairs. The view of Alicante was breathtaking. The city lights twinkled like stars in the distance. There was nothing to obstruct our view, as the *chalet*, or beach house, was the only structure between us and Alicante, six kilometers away. Framed by the arches over the terrace that surrounded the *chalet*, Alicante sparkled like a jewel.

"Do you like it?" queried Pierre.

"It's incredibly beautiful," I responded, sucking in my breath in admiration.

Pierre showed us the four bedrooms, and I made the rounds with him until everyone had found a place to sleep. He had saved the last and best bedroom for us. The shuttered windows overlooked the sea. Its gentle lapping sound would lull me to sleep. But first....

I slept with Pierre that night on a peasant's straw-stuffed mattress. I wanted to see if he filled the bill for a husband, because, after all, a mere fortune was not enough. I had to sleep with the guy.... I had to make sure.... And true to form, he knew how to make love. The deal was done as far as I was concerned. I wanted to marry Pierre. Money plus good sex plus good times equalled marriage, as far as I was concerned.

If you have to get married, you may as well marry someone with money, I had reasoned before enrolling in the Foreigners' Program at Madrid. Knowing that mostly rich people attended this kind of program, in the back of my mind I was thinking of snaring a rich husband. *Anything* had to be better than working at the Department of Employment. My feminine logic was clever and calculating, perfect except for one thing. I had never really wanted to get married at all.

Last year, when I was the tender age of twenty-two, my mother had shamed me by calling me an old maid. Working did not appeal to me after my experience at the Department of Employment, so this congenial son of a millionaire seemed okay to me. Besides, we were having the time of our lives.

I was unprepared for the clear, nearly turquoise-blue water that sparkled like crinkly sugar candy under a startlingly clear, azure-blue sky. The Mediterranean stunned me with its sheer beauty when I got up the next morning. I walked out onto the terrace into something that looked like heaven. Veronique and the small Manolo pointed enthusiastically at the sea about fifty feet down the hillside from the *chalet.*

"Let's go swimming!" Veronique shouted.

"I didn't bring a bathing suit!"

"It doesn't matter!" Veronique dashed inside and I followed, determined to go swimming in that clear, translucent sea.

I opened my suitcase and found some black panties and a sleeveless jersey. "These will do," I thought, and although I had never swum in my underwear, I put them on. Pierre followed me and put on a Speedo-type bathing suit that European men wore. It barely covered him. His tight little ass stuck out jauntily. We looked at each other and laughed. Then he took me by the hand and led me down the rocky slope to the beach. The others were already there.

"This is jolly fine!" intoned Geraldine in her clipped British accent.

"Yes, jolly good!" agreed her friend Caroline.

"Follow me!" shouted Pierre. He started swimming toward a rocky prominence. We watched him, and I started to swim after him. His head popped out of the water to see if everyone was coming. "*Allez-y!*" He exhorted in French. "Follow me!"

The Manolos and Veronique and the British girls swam

gamely after us. Deliciously clear and warm, the water caressed our smooth bodies.

"No wonder everyone vacations on the Mediterranean," I thought, while the bathtub-temperature water sent sensations of pure pleasure coarsing through my veins.

Pretty soon we found ourselves in a sea cove. There was a small, rocky beach with high, craggy cliffs on either side. As we got to the beach, Jean Paul suddenly appeared at the edge of the rocky prominence above the cove.

"*Mon dieu!* What are you doing there?" He shouted down to us.

"*C'est merveilleux ici!* It's marvelous here!" yelled Pierre. "Come join us!" Jean Paul looked dubiously at the steep cliff separating us from him.

"I'll bring you some wine," he bellowed and disappeared. Pierre scaled the cliff and stood atop it. I carefully found foot and hand holds and joined him.

"Come on, you guys!" I yelled to everyone on the little beach. "The view is great!"

The others started climbing and had just reached the top when Jean Paul rounded the bend pushing a small rubber raft in the water with two bottles of red wine on it. We saw him and cheered.

"*Allez!* Jump!" shouted Pierre. We looked down at the crystal-clear water below, and back at him.

"Come on!" Then he jumped. "*Vive la France!*" he yelled and then landed with a splash and disappeared for a moment. He surfaced and beckoned to the two Manolos to follow suit.

"I can't jump. I'm afraid of heights!" yelled Manolito, the unflinching driver who was fast becoming Pierre's best buddy.

"The water's not very deep. We'll help you, come on," yelled Pierre. "For the honor of Spain!"

The taller Manolo suddenly jumped and shouted, "*¡Arriba España!*" His head disappeared into the clear blue water, and we watched as he did a somersault and then surfaced, treading water and looking up at us expectantly.

The two British girls jumped together, holding hands. "God save the Queen!" they shrieked, laughing as they landed on their bottoms, legs outstretched.

Manolito was still on the cliff, looking nervously down at us. Then he shut his eyes, yelled, "*¡Arriba España!*" and jumped. He came down with a big splash and we grabbed him and helped him to shallower water, where Jean Paul was waiting with the wine raft. The bottles were quickly opened and passed all around. Everyone took a big swig and yelled, "*¡Arriba España!*" or "*Vive la France!*" or "God save the Queen!" Finally I shouted "America the beautiful!"

Then Pierre scrambled back up the cliff and exhorted everyone to jump again, teasing and cajoling us. Up and down we went until we were really hungry and a bit drunk.

"Let's get something to eat!" shouted Pierre and we all agreed. Everyone swam back to the *chalet* and went inside to dry off and get dressed. I dressed quickly, hardly believing this was November. It had been raining and cold in Madrid!

Outside on the terrace, the perfect sky blended into the hillside on which the *chalet* was perched, the only structure jutting out of the rugged coastline for several miles. Its pristine beauty awed me. An isolated olive tree stood sentinel on the lee side of the beach house near the terrace.

Even in my most perfect fantasies, I had never imagined a place as serenely beautiful as this stretch of white sand, flanked by dry, rugged terrain, with only cacti and scrub bushes for vegetation. It had a stark, untouched beauty that took my breath away. I experienced something akin to a religious revelation, perhaps an epiphany, for the *chalet* and its surroundings took on a special significance to me, like a citadel or holy site where Pierre and I, once married, would spend our summer vacations.

Pierre interrupted my reverie on the terrace, bounding out of our adjoining room with his customary vitality.

"Come on, Geeny! Let's go to the farm!"

"The farm?" Suburban child that I was, a farm didn't sound that interesting. "How about some food first? Like lunch?"

"No, no, you must see the farm. We have a family farm that is over two hundred years old, where the whole family unites every summer! It's a wonderful farm! We can have lunch there."

Everyone piled into our two tiny cars and followed Pierre dutifully over the dirt road back to the highway and back another kilometer to where Lo Cruz, the farm, lay. "Lo Cruz" had been the original name. It was part of the Valencian dialect that had been spoken here before Castillian was named the official language of Spain by the rulers in Madrid. It meant "the cross," but was spelled with an *o*, rather than an *a* as in Castillian Spanish, hence, Lo Cruz.

We drove over some railroad tracks on a dirt road to get there. With great reverence Pierre showed us the old stables, the rooms where bread and wine used to be made, the pig sty, the kitchen with a wood-burning stove.

Some peasants, friends of his since childhood, offered us lunch, and we ate the simple macaroni noodles with tomato sauce as if they were the rarest delicacy.

"Pierre, can we go to Alicante later? I'd like to see the town." Jean Paul angled his craggy French features in our direction.

"Let's go!" Pierre jumped to his feet, his wiry frame ready for action, delighted at a request to see Alicante.

As we drove the six kilometers to Alicante, a town that had paid its taxes of one hundred maidens yearly to the Arabic conquerors of Southern Spain during the middle ages, Pierre pointed out an incredible grove of palm trees and other local points of interest for which he said Alicante was famous. Then we sat on the esplanade that cut through the center of town, bordered by fantastic mosaic tile work and dotted with high, swaying palm trees. We ordered *horchata*, one of the local specialties, a drink made from rice that looked and tasted a bit like thin milk.

"Let's go back to the *chalet* and fix dinner," suggested Pierre. "We can cook it on the bunsen burner in the kitchen."

"What shall we get?" asked Geraldine. "Roast beef?"

We laughed. "Come on. Let's go to a grocery store and see what they have."

Lines of sausages hung from the ceiling of a small corner store—there were no supermarkets in Alicante in 1965—and lots of canned goods and macaroni and spaghetti noodles lined the shelves. We also bought several bottles of the excellent local table wine, rich with no aftertaste, as good as any I had ever tasted and only twelve cents a bottle.

"Let's fix some spaghetti," Geraldine's clipped British accent intoned. "A traditional meal." We laughed and bought the necessary items.

Cooking spaghetti noodles on a bunsen burner proved easy enough once we got it lit, and I managed to make sauce from our fresh tomatoes, basil, and sausage.

"Hurry up, Geeny, I'm hungry!" said Pierre, who always had a ravenous appetite.

"Okay, okay! It's ready! Just set the table!"

Pierre and Manolito had put two tables together on the terrace so we could have a view of the coast while we ate. We were shaded from the sun by the arches that supported the roof over the terrace. A slight breeze cooled us as we sipped the pungent red wine.

Manolito, always helpful, found some plates and napkins.

"Where are the knives and forks, Pierre?" he asked.

"They're…" Pierre opened and shut cabinets above the tile counters in the kitchen to no avail. There were no drawers, much less knives and forks.

"How are we going to eat the spaghetti?" wailed Jean Paul, dismayed. I laughed to myself thinking what he must be going through, a Frenchman, a world-class member of the bourgeoisie. I looked at the table set with white plates, glasses, and red-and-white napkins. I started serving the spaghetti, and everyone sat down expectantly. I sat down, too, and looked at all that good food. The rich aroma of tomato sauce and basil reached our nostrils. We were all ravenous. We tried eating with our hands, but the noodles were too slippery to eat with our fingers. Then I picked up my glass and scooped up some spaghetti. I gulped it down. Some of the noodles spilled back into my plate, but most of it went down.

Everyone stared at me at first. Then they gleefully followed suit. Pretty soon we were all downing glassfuls of spaghetti. It slid out of our mouths and back into the plates. Slimy noodles and red spaghetti sauce slid out of the corners of our mouths. We looked so grotesque that we began to laugh at one another.

Pierre and I laughed until our sides ached. After we cleaned off the tables, I jumped on top of a chair and started to dance the flamenco. He joined me. Geraldine got out a camera as we cavorted on top of the table. She got some shots of us, Pierre and me dancing a clumsy flamenco and howling our own version of the music on the table top. Manolito and Veronique joined us.

Pierre and Manolito were becoming fast friends. They both loved fast cars and parties. Whenever we drove, they raced with each other and played games that would have been dangerous if there had been any other traffic, but there wasn't. Our paradise was sparsely inhabited by moving vehicles.

The party lasted for an entire four days, never letting up. One of the British girls tried to dampen our spirits by throwing a temper tantrum about wanting to go home, but Pierre told her to stop being rude. She stopped, much to our relief.

The last night unfolded like a fairy tale, with Pierre taking us to one of his father's apartments in Benidorm, a nearby fishing village and tourist resort. As he unlocked the door to the modern apartment on the eighth floor of a highrise with an incredible view over the ocean, velvet covered, cane-backed antique furniture appeared—every room was completely furnished with the most exquisite furniture I had ever seen. Pierre started extolling the virtues of his father's workshop and cabinetmaker. He caught my eye, and I smiled back. It was true love.

Inseparable, we were like a couple of grown-up kids high on life and antsy for action. I wanted fun and parties forever! More important, I would never have to put up with my parents' self-pitying moaning and groaning! *Au contraire!* Pierre was proud of his entire family, even the communist, Bernarda, who had married Pierre's multimillionaire cousin, true to the flamboyant colors of her flag.

Pierre's pride became mine, and I soon shed my entire white Anglo-Saxon Protestant heritage of gloom and doom, whimper and moan and *never* impose on anyone (for fear you might have to pay them back). Thank God. I could breathe at last. I could be my irreverent self. I grabbed Pierre and kissed him hard on the mouth. He looked mildly surprised, then smiled and kissed me back.

"Do you like this, Geeny?" he asked.

"Yes."

"Vraiment? An American?" he smiled slyly.

"Yes, an American," I replied, not understanding how much the French looked down on Americans for bad manners, taste, and a whole assortment of what he would later refer to as "a lack of education or breeding." For the French and Spanish did not mean just school-acquired education, but the whole ball of wax acquired throughout a lifetime. Taste, manners, yes, a very different concept that did not even disdain to look at the "bottom line."

"I'm exhausted," I declared.

"So are we," echoed Veronique and Manolito. The others nodded their heads dully.

"Maybe we can get some sleep tonight," pleaded the now-tranquil Caroline.

I smiled sweetly at her. "Yes, it's time to bed down for a change. We have to drive back to Madrid tomorrow, so we need some rest," I agreed.

"You can sleep in the living room and two front bedrooms," said Pierre, giving instructions in his usual easy-going manner.

Everyone quickly bedded down, and after they were sound sleep, Pierre and I snuck in a "quickie" in the back bedroom. After we were through, a mischievous idea seized me. In keeping with the spirit of the weekend holiday, why not play a practical joke on everyone? Why not wake them up with our rallying cry, "*¡Arriba la fiesta!*"

I nudged Pierre, who rolled over indulgently. "What do you want?" he asked.

I whispered my "brainstorm" into his willing ear, and we got up and walked around, inspecting our sleeping friends. They were really zonked. Manolito and Veronique were in one of the bedrooms. They, too, had become lovers during our four-day sojourn on the Mediterranean. Jean Paul and the taller Manolo slept on the floor in the living room, while Geraldine lay crashed on the velvet sofa. Caroline was nowhere to be seen. Four days and nights of non-stop partying had exhausted us.

Pierre and I looked at each other and giggled. Almost delirious from lack of sleep, we counted to three under our breath and yelled in unison: "*¡Arriba la fiesta otra vez!* Start the party again!"

Manolo and Jean Paul woke up, rubbed their eyes and looked dully at us.

"*¡Arriba la fiesta otra vez!*" I cackled wildly with Pierre. We kept shouting "*¡Arriba la fiesta!*"

Suddenly the tall Manolo chorused, "*¡Arriba la fiesta!*" and started doing the flamenco as he yelled. Veronique and Manolito came sleepily out of their bedroom, she hulking over him as she was not a small Frenchwoman, and smiled. Then they burst into full party action, laughing and dancing the flamenco.

I couldn't believe that everyone had rallied so fast. I would have been furious. I really wanted to go to bed and get a good night's sleep.

I pulled Pierre aside and whispered, "Let's tell them it was just a practical joke now."

He smiled back at me and then announced, "We were just kidding. We're too tired to party anymore. Let's all go to bed now."

The rest of them looked at us in disbelief, but by this time they had come to expect anything from Pierre. Everyone nodded their heads and lay back down to go promptly to sleep, Pierre and I included. But from that time on, whenever things got a bit dull in Madrid, all anyone had to do was yell "*¡Arriba la fiesta!*" and people would spontaneously break into song, dance, and laughter.

Manolito was particularly happy the next day, probably because Veronique had become his lover. He took his radio with him to get something downstairs, and as we looked out over the balcony at the breathtaking view of the Mediterranean Sea a few blocks in front of us, he came waltzing up the entrance steps singing to a song his radio was playing. Unaware that his antics were being watched, he kept dancing to the tune on the wide mosaic porch downstairs.

A mischievous idea came to me. He was so cute and small and vulnerable down there...and he never got mad...why not douse him with a bucket of water? I had seen a bucket in the laundry room at the far end of the apartment. I ran to get it.

"What are you doing, Geeny?" asked Pierre as I filled the bucket with water.

"I'm going to see if I can hit Manolito!"

I ran to the balcony and heaved the water over. We watched as it hit Manolito squarely on the top of his head. He looked up and shook his fist at us, then hunched his shoulders and started laughing at us laughing at him. What else could he do? After I accidentally hit him in the face again at a restaurant with a glass of water that I swear I thought was empty, we called him Manolo *mojado*, or wet Manolo. He took it in good grace, and soon he and Pierre and I were the best of friends, along with Veronique and Jean Paul. I could not count the friends I had in those days.

I further distinguished myself later on in the evening by downing an entire bottle of wine at one swilling. Then the thunderous and passionate plaint of the flamenco music a local guitarist was playing in a local tavern overwhelmed me. I jumped up on one of the tabletops in the tavern and danced with fluid abandon. Caught up in the passion of the music plus the wine, I was one with the moment. Startled by a cacophony of applause, I looked into the eyes of men no longer intent on drinking their wine. They soon joined us in dancing an improvised flamenco on the tabletops.

With high spirits we piled back into the tiny Fiats to drive back to the beach house and then to Madrid. The solitary olive tree beside the *chalet* stood out like a lonely sentinel as we drove down the rutted road to the highway.

Four hours later we arrived in Madrid.

☼ THE YEAR OF FREE SPIRITS

CONSCIOUSNESS SEEPED SLOWLY into my brain. Someone's hand was on my shoulder, shaking it.

"Geeny, Geeny! Wake up! We are in Madrid!"

Pierre grinned happily at my inert form, my matted hair, my rumpled pants and jersey. I looked up at him groggily. "We're back? Already?"

"You slept the whole way."

"Too much wine…" I remembered, dimly.

I sat up and shook my head to clear it. Pierre's car was parked in front of a modern apartment building at the end of a cobblestoned street. The early morning air was clear and warm. Madrid still slumbered, silent and beautiful.

Veronique and Jean Paul were taking their bags out of the back seat.

"You have to spend the night here, Geeny, with us. The *portero* will not let you into your new place."

Now I remembered that I was in the middle of a move—from stuffy old Señora de la Valle's rented room to a five-bedroom apartment I had rented with some other girls, students like me.

"Okay. Let's go!" I got out of the car.

Pierre called to the *portero*, the night watchman who let people into the apartment building after ten o'clock. After the evening meal, when the women put their children to bed, the wrought-iron gates that elegantly decorated the buildings during the daytime were locked, protecting all within. Young women lived with their parents until they got married, so the only people out in the streets after ten o'clock were foreigners and an occasional Madrileño taking a stroll or a *copa*, a drink of cognac. It was so different from the

46

United States! In California, girls left their homes when they were eighteen to go to school or to work. Some got married, usually the poorer or pregnant ones. Pregnancy! That was for the other women, not me, I had decided quite a while ago. Lucky for me, the "pill" came out the year I lost my virginity. The summer I turned nineteen, I had a hot and heavy fling while visiting my aunt in Arlington, Virginia. Bobby Sanders tried to "make it" with me in the back seat of his car after we danced the Pony for three hours at the Hayloft in Washington, D.C. We couldn't take our eyes off of one another as we writhed to the pulsating music of a rock and roll band. They kept playing "Tossing and Turning All Night," and Bobby insisted that's what he had done last night because he wanted "it" so much.

I wanted "it" too, but thanks to my mother's strong grip on me and iron-clad moral values, I had no intention of "doing it." Greedy little hands and fingers had explored my bras and panties for several years, but they got no further. It was as if I were wearing a chastity belt. I'll never forget Tommy Potter, who asked plaintively, "Just one inch, just let me put it in one inch." We were the closest I had ever come to doing "it," but his parents had arrived in the nick of time. Tommy hid me in his clothes closet, where I stood straight as a stiletto trying not to make a sound while hangers fell all over me.

When I wouldn't do "it" with Bobby, he got mad at me, called me a "penis tease." I genuinely liked him, and his anger shook me up. On the way home to California in the plane, the virtue of virginity suddenly lost its charm. It wasn't worth losing friends for such a silly thing, and I decided to do "it" with my next boyfriend. When I offered no resistance, my next male friend refused to believe I was a virgin. Men wanted women to put up a fight, play hard to get, all that tripe. Cynicism arrived full blown in my consciousness as I protested my former innocence. People prefer lies to the truth, I decided. White lies that make life less "disagreeable." The more I realized this, the feistier and more blatantly honest I became. Angry with people for wanting me to pretend, for wanting everyone to pretend, I always stood firmly for the truth as I perceived it. My popularity dwindled. I developed a point of view, a mind of my own. This aspect of my personality disappeared in Madrid, where I could only communicate as a foreigner, and where, among foreigners at least, I found much less hypocrisy regarding sex than in the United States.

The *portero* rounded the corner carrying his lantern and heavy set of keys. He searched through them for the one to Pierre's apartment building and then opened the heavy wrought-iron grating with a squeaking turn of the master key. Pierre handed him some *pesetas*, or pennies, and the man respectfully tipped his beret and said, *"Gracias, señor."*

Up the elevator we went, still full of excitement and laughter from our adventures on the coast of Spain. Heady from our adventure, Pierre draped his arm over my shoulders and Jean Paul leaned against the elevator wall, a diabolic look in his eye. Veronique stood quietly next to us.

"You were really drunk last night, Geeny," laughed Pierre. "You danced on tabletops in a bar!" He put his arm around my waist and hugged me close.

"He's making this up, isn't he?"

"No, no, and everyone else got up and danced with you," said Veronique.

"Like this?" I started doing the flamenco in the elevator. It moved. Pierre put his hands on my shoulders and tried to stop me.

"Geeny, you're shaking the elevator!"

"Do you think it will fall?"

"It might if we all jump at the same time," said the usually taciturn Jean Paul. Suddenly he leaped high in the air. His gaunt frame landed hard on the elevator floor. The elevator bounced a bit.

"Stop it, Jean Paul!" I yelled, frightened.

"Come on, don't worry. Nothing is going to happen." Jean Paul jumped again just as we arrived at the eighth floor. The elevator stopped moving and the door opened, much to my relief. Jean Paul was full of surprises.

Pierre got out and took my hand. He led me down a corridor.

A mahogany door loomed at the end of the winding corridor. "Is this going to be like Benidorm?" I wondered, half expecting to find a fully furnished apartment waiting for us.

Pierre opened the door to a long hallway leading to a new but nearly empty living room save for an old baroque dining room table and chairs. The apartment looked barren compared to the one in Benidorm. I sniffed. I could still smell the varnish on the floor. Like a new car, the last coat of finish still permeated the air.

"I got them at the flea market!" enthused Pierre, waving his hand in the direction of the furniture.

The heavy antique table and chairs contrasted oddly with the sterile, modern look of this apartment, very different from the one in Benidorm. Then I saw the terrace overlooking the rooftops of Madrid with a view almost to the Navacerrada Mountains.

"Look at the view!" I squealed and ran out onto the terrace to look at the splendor of Madrid. Red tile rooftops and apartments with open courtyards lay quietly beneath me. Madrid, an ancient town dating back to medieval times, slumbered fast asleep before the first traces of dawn. The others followed me. Suddenly a small Fiat sped into view and the driver slammed on the brakes. Manolito got out and looked up at us.

"*¡Hola!*" he shouted from below. "Let me in! I don't know where the *portero* is!"

We laughed and shouted back not to worry.

"Don't worry! I'll let you in," yelled Pierre. He took off at a fast trot to go down and unlock the door for Manolito. They came back talking as merrily as if they had just woken up from a good night's sleep.

"Isn't Pierre's apartment great?" I yawned. "But where are we going to sleep?"

"Sleep?" chorused Pierre and Manolito. "You slept all the way back! *¡Arriba la fiesta!*"

"Now? At four in the morning?"

"*Eh, bien,* I have to teach at nine o'clock," said Veronique. "I'm sorry, Pierre, but I have to go to bed."

She smiled as Manolito gave her a sexy look. She took him by the hand and led him to Pierre's bedroom. Pierre scratched his head, perplexed. The premature creases around his mouth made him seem a bit sad, a sadness he masked well. His tousled hair and stooped shoulders made me feel sorry for him, so I held his hand. He smiled at me.

"Now there is no place for us to sleep…Well, Jean Paul, you can sleep on the living room floor with some blankets and Geeny and I will…." I looked at him expectantly. "We will sleep in the other bedroom."

He took me by the hand and led me to an empty bedroom with a parquet wood floor.

"Isn't there a bed?" I asked.

"No, Geeny, we will have to sleep on blankets, too."

"I can go to sleep on a floor." I surveyed the parquet flooring. It looked clean and nice.

Pierre bustled about and found a quilt and some blankets and we bedded down to catch a few winks, not without a quickie, of course. That floor was harder than I thought.

Morning came quickly, at least for Veronique, who had to teach. The rest of us got up late and decided to have *cafe au lait* at the Retiro, a beautiful lake in the center of Madrid, where we could relax and rent paddle boats. Later on Pierre would take my suitcase over to my new residence so I could move in.

The Retiro was lovely, a large, deep-blue lake in the middle of a cosmopolitan capital of Europe. We ambled along, Pierre, Manolito, Jean Paul, and I. We rented paddle boats.

"¡*Arriba la fiesta!*" Pierre shouted, and we were off and paddling furiously, Manolito and Jean Paul following Pierre and me. I watched the broadleaf trees that lined the shores, the people pushing babies in prams or eating lunch at an outdoor restaurant. Pierre slowed down and we smiled broadly at each other. A feeling of fullness, of delight, enveloped me as he shared my happiness. We were glad we had found each other.

Some more of Pierre's friends came over that night, and

we spoke many languages. Peter was from Hamburg, Germany, but his Spanish was already very good. He could converse easily in it. I could barely understand the two Manolos, but their smiling faces and willingness to repeat sentences helped me.

"So what is the difference between Catholicism and Protestantism?" I wanted to know.

Manolito tried to explain it to me in Spanish, and Pierre and the others tried to help me understand, but I was dense, or Protestant, or something. I couldn't figure it out.

"We both believe in the same things, don't we?" I queried.

"*Aparte de la virgen María,*" Manolito earnestly explained. "Except for the Virgin Mary."

I was still completely in the dark. "But we believe in Mary. She was the mother of Christ!" I said, naive as could be about the importance of Mary in the Catholic religion as compared to the Protestant religion. Everyone could see my naivete as well as my good intentions. But Manolo and I could not surmount the language barrier.

Pierre, who had been raised outside of religion by a Catholic mother and Lutheran father, was trying to translate for us.

"It's because in the Catholic religion the angel Gabriel announced to Mary that she was going to be the mother of God," said Pierre. Manolito's brown eyes shone brightly under long lashes as he waited for my response.

I thought quickly and said, "So how did she find out in the Protestant religion?"

By now everyone in the room was listening to our conversation. Pierre and Manolito looked at each other and hunched their shoulders skeptically. They didn't know.

"Maybe she skipped a period!" I announced. That brought down the house. Everyone laughed uproariously. I still didn't know what the difference was, but who cared? I was having the time of my life. And everyone loved me.

Peter, the German, told us how the streets of Hamburg had boiled during the bombing by the Allies during World

War II. The heat from the bombs had fried everyone to death. This was the first time I had met a German and heard about the bombing of Hamburg.

"Do you mean innocent German people were killed?" I asked earnestly.

Peter smiled sadly and said, "Everybody was killed."

"But mostly Jewish people," I said, somberly.

"This was Hitler," he responded. "The young people of Germany had nothing to do with World War II. Now we give amnesty to all political refugees and do not persecute anyone. Fourteen million people died in World War II. Many were German."

I nodded my head thoughtfully. Although I didn't know too much about wars and the history of Europe, I wanted to know more. We stood around the only piece of furniture in the room, the long, antique wooden table that Pierre had purchased at the *rastro*, or flea market. Suddenly, Peter took a pencil and piece of paper and began drawing on it. Everyone looked on with interest as he drew a graph. Veronique and I looked at each other as he started to explain his theory.

"You see, men are naturally superior." He drew an arrow that pointed upward.

"No," I interrupted. I took the pencil from his hand and drew an arrow pointing downward. "Women are superior."

Peter grabbed the pencil and pointed the arrow upward again. Veronique took it and drew a line with the arrow pointing down. Pierre, Jean Paul, and the Manolos looked on.

"*¡La flecha arriba!* The arrow upward," laughed Manolito, taking the pencil and drawing a line with the arrow pointing up again.

"*¡La flecha abajo!* The arrow downward!" cried Veronique, taking the pencil and making the arrow go down again.

"*¡La flecha abajo!*" I laughed.

Everybody laughed, and we all shouted *la flecha arriba* or *abajo*, depending on whether we were male or female. Suddenly Jean Paul started holding his sides and rolling on the floor. "*¡La flecha abajo!*" he howled, laughing uncontrollably.

Pierre turned on his record player and Ray Charles' song, "Wha'd I Say" began to throb in the night. Everyone shouted *"arriba la fiesta"* and we began to dance the twist and sing "Hey, baby, wha'd I say...." Noise and shouts made it hard to hear, but nobody cared except perhaps the neighbors.

"Hey, baby, wha'd I say!" I yelled, perpetually off key.

Pierre and I twisted happily away, not caring a bit whether the arrow went up or down. We just wanted to dance and talk and laugh with our friends forever, which turned out to be one o'clock in the morning this time.

Pierre looked at me as the non-sleepover guests departed and said, "It's too late to move your suitcases tonight. Why don't we do it tomorrow?"

"Yes, let's go to bed now," I replied, always sensible about getting a good night's sleep. Then I thought of that hard floor. But I didn't care where I slept as long as it was with Pierre and his friends. I had fallen in love with all of them. I had never been so happy in my entire life. Pierre kissed me as we lay down between the covers. We fell asleep with our arms wrapped tightly around each other.

The next morning dawned late, at least for us. The louvered shutters kept the sun out of the bedrooms. Everyone except Veronique got up late. We jumped into our cars to go to the University of Madrid. Pierre and Manolito madcapped through the roundabouts of Madrid, racing and weaving in and out of traffic like Sterling Moss, the race car driver. Jean Paul and I alternately ducked our heads in mock or real fright and yelled, "We're going to crash!" Then we'd laugh.

We got to the University late. To make up for our tardiness, we raced up the four flights of stairs to Professor Misol's class in art and architecture. As we tore up the stairs we saw Peter, running down the stairs.

"¡Abajo la flecha!" I yelled, cackling like a hen.

"¡Arriba la flecha!" he reciprocated.

"¡Arriba la flecha!" shouted Pierre, charging ahead of me on the steps, his wiry form shooting forward like an arrow.

"¡Abajo la flecha!" I gasped, madly trying to catch up with Pierre. Too late. He was a flight ahead of me. The stairs led

to the top floor, where the classes for foreigners were.

"*Arriba, abajo,*" Jean Paul took up the chant, trotting behind me at a slower pace, more suitable to his laconic personality.

We arrived just as Professor Misol began to expound on the majesty of the cathedral arches in the cathedral at Toledo, Spain. "*Arcos de boveda,*" he called them. His face shone with pride as he described the evolution of the classic archways of the cathedrals in Spain from the Roman occupation of Iberia, as Spain was called in the times right before and after Christ, through the conquest of southern Spain by the Moors, until 1492, Spain's red-letter year. That was when the Spaniards chased the Moors back to Morocco, discovered the New World, and started the Spanish Inquisition, to "purify" their country.

This so-called purification was an oblique reference to the Spanish Inquisition, something the Spaniards claimed was not as bad as the rest of the world made it sound. Many Jewish Spaniards who would not change their religion to Catholicism were burnt at the stake after 1492, when the Moors were driven from Spain with the help of the Jewish Spaniards, according to Pierre. When I looked to him for further explanation, he only said, "People always exaggerate the wrongdoings of the world's richest nation."

Spain was the richest country in the world for many years, as gold from the New World lined huge vaults in Sevilla and other ports in southern Spain, so the other countries of Europe envied it. Nonetheless, Pierre's account of the Spanish Inquisition left me puzzled, but I accepted it temporarily, waiting for future edification from another source.

Pierre and I looked at each other and pointed at one of the foreign students who always wore dinner clothes to class. We laughed.

"She looks like a *pavo real,*" whispered Pierre.

"What's a *pavo real?*"

"A duck, a royal turkey," whispered Pierre.

"You mean a peacock," I announced. Everyone turned and looked at us and I shut up. I had a shrill voice like my mother's. The royal turkey held her head high with pretention and I imitated her. Pierre pinched me on the arm and said, "Not now, Geeny." He was smiling but trying to pay attention to the teacher. I looked at him as he earnestly tried to take notes on what Professor Misol was saying. Pierre's tie was tucked neatly into his heavy sweater, his wide, wiry shoulders hunkered over a notebook, his narrow hips leaned against the wall. We had been too late to class to get seats, so we stood with a few other students on the far side of the room. It was packed.

"Do you want to go to the theater tonight?" Pierre asked. "With Jean Paul and me after class?"

"Yes. What play is showing?"

"La lucha para la sombra de un burro is playing at the Felipe II Theater. It should be interesting."

"The Battle for the Shade of a Donkey?" I translated the title literally. "What's it about?" I interrupted Jean Paul.

"I don't know exactly, but I hear it's good...."

"Let's go!" said Pierre, and that decided it. Pierre's enthusiasm led our gallant band everywhere.

We took off for the theater that night, and got good seats for only 120 pesetas, the equivalent of two dollars.

The crowd bustled in. Everyone but us was dressed elegantly in black evening dresses and suits. Pierre wore his usual slacks and sweater with a white collar from his shirt underneath showing. I wore a gold blouse with a big bow tied at the neck and a brown jumper that resembled something from the *I Love Lucy* show. Pierre didn't like it. So what? The curtain of the several-centuries-old baroque theater rose, and there was a donkey on the stage with two men arguing over something. I couldn't understand very much.

"What does it mean?" I whispered in Pierre's ear.

"Shhhh!" was all I got out of him.

"Okay," I thought. *La lucha para la sombra de un burro* means the fight over a donkey's shadow. Wait a minute. I looked at the men on stage. Their fists in the air, they argued feverishly over the rental fee for one man's donkey. The donkey stood placidly on stage as if nothing were happening.

Nice donkey. But wait...they're arguing over the price of the donkey's shadow...or maybe shade? I started to laugh because it struck me funny. I heard other people laughing around me, including Pierre.

During the intermission, we got up and walked into an open-air patio where you could buy refreshments. Men and women walked amiably about, some with their arms linked, some looking up at the starry night sky. Pierre discussed the play with Jean Paul. They waved their arms in the air and gesticulated animatedly. I interrupted them, full of curiosity about the play.

"Pierre, why are they fighting over the price of a donkey's shade? You can't rent a donkey's shade!"

"It's a satire," asserted Jean Paul, our self-appointed intellectual, always suave and pensive, with a surprise waiting for us.

"They're making fun of human pettiness?" I suggested.

The theater curtain call sounded. As we walked back to our seat, Jean Paul mumbled something about "just watch the actors, Ginny," and I renewed my determination to figure out this "satire."

The red velvet curtain rose, and there stood the two men with the donkey between them again. They kept arguing, growing angrier and angrier until their fists were raised. As they circled warily around each other, the donkey off to one side, Hiroshima's mushroom cloud appeared on the wall behind them. A projector cast other frames of World War II disasters and atrocities as they began to hit each other. Picasso's famous "Guernica" painting appeared on the screen. A thrill ran through my body. This was so much more sophisticated than what I was used to in the United States. And it was so simply done, relating the everyday stupidity of men to their self-destruction on a grandiose scale.

Their eyes riveted to the stage, the rest of the audience followed the play with rapt attention.

Then the curtain fell and the applause was thunderous. I clapped until my hands hurt. Tears of emotion ran down my face. People started to stand up—a standing ovation. I stood and clapped with all my might. Pierre did the same.

After it was over we talked enthusiastically about the play. "What was Picasso's painting doing on the screen?" I wanted to know.

"Guernica was a small Spanish *pueblo* that the Nazis wiped out to a man, woman and child. Not even a donkey survived," explained Jean Paul.

"But Spain didn't fight in World War II!" I exclaimed, confused.

"The Spanish Civil War ended right before the Second World War began," explained Francois patiently. After all, I was an American and didn't know much about world history. "The Nazis practiced *blitzkrieg* on Guernica."

"What were the Germans doing in the Spanish Civil War?" My confusion was growing.

"Don't you know?"

"No. I didn't know there was a civil war in Spain. Just in the United States."

Jean Paul looked surprised. "Don't you have a degree?"

"Yes. A bachelor's in psychology from UC Berkeley." I raised my head proudly.

He raised his eyebrows, then frowned as he explained patiently, "General Franco asked Mussolini and Hitler to help him win the Spanish Civil War. He eventually even asked the Russians. He gave them the entire national treasury, all of the gold from the conquests in the New World, to pay for their soldiers and weapons."

"Oh," I said helplessly, wondering why I hadn't learned this in some course in college. World history had not been part of my psychology major, so I had never taken it, much to my regret.

We walked along the lantern-lit streets of old Madrid, its cobblestones glinting under a full moon. Nothing had been touched in this section of town for centuries. It was forbidden to tear down anything of historical value in Spain, I later learned, which was almost everything.

"Another night on the floor!" I thought. But I didn't care. I wanted to know more about the Spanish Civil War.

"Why don't we have a cognac at the Plaza del Sol?" I asked Pierre. He nodded.

"*Allez,* let's go!" said Veronique, even though it was late and she had to teach the next morning.

We jumped into our cars and headed for the Plaza, but before I could say "*arriba la fiesta,*" Pierre and Manolo stood up and started driving with their knees again. All thoughts of history and wars dissipated like so much fog in the night.

I jumped up beside Pierre and teetered a bit. I felt like I was a visiting celebrity. I waved to the people in the streets. My hair streamed in the wind away from my face. I looked at Pierre. He grinned at me. We held hands and laughed giddily. What luck to have found each other. Jean Paul was probably ducking for cover inside the car.

Suddenly I shouted, "*¡Franco es un cabrón!*", a phrase I had heard frequently. I didn't know what it meant, but it made everyone on the streets stare at us. Pierre looked at me half in surprise, half in admiration.

Then he shouted, "*¡Franco es un cabrón!*" Manolo echoed the same thing from behind with a wild look in his eyes. We drove like demons, yelling "*¡Franco es un cabrón!*" at the top of our lungs.

Pierre suddenly sat back down in his seat and motioned for me to sit down in mine. I looked at him inquisitively as a police car passed us. Why was he so worried about a ticket? He pulled into a parking space and got out of the car. The wide avenue, La Castellana, shone brilliantly. Antique lanterns on posts lit the street, whose cobblestones reflected the light in an uneven, gentle gleam.

"Pierre!" I shrilled. "I've never had so much fun."

Manolo got out of his car and came over to see what was going on.

"Geeny, we could have been arrested!" said Pierre.

"Oh, well, maybe. But we weren't hurting anyone."

"You can't yell *'Franco es un cabrón'* in Madrid! They'll put you in jail if they find out!" Pierre's voice was shrill with annoyance.

"Put us in jail?" I was perplexed.

"General Franco is a dictator," continued Pierre.

"Yes, I know." I listened patiently.

"Virginia," said Manolo patiently, softly, "My father and many of their friends spent a long time in jail for their part in the civil war. Some of them were murdered."

Wow. Jail. Murder. Manolo's father. I couldn't even imagine it. "What does *'Franco es un cabrón'* mean?'"

"It means 'Franco is a cuckold, a horny old goat.'"

"What's a cuckold?"

"Someone whose wife is unfaithful. It also means worse things."

"Oh. Well, I'll never yell it again," I said. This was not like America, I thought, or was it? The free speech movement was evolving at Berkeley right now. Friends of mine were getting arrested for holding protests for the right of free speech on the University campus. But they were not being killed. My head reeled from all of the excitement, the new ideas, the intellectual force-feeding. I felt tired.

"Let's go home," I said. Without another word, we piled back into our cars and drove back to Pierre's apartment, sitting down all the way.

☼ MOROCCO

MARIE HÉLÈNE wrapped her light summer robe around her diminutive figure and walked barefoot onto the terrace. The moon shone on her blond hair and made it gleam.

She leaned on the balustrade overlooking the garden tangled with honeysuckle, night blooming jasmine, and wisteria vines. She inhaled deeply. "How I love the smell of wisteria," she remarked, luxuriating in that evocative odor.

"Yes, it reminds me of so many things. Morocco, for example. The farm at Ouezzane...."

"Yes, the wisteria on Marc and Sifia's farm in Morocco smelled better than any on earth." She sighed deeply. "But I love this farm, too."

"Do you miss Morocco?" I asked as I stared into the depths of the tangled garden. The pungent smell of honeysuckle wafted into my nostrils. I took a deep breath of this sensual odor. Somehow everything seemed transformed tonight, more pungent, more poignant.

"It was another world, a Muslim world." She turned to me and smiled. "What did you think of Morocco, Virginie?"

"It was very mysterious, very medieval...we decided to go there for Christmas vacation. Pierre wanted me to meet his parents, since we were getting married. And me, I was ready for anything. I had never been out of Europe or the United States. North Africa held a special intrigue for me."

Marie Hélène smiled encouragement at me. I began to tell her what had happened during the five unforgettable years I was in Morocco, that almost medieval land where I received my real education.

A week before Christmas Pierre and I took off for his hometown, Rabat, the capital of Morocco. We were going to meet Jean Paul in Cadiz, an old Spanish fortress city on the Mediterranean directly across from Gibraltar. Jean Paul would give us the cook's tour of the city. Eating raw oysters at a cheap restaurant, one of Jean Paul's favorites, was to be the highlight of the tour.

"These oysters are wonderfully fresh, and they only cost ten cents a dozen," he assured us as we gazed at the beauty of the city surrounded on three sides by the sea. It was once a stronghold against marauding pirates, Moorish armies, and the many invaders of Iberia, as ancient Spain was called. Great slabs of concrete walled off the ocean and welled up into buildings, churches, and schools—a bulwark against the rough breakers of the Atlantic Ocean on one side and the Mediterranean Sea on the other. I looked out at the watery expanse of blue and thought of the endless waves crashing against this stalwart town that had lasted through so many centuries.

"America is only two centuries old," I mused. "We have such an abbreviated sense of history, of the implacability of time."

As the night fell, the stars twinkled in the heavens above us. The lights of the fortress town on the sea sparkled like tiny jewels set almost in the water. Waves smashed against the walled barrier as we looked down at the ocean from our room. Swept away by the romance of the setting, I nestled my head on Pierre's shoulder, secure in our love and plans for marriage. Everything was turning out better than I had dreamed. I had a wealthy, fun-loving fiancé and a growing sense of fulfillment.

Meanwhile, my mother kept writing about the poor Europeans, despite my description of the Moulets' wealth. "How nice that you have made a friend in Europe," she wrote. "Does he know how to drive?" She stubbornly refused to believe that anyone outside of her narrow, suburban world in the United States of 1965 could be well off. I turned to Pierre. He jumped behind the steering wheel of his Austin Mini, and Jean Paul and I got in as fast as we could. He raced through the narrow streets of Cadiz like we were on a freeway, veering this way and that to avoid collisions. Nimble and hyperactive, he always drove very fast.

I could picture him in Madrid, lining up motorcycles and then jumping over three or four at a time to show off. With his wiry body and slightly overlong arms that sometimes dangled in front of him when he hunched over, he reminded me of a chimpanzee ready to swing from the nearest vine. I chose to find these traits charming until I fell hopelessly in love with Sebastian. "*Alors,*" announced Pierre, "where is this famous restaurant you keep talking about, Jean Paul? *J'ai faim!* I'm hungry!"

Jean Paul nodded a vague acknowledgement of Pierre's complaint. He always seemed preoccupied. He inclined his lean, gaunt frame toward us, his cynical squint focused on some undiscernible object.

Maybe he is thinking about a lost love, I mused, or getting a job at the United Nations as a translator.

"The restaurant is near the port," exclaimed Jean Paul, coming out of his reverie. Jean Paul was always serious on the surface, with his manic humor lurking just beneath. "And the price is incredible! Twelve *pesetas* a dozen!" Jean Paul loved inexpensive restaurants. So did Pierre. He was really a penny pincher and rarely spent any money on me, but I assumed all of this would change after we got married. Meanwhile, I split the cost of the gasoline to his hometown in Morocco with him, willingly.

I rarely questioned my friends' ethics. After long years as the daughter of a naval officer, a navy junior whose family moved as frequently as my father's orders arrived from the Pentagon (except for the years when we lived with my grandmother to save money), I readily embraced all new friends. They would soon become my new support system, to whom I would remain loyal until our next move.

In looking back, I remembered these uprootings, often accompanied by anguished tears, like the time when the ship pulled away from the dock full of my friends waving goodbye in Pearl Harbor. In a last gesture of despair, I tossed my beautiful Hawaiian lei made of fragrant plumeria flowers onto the churning waters as the huge ship's horn blasted a last warning and pulled away from the dock. They said that if you threw a lei onto the water, you would come back someday. I fervently hoped so, especially after the boat docked in Los Angeles and the snobbish kids at University High School ignored my smiling face for a year. I attributed my lack of popularity to a sudden outbreak of acne, but really the kids were just snooty.

I looked up and saw Pierre watching me with interest. I snapped back to the present.

"I crave oysters!" I announced, even though I had never eaten an oyster in my life. "Only ten cents a dozen! I've never heard of such!" Everything was so inexpensive in Spain. We lived so well here, and for so little. Only the gas was more expensive than in the United States. Pierre had taught me the meaning of "Dutch treat." At first I was shocked that he expected me to pay my way all the time, but I quickly got used to it. I didn't mind.

Besides, once we get married, I won't have to worry, I thought, dreamily.

Pierre followed Jean Paul's directions to a small, dimly lit restaurant, a bit dingy, perhaps, but laden with the romantic atmosphere of the ocean, of countless fishermen's voyages into the perilous waters of the Atlantic Ocean to bring back our seafood suppers.

A big, burly waiter approached us, a slimy towel wrapped around his massive arm. We quickly ordered three dozen raw oysters, and he smiled knowingly, then left to get them. He brought them in a big basket and started opening them in front of us, using his toweled arm to wipe a sharp knife on. I opened my eyes in astonishment.

"Why is he doing this here?" I turned to Pierre.

"To show us they are fresh, still alive," he answered with a worldly air of omniscience.

The waiter put some of them on our plates. Jean Paul began to expertly pick them out of their shells. He squeezed some lemon juice on the meaty portion of the shellfish, and then, with an air of great satisfaction, slurped them down.

"*Ils sont bons!*" he declared, wiping his mouth on a napkin. "They're good!"

I looked down at the raw, viscous, pulpy oysters on my plate and hesitated. I had never eaten a raw oyster in the United States. The waiter hovered near me and noted my concern. With a big smile he squeezed lemon juice on a big, fat oyster. It moved a bit. My eyes widened in astonishment.

"*¡Estan vivos!*" he proudly announced. "They're alive!"

"Are we supposed to eat them alive?" I asked Pierre, incredulous.

"Of course, Geeny! That way we know they are fresh!" He went back to gulping down large quantities of oysters. Pierre's appetite, like his smile, never faltered.

"Oh, okay." I smiled gamely and pried one loose from its shell and downed it. It felt slippery and gooey, but tasted salty and deliciously tangy. With the enthusiasm of a born gourmet, I started downing as many as I could. After all, I rationalized, they were only ten cents a dozen! My bargain-loving mother would have been proud of me.

We swilled down some good white wine and felt even better.

"So you're taking the train at the crack of dawn tomorrow, eh, Jean Paul," intoned Pierre, glowing from the wine.

"*Eh, oui,*" replied Jean Paul. "I have to visit my mother for Christmas."

"And we're going to take the ferry to Tangier!" I chimed in. "To Morocco!" I glowed with happiness.

"Yes, then we have about a four-hour drive to Rabat. My parents are expecting me," said Pierre. "I sent them a telegram so that my mother wouldn't worry."

Pierre's mother had a delicate state of health, or at least of mental health, and had spent a year in a Swiss sanitarium to regain her sanity. When Pierre had visited her there, she said she didn't even want to see him.

"What made her break down?" I asked Pierre, full of curiosity.

"I don't know, Geeny. She finally regained her sanity, but the treatment cost my father a small fortune. If it had gone on much longer, it would have broken him. But he would do anything for my mother."

He looked at me for a moment with downcast eyes. They began to sparkle as he described Françoise. "My mother can be very...um," he hesitated, "what I think you call high-strung in English, but really she is a brilliant woman. She has written a book of poetry and novels and was one of the first women in Spain to receive an advanced degree at a university, a degree in Latin. She was the first woman to own a Model T in Spain. She knew Garcia Lorca!"

"Really," I replied, truly impressed. Lorca was my favorite Spanish poet, indeed, his descriptions of lithe, alabaster-skinned young men of intense passion had drawn me to Spain. Later I learned that he was homosexual and that these young men had perhaps been his lovers.

"Yes," Pierre went on, always eager to describe his family's accomplishments. "My uncle was Pedro Salinas, also a famous poet of the generation of 1927. He married Margarita, one of my aunts. My mother spent a summer with them in Santander, when Federico would come over to play the piano almost every night. He even dedicated a poem to Solita, who was just a little girl then. Lorca loved children!"

"And your mother?"

"She has always loved me very much. I'm her only child!" Pierre became almost reverent when he talked of his mother, and I realized there must be a strong bond, a very special love between them.

Françoise was not an ordinary woman, I decided, mostly due to her family's enormous wealth, but also due to her intellect and nerve, which had failed her at least temporarily. I looked forward to meeting this worldly and probably very eccentric woman.

We slept soundly at our cheap hotel that night and awakened early to catch the ferry to Tangier. The crisp ocean air smelled salty. A stiff breeze ruffled my long, now-tangled hair. The seagulls flew overhead, shrieking and fighting for food. They trailed the huge boat to eat the garbage that swirled behind it, a kaleidoscope of colors and motion. Our car was parked belowdecks. Pierre and I went inside the bar to have a drink. The boat's whistle sounded loudly and we lurched forward. My stomach lurched, too.

"I'll have a cognac," said Pierre.

The waiter looked at me expectantly. I looked back and hesitated. My stomach felt queasy. The boat was rocking back and forth. My stomach pitched with it.

"I must be seasick!" I said. "I'll have to sit this one out."

As the ferry plowed past Gibraltar through the choppy waters of the Atlantic that separated us from Tangier, I felt like vomiting.

"I'm going to be sick!" I groaned.

"Let's go out on the deck to get some fresh air," suggested Pierre. We quickly went topside, where I breathed in great draughts of exhilaratingly fresh ocean air. Effortlessly the seagulls dipped and soared gracefully above us. Then I had to throw up—over the railing. How romantic.

Soon Tangier loomed ahead of us, a white-walled city perched on the brilliant blue ocean. The sight would have thrilled me but for the bitter taste of bile that remained in my mouth. Plaintively, I looked at Pierre like a sick dog, then went over to the boat's railing and threw up again, leaning as far over as I could without falling.

Pierre stood up and followed me. "Geeny, you are not well," he exclaimed as I continued to barf over the railing, my face red and hair a tangled rat's nest.

He put his arm around my waist as soon as I stopped and led me to his car. We were packed like sardines belowdecks in a long line of cars waiting to drive off the ferry into Morocco. And I felt rotten. I slumped down in my seat and tried to sleep as Pierre drove the car off the ferry, passed customs, showed them our passports, and started the four-hour drive to Rabat. It was getting dark. Pierre was driving fast, as usual.

Suddenly I woke up with a distinct pain in my stomach. I looked over at Pierre, whose eyes were riveted to the road ahead of him.

"Pierre," I mumbled, "stop the car. I have to throw up."

Pierre screeched to a halt and I half rolled, half walked

out of the car and immediately heaved the contents of my stomach onto the dirt shoulder of the road. Pierre waited while I vomited.

"Geeny, Geeny, hurry up! My mother is expecting us!" he said, with a note of anxiety I had never heard before in his voice.

I wiped my mouth on my sleeve and nodded dully. Pierre was already gunning the engine as I clambered back into the car.

He took off at top speed. I still had to throw up. This was not seasickness. I knew it was food poisoning from the oysters.

"Pierre, Pierre, you have to stop again. I'm going to throw up!"

"Open the window, Geeny!" he shouted. "I can't stop! We're already late, and my mother will be hysterical if we're too late. She's very nervous!"

Obediently, I rolled down the window and threw up on the side of his fast-moving car. He did slow down a bit, but not much. I pulled my head back in and rolled up the window, oblivious to everything except the churning in my gut and the stench of vomit. I slumped into a fitful slumber. One session of vomiting-out-the-car-window later, we arrived in Rabat, the capital of Morocco and Pierre's hometown. His parents were waiting for us.

Pierre embraced his mother warmly, and talked to his father. I shook hands with them woodenly, hardly even seeing them.

"Geeny is not well. *Virginie ne va pas bien,*" said Pierre in French.

I smiled feebly and nodded my head.

His parents noted my stricken condition and then quickly led me down a long hallway to an enormous bedroom. They whispered something in French and left me to sleep in peace.

The next morning I got up to go to the bathroom, still feeling sick to my stomach, swearing to myself I would never eat another oyster as long as I lived. Slowly an enormous man's shadow, a veritable hulk, rounded the corner, and I heard Pierre's father say, "What a glorious morning!" with a German accent. Big Tilman, as Pierre's father was often called, was in the best of spirits. Then a pair of very blue eyes met mine and I smiled despite my upset stomach. A mountain of a man smiled down at me.

Pierre's father was German, or had been until the French conquered Alsace-Lorraine, the region of Germany his family had lived in. It became part of France overnight when General Vichy signed the Treaty of Versailles in 1917. Not long after that, massive land grants were offered to any Frenchman who wanted to go to Morocco, then a protectorate, or colony, of France.

Tilman and his brother Marc took off and staked a claim of one thousand acres, where they planted orange trees and built a farmhouse. The farm flourished. Tilman went to the University of Algiers to study agriculture. There he met and courted Françoise, the daughter of a well-known immigrant from Spain who had amassed a vast fortune in Algeria in factories, apartment buildings, and farms.

Françoise was as small, fragile, and dark as Tilman was tall, robust, and blond. She was high-strung and nervous, Tilman easygoing, with a good sense of humor and solid nerves. She often wrung her hands nervously while talking, as her dark eyes darted nervously about. Tilman was as solid as the Rock of Gibraltar. He rarely moved. Françoise and Tilman were thus well suited emotionally, each making up for the other's strengths and weaknesses. Tilman also invested her money skillfully. Françoise had inherited a small fortune from her father, who had died a few years before she married.

When Françoise got tired of living on Tilman's farm in Ouezzane, a remote province in Morocco near the Rif Mountains, she sold one of the apartment buildings she had inherited and they started their antique store, Art et Style, in Rabat. Business boomed, and they rented one of the most elegant apartment flats in Rabat for the sum of seventy-five dollars a month. Rabat, like all the capitals of Europe, had rent control, so, twenty-five years later, they still paid a trifling sum for a magnificent apartment. In Europe, you rented with the intention of staying for many years, secure in the knowledge that your rent would not be raised.

Tilman also designed expensive homes, which he sold at a profit to Europeans and Americans who resided in the capital of Morocco. He contracted local help, which he paid only a dollar a day. I soon learned the Moroccan laborers were eager to work for him because wealthy Moroccans paid even less, or nothing at all. Some just fed their workers and gave them used clothing. Tilman had his gardener dig a swimming pool for one of the estates. It took Ahmed an entire year to finish the pool, but Tilman didn't care. He was never in a hurry, unlike his nervous wife. These houses were called villas in Rabat, which was appropriate for the lavish structures surrounded by high, thick walls that usually had broken glass stuck in the top to discourage thieves. When caught, the beatings they received at the hands of the police discouraged them even more.

Breakfast was a real challenge for me that first morning, not so much because of my queasy stomach, but mainly because of the pearly white tablecloth on which I kept dripping the thick, rich, blackberry jam. I was used to plastic place mats in the United States...and the jam was so good! But every time I attempted to take a bite of toast, the jam spilled onto the tablecloth.

"¡Lo siento mucho! I'm sorry!" I said to Françoise, who spoke her parents' native Spanish as well as French, the language of her culture, the official language of Morocco and Algeria during the French occupation.

"Tilman makes wonderful marmalade," my mother-in-law-to-be confided in me. "Don't worry about the tablecloth. One of the maids will wash it." She always talked as if she were telling you something meant only for you. Her warmth was infectious, and I smiled into her dark brown eyes, crinkled with a mature charm, the charm of a woman of the world who knew when to attract and when to repel with equal dignity.

Her hairdo was unique. She had small, curly fringe bangs, and then the rest of her hair was swept from the back toward the front to hide a small bald spot on the top of her head. It created an unusual effect, but it suited this woman dressed for breakfast in an elegant gold-and-orange dress with a large pearl necklace. Her attire and mannerisms were refined to the point of seeming affected, especially if she got nervous, which she frequently did.

Later on in the day, she took me aside and sat me down opposite her in their opulent living room full of Empire and Louis XV and XVI French antiques and the most stunning chandelier I had ever seen. We sat on white and gold brocade arm chairs with a delicate mahogany tea table between us, but we didn't drink tea. Françoise had more important things to do—she had to tell me about their life in Morocco.

"We imported the chandelier from Venice," Françoise stated with pride. "The craftsmen there are the best." She paused, then gave me a penetrating look. "Of course, we must leave because of the Arabs. We will not be able to take everything with us." She showed no particular emotion. Apparently this was something she had accepted.

"Where are you going?" I asked. Pierre hadn't mentioned that his parents were leaving Morocco.

"To the farm in Spain," she informed me with her austere dignity. "Tilman and I are building a house, a villa, on some of our land near the farmhouse."

"And Pierre?"

"He will come with us, of course," she intoned. There was no hesitation in her confident voice.

"Oh," I commented, my mind a blank. I had never talked to anyone this regal. I didn't know how to react.

Then she took my hand in hers and looked intently at me. I met her gaze, wondering what this was all about.

"Virginia," she said in Spanish, as I had not yet learned to speak French, "I do not love my son." She stared at me intently.

My eyes widened. "Really?"

"I adore him!" She spoke with the conviction of a woman used to speaking her mind with ease and confidence, even if what she said was shocking or disagreeable, a rich woman used to money and the privileges accompanying it.

Her resolute declaration stunned me momentarily. My mother had never told me she loved me, and here was a woman who told me, a near stranger, that she adored her son. I couldn't fathom why she would say such a thing, but I knew one thing: Françoise was a woman who would never hide her feelings from me or anyone. Here was a woman to contend with, a woman of spirit, a woman unlike any I had ever met. I enjoyed her honesty, her strong will, and chalked anything unusual up to her mental break a few years ago.

I felt she was probably still a bit unbalanced. I would handle her with care.

"Virginia," she continued, "I must warn you."

I looked politely into her eyes, now serious with discretion.

"People outside of Muslim countries do not know their culture, so I must tell you. They still buy their brides here. There is a bride price established, and the groom must give that to the bride's family. If she wants a divorce, she cannot keep her own children. The men have all the rights."

"What happens to a divorced woman?" Now I was concerned.

"She must go back to her family and her family must give the husband back everything he paid for her: sheep, camels, gold and silver jewelry, everything."

We looked at each other somberly for a moment. The idea of women being bought and sold stunned me into silence.

My mother-in-law put her hand on my arm and whispered into my ear, "Never marry in Morocco, Virginia."

Before I had time to ask her about my marriage to Pierre, my enterprising husband-to-be arrived.

Pierre came into the room and started to straighten the bed he had made last night on the authentic Empire-style living room sofa. I realized that these were true antiques, some of them dating back to the seventeenth century. While my family had busied themselves trying to acquire tasteless new furniture (and plastic flowers, which I hated), the Moulets reveled in the old, the antique, the authentic. This pleased me immensely. It felt solid. It felt right.

Pierre's father entered the room and laughed at him.

"Make your bed in the bedroom with Virginie, Pierre!" he guffawed, a teasing look in his eyes.

Pierre's face flushed. We exchanged startled looks.

"Oui, papa," he replied, his head turned away in embarrassment.

I smiled in spite of myself. "Of course, he should." I declared. "After all, we're engaged to be married."

Pierre dutifully gave his sheets to the maid and moved his things into his room.

His parents' open-mindedness about our affair astounded me. I felt accepted and unashamed. These people were worldly. My parents would have died before they let me sleep in the same room with Pierre under the same roof as them.

In fact, they put us in separate bedrooms when we went to California to get married. They also refused to give us a wedding because Pierre's mother was Spanish. They considered him a foreigner, an outsider, and too dark for us, even though he was white. He had a "suspicious" blood line, and also they wanted to punish me for landing such a rich husband, a foreigner, whom they normally enjoyed looking down on. They couldn't do this with Pierre, who was richer than they. So they decided he wasn't white enough for them in order to snub us and to feel better about their own lack of education, travel, and world knowledge. Also, in their circles, if you weren't "lily white," people looked down on you. You lost points in the status game.

"But Pierre is white!" I protested to my mother.

He doesn't look like we do," she had snipped, her chalky-white brow furrowed and angry.

I was used to my mother's almost unbelievably small mind, and didn't answer back. It was useless anyway. To find the opposite attitude in Pierre's parents was liberating. I basked in an acceptance I had never felt in my own biological family.

Pierre sat on the bed and gave me a funny look.

"What's the matter, *cheri*?" I asked.

His cheeks suddenly bulged as he if were about to throw up, and he turned a bit red in the face.

"You're not...."

He bolted from the room and made it to the bathroom just in the nick of time. It was the oysters' revenge.

Later on in the day, when he was feeling better, Pierre brought a large, original oil painting into the living room.

"My parents want to give your parents a gift," he explained.

I looked at him curiously, then at the painting. It was a splendid portrait painted in the grand style, reminiscent of Rembrandt. The artist had chosen a handsome Arab as his subject.

"Heidekoper is a Dutch artist who lived and painted in Morocco for a long time," continued Pierre. "His works are on display at the Haye."

"The Haye?"

"That is the national art gallery in Holland." Pierre looked at the portrait with reverence.

The painting was of a dark-skinned Arab, but the brown tones the artist had chosen were luminous. The portrait was magnificent. I knew it was very valuable. Then I thought of my parents narrow-mindedness, their racist attitude. I shook my head.

"Pierre, I love the painting, but my parents don't appreciate art." I thought of the pictures of mountains and lakes in our house in which the snow sparkled like bright confetti. The skies were bright blue and there was no subtlety of hue or evidence of real artistry. "They will just see a picture of a dark Arab and sneer at the color of his skin. They would never hang a picture like that in their home."

"What is wrong with your parents?" asked Pierre, astounded. "This is a valuable painting."

"They are very narrow-minded, Pierre. They've never traveled. All they know is what they see on television and what their friends consider important. They're small-minded."

"What about this painting by Heidekoper?"

"Tell your parents thank you very much, but it would be a waste to give it to people who can't appreciate its beauty."

"Are all Americans like this?" Pierre could hardly believe what I was saying.

"No, not all of them," I said quietly.

Pierre looked at me thoughtfully, then placed Heidekoper's masterpiece against one of the armchairs.

I forgot about the incident, although I thought it was nice that his parents would want to give mine a present.

Our stomachs recovered, and Pierre took me to Club Equestre, the horseback riding club that he and all of his friends belonged to. They had grown up riding horses, playing tennis, going boating. This was a new world for me!

A Moroccan dressed in shabby but comfortable European pants and a shirt saddled an old, trusted horse for me.

Monsieur Piet, the aged and fabulously wealthy president of Club Equestre, laughed when Pierre told him about my lack of expertise.

"Don't worry," he said. "Avril only runs away once a year, on her birthday!" His wizened hand motioned toward the old horse the Moroccan stablehand had saddled.

Everyone laughed, and then Pierre changed his mind.

"Take off the saddle," he ordered the stablehànd. "Geeny, I'm going to teach you to ride bareback."

"Bareback?" I said, incredulous.

"You'll learn balance that way," said Pierre. "I'll hold the horse in a steady gait with a long rope."

He took the horse by a loose bridle and led it to the corral with me following. I wore some borrowed horseback riding boots and an old pair of blue jeans. I had never ridden anything but amusement park ponies in the United States, but as usual I feared nothing. Tedium scared me, but not riding bareback.

"She should have a riding hat," Monsieur Piet frowned at Pierre.

"We'll buy her one in Spain," said Pierre, nonchalantly. "I'm just going to teach her to ride without a saddle now, for balance."

We walked to an empty space in the corral to conduct my "lesson." Pierre helped me onto the horse's back. I sat high and looked out over the countryside. Green eucalyptus trees hemmed in the club like silent sentinels. It had just rained, so everything had turned a gentle hue of green in this semi-arid country. The weather was crisp. Nestled on the Atlantic Ocean behind fortress walls, Rabat was humid, not at all a desert, and tended to be foggy in the evenings and resembled California. The Sahara Desert was further south, past the high Atlas Mountains, where we planned to spend New Year's skiing.

Pierre gave the horse a swat on its rear end. Avril started loping around him in a large circle, guided by the long rope he held loosely. The big animal surged beneath me. I bobbed up and down on its back like a cork in the ocean.

"No, no, Geeny, not like that!" shouted Pierre. "You must hold the horse tightly with your thighs and follow its movements."

I obediently squeezed Avril with my thighs, although I doubt that the horse noticed. It did stabilize my posture, and soon I was not "bobbing" so objectionably.

"That's better!" exhorted Pierre. "Now, *au trot.*"

The horse started moving faster. I squeezed the big creature harder with my thighs. My body swayed agreeably in time with Avril's gentle trot, and it seemed pretty easy. After a few turns *"au trot,"* Pierre announced *"au gallop."* The horse started to gallop in circles. I squeezed it as hard as I could and synchronized the undulations of my pelvis with the big animal's movements. Then Pierre gave Avril a gentle flick of the whip and the beast leaped forward.

"Not so fast!" I yelled.

"Just squeeze with your thighs, Geeny!"

"Goddamit, Pierre, I...."

The ground hit hard and everyone looked at me. Pierre laughed. I was too angry to feel any pain.

"You bastard, fucking asshole...shit!" I yelled at the top of my lungs. My body reverberated from the fall, but my fairly well endowed ass had cushioned the blow.

"Geeny, watch your language!" said Pierre, shocked.

I got up, brushed myself off, and walked over to him.

"Screw you!" I said.

Pierre registered shock and embarrassment in front of his friends. Here he had thought he was going to show off his American fiancée, and I had put on a bad show. He was furious.

"Geeny, you can't talk like that here!"

"Oh, yeah? Who says I can't?" I stalked toward the stables. I had had enough.

"You were doing very well. You should have kept going!"

I turned and confronted him and the horse, which ate grass nearby, contented as a cow. They both looked at me balefully. "Damn it, Pierre! I've never ridden a horse in my life, much less bareback. What do you think I am, a gymnast?"

"Maybe you need lessons," Pierre's tone softened.

"Maybe I do!"

Suddenly, a huge commotion arose as a Rolls Royce with an entourage of Moroccan military cadets on motorcycles arrived in front of the club. All of the Moroccans ran to the front of the club and prostrated themselves on the ground. The Europeans who had been sitting at the bridge table inside the club stood up and stared nervously at the sight.

"Stand up straight, Geeny!" Pierre grabbed me and brushed the dirt from the seat of my jeans where I had hit the ground.

"Why?"

"It's the king! If he comes this way, bow!"

"Bow? How do you bow?"

Pierre pushed me roughly from the waist and I executed an involuntary bow.

"Wait a minute! I'm an American citizen! I don't have to bow!"

"Geeny, everyone bows before the king. He is all powerful in this country. He takes what he wants from our store for the palace and says it's taxes."

"That's outrageous!"

Suddenly, an impressive man dressed in horseback-riding clothes, elegant with white jodhpurs and a black riding crop, appeared on a pure white stallion. His handsome brown face smiled at me, and I smiled back. Then I bowed briefly and watched him trot by, accompanied by his cadets.

Thrilled to the core of my being, I shouted, "Pierre! A real king!" Head still bowed, Pierre looked at me out of the corner of his eye. Then he slowly raised his head and put his arm around my waist. He steered me toward the clubhouse.

"You must be careful, Geeny."

"Why?"

"If you act too eager, the king may request your presence in his palace, alone."

"You couldn't come with me?"

"And I might never see you again."

"Oh," I responded, not believing him.

People ran about excitedly talking in French and Arabic.

I couldn't understand a word of what they were saying, but I knew it was about the king.

"What are they saying?" I asked Pierre.

He took his arm from my waist and smiled at me. "We're invited to his birthday party at his summer palace."

"Do you think we'll get to go?"

"It's not until this summer. Perhaps, if we're back from America in time."

Forgetting about the incident with the horse, I threw back my head and laughed, then hugged Pierre.

"Let's go!"

Pierre smiled at me. "If we're here, we'll go."

I could hardly wait. This would be an event more exciting than getting married, I concluded, silently.

The clubhouse took on a surreal aspect. I felt like the world was so wonderful that I would burst. That night before going to sleep, Pierre groped for me under the covers and we made love. It was over in the blink of an eye, something I was getting used to. I thought of the horseback riding incident. It reminded me of his impatience in bed. *Allez, au trot, au gallop,* boom! All fall down. I reminded myself of his basic human goodness, his kind heart; besides, we planned to spend a year traveling through Europe, the United States, Mexico....Our goal was to work a bit in the U.S. and then make it around the world, stopping in Thailand to visit our good friend Alex from London. I pushed any pessimistic thoughts out of my mind, turned over, and went to sleep.

We had a wonderful Christmas vacation in this exotic but also oppressive land. Pierre and I continued to make plans for our trip to the United States.

✡ THE FARM IN OUEZZANE

THE FEEBLE EARLY MORNING LIGHT filtered into our bedroom through the slatted window shutters. I dimly perceived an eerie, undefinably beautiful wail. A strong and persistent lament, it sent shivers through me. Even though it was only six o'clock in the morning and I was a stubborn sleeper, I got up and went out onto the balcony of our bedroom to hear better. The wailing, soulful cry persisted. I listened for a while, then climbed back into bed with Pierre. When we both woke up, I asked him what I had heard.

"That was the *imam*, the holy man who calls the Islamic people to worship each morning, Geeny," he explained drowsily.

"You mean they go to church at six in the morning?"

"To the mosque."

"Why?"

"To pray to Allah."

"They must be crazy!"

"No, just Muslim. They are very religious, Geeny."

"I'll say!"

Pierre started to fumble under my nightgown, but I was too quick for him this morning. I bounded out of bed and dressed quickly, putting on light-green culottes and a pale-peach blouse.

"I'm going for a walk before breakfast," I announced.

"Don't take too long!"

"Don't worry!"

Venturing through the central part of Rabat, I found clean streets lined with well-trimmed orange trees. There were high walls surrounding most of the buildings, blocking one's view of the interior courtyards. At the foot of one sat a man swathed in a burnoose, a voluminously loose garment that covered his entire body. His arm outstretched, he chanted in what I thought must be Arabic. He also wore the traditional turban, a cloth wrapped around his head. Squinting up at me in the sun, his grizzled face broke into a smile.

When I left for Spain in 1965, the United States did not have beggars, or street people as they are now called. I dutifully opened my purse and put a *dirham*, a Moroccan coin worth about twenty cents, into his begging bowl. He nodded his head and chanted something. Maybe he was asking Allah to be good to me! I smiled at him and he smiled back.

"He's nice," I thought.

Well-kept and orderly shops flanked the sidewalk for the next few blocks. A wide avenue with a huge mosque at the end caught my eye, and I turned onto it. Silent Moroccan women passed me wrapped like mummies in their grey *jallabahs* with caftans underneath. They were discreet and mysterious. Most, but not all of them, wore veils. Perhaps they had been praying, I surmised, but I was not sure. I could not speak to them because of my lack of French and Arabic. They seemed not to notice me, so I kept walking.

I knew the Moulets' antique shop, Art et Style, was straight ahead on Avenue Allal ben Abdullah, so I walked until I came to it. Small but bursting with furniture covered with rich, vividly hued velvets and shimmering mahogany tables, chairs, china cabinets, and occasional pieces, it gleamed like a jewel. Half a block from their opulent store, another beggar held out his hand. This man wore a white European shirt and Western-style pants. No turban. Dishevelled but not dirty, he looked somehow debonair in his modern clothes. His face was a light brown color. His brown eyes sparkled as he smiled at me. Something that resembled graffiti caught my attention. It was something written in Arabic script almost directly above his head. I looked at the curiously formed letters. His eyes followed mine. He started to try to erase it with his bare hands.

I grinned and shook my head. He looked contrite, then grinned back at me.

I opened my purse and searched for some more *dirhams*, but I didn't have any. I looked at him apologetically and said, "I'm sorry. I only have American money. Would you accept a dollar?" I pulled a dollar bill out of my wallet to show him.

He nodded his head enthusiastically and said, "Thank you!"

"You speak English!" I was surprised.

"Yes, speak English," he replied. "You visit *le Maroc*?"

"Um, yes," I answered, fascinated by this initial contact with a real Moroccan beggar. Always on the prowl for new experiences, I liked this man instantly.

"I'm visiting my fiancé's parents! They're very rich. They own that antique store!" I pointed to Art et Style a half a block away.

He looked surprised and pointed down the block, "That store? That store over there, *mademoiselle*?" he asked eagerly.

"Yes, it's called Art et Style," I replied, happy to have something to talk about. That he was a beggar made no difference to me.

"Can I go by there?" he asked, politely.

"Yes! They have lots of money!" I enthused.

He smiled at me and we shook hands. I left feeling elated. I had made a friend, a Moroccan friend!

Breakfast was on the table when I returned. I took my seat and started heaping marmalade on my toast.

Then I turned to Françoise, my mother-in-law-to-be. "I just met the nicest beggar," I said in Spanish, the only language we had in common, as I could not yet speak French.

"*Quoi*? What! A beggar!" Françoise spilled some of her coffee nervously. "You didn't give him anything, of course!"

"Well, just a dollar..."

Françoise said something to Tilman in French and they began to laugh heartily. I wondered what was so funny.

Pierre translated for me. "They are laughing because you gave a whole dollar to a beggar. They would be angry with you if you weren't so naive."

"But he spoke English and he knew where your shop was...."

Françoise, Tilman and Pierre exchanged amused looks.

"Now he will come there everyday to ask us for money, Virginie! These people are relentless! You must beware of them!"

My vision of the friendly Moroccan beggar melted slowly as Françoise recounted horror stories about beggars. They crippled their children from birth so they could become professional beggars, they stole from each other...some were leprous....

"But this man was really nice!" I insisted.

Françoise looked at me with a distinct air of superiority. She ran her hand along the back of her eccentric coiffure, then declared, "*Sal race!* The Arabs are a filthy race. The scourge of the earth." I blinked at her in disbelief. She saw my doubt and redoubled her efforts to convince me that the Arabs were the worst people on earth. I looked at the curly black hair fringing her face, her olive-hued complexion, and thought, She looks a lot like an Arab. Is this why she is criticizing them so vehemently? Worse, her racist remarks reminded me of things my mother had said about blacks. I put down my napkin on the table and excused myself.

As I left the room, I heard Françoise say, "*Elle est Americaine. Elle n'en sait rien.* She is American. She knows nothing." I ran into the bedroom and buried my head in my pillow. Pierre followed me and tried to explain.

"Geeny, you must be careful. These people might try to take advantage of your naiveté."

"He was really nice, Pierre, you don't understand!"

I didn't want to listen to advice. I wanted to live, to experience, not to judge and recoil from life. Experience would be my teacher and damn the consequences. I would find out for myself.

The next day Pierre took me to the Arab market place, the *medina.* He showed me schools where the children sat chanting on the floor in front of the teacher.

"They are learning the Koran, Geeny. That is all they teach in these schools."

"Hmm," I muttered, refusing to comment.

Then he led me through the crowded *medina*. This Arab market place, which dated from before Christ, bristled with life. The passageway was too narrow for cars, but men and women in caftans and burnooses hastened past me. Children ran after their veiled mothers. Beggars adorned the entrance. These particular beggars had their legs turned under them. They had been crippled at birth in order to beg, Pierre informed me.

"Your mother already told me about them," I snapped, coldly. Once was enough.

Donkeys laden with vegetables, spices, caftans, and other commodities lurched down the narrow alleyway until we turned into an alleyway littered with brightly colored stalls with caftans, bronze pots and pans, and an occasional animal carcass in front of a butcher's stall that beckoned us to enter. Life teemed abundantly in this richly populated microcosm, this ancient marketplace.

My heart beat with anticipation at every turn. The women walking silently by in caftans intrigued me. They looked quickly at me, then away. What must they be thinking? Some wore their veils just below their nostrils.

"How come they're wearing their veils like that?" I asked.

"Probably so they can breathe better, Geeny," said Pierre, as he propelled me toward some brightly colored spices laid out like a painter's palette next to one another. The rich aroma of saffron reached my nose. My senses mutinied under the assault of such a riot of color and smell. I felt a bit giddy.

"Some of these are poisonous," intoned Pierre. "You must be careful."

"Hmmm..." I hated caution. "Pierre, I love it here! It's so different from Europe or the United States!" I felt like Alice in Wonderland—like I had just stepped through the looking glass into a totally new and exciting world.

We entered a crude shop full of children weaving brightly colored Moroccan rugs. The colors transfixed me.

"These children are orphans, Geeny," continued Pierre. "They must do this for a living. Otherwise they will not be fed."

"Nice rugs," I commented. "The children are learning a trade that will help them in life, aren't they?"

Pierre frowned and led me to an open space where various merchants displayed their wares, including a fellow with some human teeth on a piece of cloth on the ground. Above him hung a sign with pliers and a tooth on it.

"Look at these teeth, Geeny." Pierre pointed to a grimy carpet and I looked intently at the rather grisly assemblage of teeth.

"They all have roots." Pierre picked one up. I winced. It was yellowed, and there was still a blood stain on it. The Moroccan "dentist" smiled at us. "He doesn't show the ones without roots. The ones where the whole tooth wouldn't come out and the roots were left impacted in the mouth to fester and decay. The poor people have no choice but to go to this man when they have a toothache."

"I see," I muttered. My stomach felt queasy again. I looked away from the gritty carpet with its dubious advertisement of dental hygiene to a more appetizing display. I saw caftans hanging outside of a shop—deep blue, green, purple—gorgeous velvet caftans that a princess would be proud to own. A plump, smiling young Moroccan woman hovered just inside the doorway. I spotted a particularly beautiful caftan and she grinned at me.

"Let's go in there!" I left the display of teeth and entered into a world of rich velvet gowns trimmed with gold and silver embroidery. They were beautiful. The plump, smiling woman approached me.

"*Bonjour, mademoiselle,*" she said.

I shook my head. "I can't speak French. I'm sorry."

She smiled even more broadly. "I speak English. I spent a year in Switzerland, where I learned English. My name is Khadija."

"Really? You have traveled?"

"Yes. Not all Moroccan women stay at home." She and I exchanged approving looks as Pierre walked in, scratching his head, wondering what to do with his headstrong American fiancée.

"Pierre, this is Khadija," I exclaimed. They shook hands.

"*Enchanté,* nice to meet you," said Pierre. He walked over to a rack of velvet caftans and began to finger the material. Pierre could not resist appraising another merchant's wares. Khadija smiled and rubbed her hands together.

"Pierre, I want a caftan!"

Khadija held up a gorgeous royal-purple one trimmed with exquisite gold braid. Her dimpled face lit up with a radiant smile.

"Geeny, these are very expensive," he said, plaintively.

"How much are they?" I asked Khadija.

"One thousand and forty *dirhams.* They are of the finest...."

"We have to look in some other shops," Pierre interjected quickly, tugging me by the hand. I looked back at Khadija as she watched me leave with regret.

Pierre steered me to another shop full of cheaper caftans, cotton and nylon ones.

"Why don't you pick out one of these, Geeny?" he asked. He smiled his gregarious, infectious grin.

I smiled back. A cornflower-blue caftan with a white embroidered trim around the neckline and down the front caught my eye. I picked it up.

The shop owner eyed me, then approached me anxiously. "Fifty-five *dirhams, mademoiselle,*" he said. That was about fifteen dollars. He hovered over me as I fingered the cloth. It was made of slick, cheap cotton.

Pierre gave me an apprehensive look. I tried it on. It slid easily over my hips and looked very nice. It wasn't made of velvet, but the color made my eyes look very blue.

"What do you think, Pierre?" I turned and smiled at my erstwhile fiancée. He fingered it and frowned.

"*Douze dirhams,* twelve *dirhams,*" he said to the shop owner.

A pained look distorted the shop owner's thin face, as if he had just sucked on a very sour lemon.

"I'm sorry, *monsieur.* This caftan is very well made. Just look at the fine embroidery." He paused and smiled at us, an unctuous smile, but it was better than the sour lemon look. I smiled back, hopefully.

Pierre frowned at me. "Geeny, don't smile! He'll raise the price."

"*Quatorze dirhams*," said the shop owner.

"*Treize*," said Pierre, stubbornly. Thirteen.

I looked anxiously at the merchant, trying not to show that I wanted that caftan. He read my face and held fast to his bargaining price. "*Quatorze dirhams*," he insisted. Fourteen *dirhams*.

"Pierre, that's only about twelve or thirteen dollars," I interjected. The shop owner rubbed his hands together in anticipation. He could almost feel those *dirhams*.

"Geeny, don't interrupt me when I'm bargaining!" Pierre raised his voice an octave and looked truly vexed with me this time. "*C'est trop haut.* It's too much." He abruptly turned and walked out of the store. I followed, reluctantly. I wanted the cornflower blue caftan!

"But Pierre, it's so pretty. I'll pay for it! Just..."

"Geeny, that isn't the point. You always leave and then come back to get the price you asked for."

"What if they won't give it to you?"

"This is the way things are done here, Geeny. This is not the United States." His big, sweet eyes begged me to understand.

"Okay. It's not like America. But that's an awfully pretty dress for just twelve dollars or so."

"Geeny, you are too frivolous."

"Why? Because I want a dress? Can't I bring home a souvenir of this country? Can't I wear it to parties?"

"No, Geeny, you don't understand. We have to get the right price." Pierre's eyes implored me to listen, to understand his way of doing things. As usual, impatience overtook me. I didn't want to understand. I wanted the cornflower-blue caftan.

"Let's go back, Pierre! I really want that dress! Please. I'll pay."

"Geeny, we're going to go back."

I smiled at him. "Then let's go!" I slipped back into the store and said without hesitation, "Fourteen *dirhams!*"

The merchant understood my English and started wrapping the caftan with the pretty white embroidery in tissue paper for me. He grinned broadly.

"Geeny, this is when you lower the price, when you go back." Pierre groped for words. He paced back and forth nervously as the shop owner quickly wrapped the caftan.

"Oh. Well, we got it for fourteen *dirhams!* Isn't that good enough?"

It was hopeless. I could care less about the difference of a *dirham* or two, and Pierre staked his honor on it. An impasse stood between us. The merchant handed me the caftan and I thanked him.

"*Baraka,*" I said as deferentially as possible. That was the only Arabic word I knew.

The store owner's eyes lit up and he bowed deeply to me. My heart accelerated as a thrill coursed through my being. Pierre smiled at my childish delight and heaved a deep sigh—of relief, I thought, or maybe resignation. I smiled back at him and kissed him. The impasse was over. But from that day on he said I was heedless.

That evening I proudly put on the caftan to wear to a party at Club Equestre, the horseback riding club. From behind one of the younger men at the party, Michelle, one of Pierre's friends, who was wearing a *decolté*, a low cut, tight-fitting European dress, came up to me. She fingered my caftan rudely.

"Just cotton, eh, Virginie..." she said.

"It is a beautiful cotton!" I replied. I held my head high and felt very elegant. I looked at the other women, all dressed to the nines in black silk evening dresses and elegant crepes. I didn't care. Once I had acquired something, I stubbornly preferred it. I never compared it or myself to anything or anyone else. What for?

I usually got what I wanted, and once I had it, treasured it for years to come. Pierre looked at me and I smiled at him. I was that way with men, too.

Actually, I just wanted to get married and not have to worry about finding a husband, dressing in a particular way or trying to please a man ever again. And with Pierre I thought I had it all.

The next morning dawned crisp and clear, much like any other day in Rabat. The climate reminded me of Santa Barbara, warm and sunny. The orange tree-lined streets of Rabat were clean and elegant. The city spun around a big traffic roundabout full of small European cars, rich Moroccans in Mercedes Benzes, tiny taxi cabs that would take you anywhere in the city for a quarter, and donkey carts that all swirled around the hub of the city and then got off on one of the tributary streets. Past the imposing official government buildings built of granite inlaid with mosaic designs whirled this kaleidoscope of vehicles. Most of the buildings had brass Arabic letters on them. On the surface, Rabat appeared to be an agreeable mixture of French and Moroccan architecture and culture.

I stretched lazily next to Pierre and looked at the clear sky. He turned over and smiled at me. "We're going to the farm today."

"Oh? What farm?"

"The farm in Ouezzane my father and his brother started many years ago. I lived on it until I was eight, when my mother got tired of the country and they decided to come to Rabat and start the shop."

I sat up and slid out of bed into my bedroom slippers. "I thought you only had a farm in Spain."

"No. This is the one my uncle Marc lives on with his Moroccan wife, Sifia, and my cousins, Lassan and Marguerite. Marguerite is marrying a French civil servant next month."

"You never told me about them."

"We don't see them that often. But we'll spend the night there tonight. So get ready!"

Amina, Françoise's Berber maid, who arrived every morning at eight-thirty dressed in a traditional caftan and long, elegant black gloves, served the *cafe au lait*, toast, and marmalade. I smelled the rich mocha coffee (the best, according to Françoise) and inhaled deeply. I loved the smell of coffee better than the taste, but then I was American, and I hadn't acquired French tastes yet.

Françoise leaned forward and smiled graciously. I knew this meant she was going to divulge something interesting. She didn't disappoint me.

"We're going to the farm," she said, as if telling me a state secret. "That is where Pierre was born."

"Oh?"

"France gave away land after they became the protectorate of Morocco in 1912. It was after World War I when my husband and his brother Marc became French citizens, so they came to Morocco and claimed 1,000 acres. We met later at the University of Algiers when Tilman was studying agriculture."

"Why did they become French after World War I?" I asked, confused.

Françoise smiled, her slightly bucked teeth protruding as she arched her back and straightened her spine proudly. "Because they were from Alsace-Lorraine, the part of Germany that France won back in World War I."

"Won back?" I was confused. I'd never heard of Alsace-Lorraine until now.

Pierre looked at me and started to explain. "Geeny, France and Germany fought many wars over the rich valley of Alsace-Lorraine. My father was German until 1917, when, at the end of the war, the Germans had to give it back to France. So he became French automatically."

I took a drink of coffee. "The history of Europe is very complicated!"

"Yes, of course. Europe is thousands of years old," continued Pierre.

"And your uncle married a Moroccan woman?"

Françoise narrowed her eyes and Pierre explained, tactfully. "They never got married because he was Protestant and she is Muslim. They just had children together. But it is like they are married. Maybe better...since she is..." Françoise hesitated.

"Really?" I laughed. Marc and Sifia's unconventional union intrigued me. I couldn't wait to go to their farm.

I slipped into some comfortable clothes and went into the living room to wait for the others. Yellow silk brocade curtains with gold tassels, an Empire sofa covered in a lovely salmon-colored velvet, a Venetian chandelier, the thickest rug I had ever walked on, a huge Moroccan one with exquisite colors made from natural dyes, decorated the Moulets' beautiful main room. I had never seen so many exquisite furnishings outside of a museum.

"*Allez*, Geeny, we're ready to go!" called Pierre. I jumped up and we walked down the spiral staircase to the car. A lot of the wrought-iron railing of the staircase was missing. Françoise gestured toward it. "*Les Arabes*...the Arabs come and saw if off at night, piece by piece. Look. They've gotten to the second floor."

I steeled myself for more *sal race* or anti-Arab talk. But the conversation as well as the ride was pleasant. We drove inland, away from the ocean to the countryside, which was mostly arid land except for occasional rows of palm trees leading to a farmhouse and orange groves.

"The French planted all the orange groves," announced Françoise proudly, as if she had done it herself. Tilman and his brother have a magnificent grove at the farm."

I looked out the window and saw occasional burnoose-clad Moroccans on donkeys, but mostly semi-arid countryside with an occasional oasis of palm trees. After a long ride of about four hours, we arrived at the farm. The spacious, two-story white-frame farmhouse was on top of a hill. The first thing I saw was a peacock. "How gorgeous!" I said as the bird strutted about fanning its enormous blue-green plumage.

"Be careful, Geeny," admonished Pierre. "They bite."

"A peacock bites?" I couldn't believe it. Everything in Morocco had a hidden danger, according to Pierre and his mother, I thought with a trace of annoyance.

A robust, tall, balding man in remarkable shape for his age burst out of the farmhouse. Tilman walked over to his brother and they embraced heartily, thumping each other on the back. Then they started speaking in a language I couldn't understand.

"What is that?" I asked Pierre.

"German. They always speak their native language together."

"Oh."

A well-rounded, dark-haired woman with pale brown skin and pinkish cheeks came to the door and smiled. Her harem pants were covered by a pretty caftan belted at the waist by an intricately woven silver-and-gold belt. This was Sifia, his Moroccan wife. A pretty girl, about seventeen years old, who looked very Aryan with blond hair and blue eyes, stood beside her and waved. This was Marguerite, Marc and Sifia's daughter. She had her father's complexion and her mother's smooth sleekness. Pierre told me the Frenchman she was going to marry had been doing his three-month civil service internship in Ouezzane when they met.

Françoise got out of the car and shook Marc's hand, then walked over to Sifia a bit stiffly, her high heels catching in the earth beneath her feet. She looked out of place in an elegant wool suit, I thought. I was glad I had worn pants and a loose blouse. After all, this was a farm. Françoise and Sifia embraced, then bussed each other on the cheek. Françoise talked to her warmly, but I detected a sort of professional warmth, full of tact and grace and condescension. Marguerite hung back discreetly until Françoise went up and bussed her dutifully on the cheek, somewhat coldly, I thought.

Then the noise of a horse galloping up the hill distracted me. A young man rode it with a loose elegance.

"Hey, Lassan!" shouted Pierre, running over to meet his cousin. "*Comment ca va?* How's it going?"

Lassan jumped off his horse, nuzzled it affectionately, and then it loped over to where we stood. I looked at the beautiful beast in awe. Carefully groomed, its sleek, strong contours reminded me of a racehorse. Pierre jumped on its back and trotted it around the courtyard, waving and laughing at us. I waved back. Then I turned to look at Pierre's cousin, Lassan. He was handsome. He had his mother's dark hair and honeyed complexion coupled with his father's tall, lean good looks. His smile was contagious. Pierre jumped off his horse and introduced us. We laughed and shook hands.

The brothers and their wives started to walk toward the farm house, and we followed them in. The mosaic tile floors and sofas arranged on the floor with many soft, plumped-up cushions looked cool and inviting. Sifia, who spoke only Arabic, motioned for us to sit down, and we did. A maid brought us some mint tea, the traditional Moroccan tea, in a silver teapot and served it in the porcelain cups arranged on the large, round, intricately etched silver coffee table in front of us. Then she brought us a dish of water with soap and a kettle. Pierre washed his hands and then dried them with a towel offered by a second maid. We all went through this ritual, which was traditional before eating a Moroccan meal.

A huge, steaming bowl of couscous, a kind of semolina, white and soft, was placed in the middle of the round table, as well as a huge dish of steamed vegetables—yellow squash, zucchini, carrots, and garbanzo beans with big chunks of lamb and a reddish sauce called *camoon* on the side. Everyone looked at me, the American, and waited for me to serve myself. I looked at Pierre for instructions and he laughed. There weren't any serving spoons or silverware!

"Here, Geeny!" He took a bit of couscous in his hand and made a ball out of it and tossed it into his mouth. Then he picked a choice piece of meat and vegetables from the main plate and dipped them in the *camoon* sauce. "Delicious!" he proclaimed, and everyone dived in and began to eat with their fingers. I hesitated, then tried to make a ball out of some couscous, but I was too clumsy. Pierre wolfed down couscous like a pro, but Lassan gave me a sympathetic look. I smiled and he smiled back. With great refinement, he took some couscous in his hand and rolled it around a few seconds until it formed a small ball, then put it in his mouth. His dazzling smile reappeared and I nearly dropped the couscous I had been wadding into a sticky ball in my hand. I did the same and managed to get some down, although I spilled a bit in my lap. Everyone laughed at my clumsiness. I looked up for help. Suddenly Sifia clapped her hands and the maids brought out the silverware. Everyone laughed at my antics, including me. I felt very happy to be with them. "You didn't do too bad for an American!" joked Pierre.

"Just give me a fork!"

Sifia said something in Arabic, and suddenly one of her maids appeared with forks. I took one and started eating the delicious couscous with a vengeance.

Pierre looked at me and smiled. His eyes sparkled with warmth, and a dimple appeared on his cheek. I smiled back, loving his eyes, his dimple, all of him. How had I landed such a great guy? He continued to eat with his fingers, the Moroccan way. Only Tilman, Françoise, and I used silverware.

"Does it taste better that way?" I asked, trying to tease them a bit.

"Much better!" exhorted Lassan. "The oils from your hands mix with the food and form a savory mixture. That is why Moroccans eat with their hands!"

"Really?" I was always gullible.

"He's making fun of you, Geeny," said Pierre.

"Oh."

Lassan smiled at me. "Not really," he said. "It's just that foreigners often make fun of the way Moroccans eat."

I thought for an instant. "It must save money on silverware...and there are fewer dishes to wash!"

He laughed and turned to his mother, who also smiled broadly. I sensed they liked me, and I liked them for it.

Sifia must have been a raving beauty in her day, I imagined, noting her still-flawless skin and almond-shaped eyes. She was large, but very curvaceous, as much as I could tell from the caftan that she wore so gracefully.

Then Lassan put a piece of lamb in my mouth. I opened my eyes wide with surprise and chewed it up and swallowed it. Everyone laughed at me.

"Is that another Moroccan custom?" I asked, wondering what might be next.

"Yes," smiled Pierre's smooth-skinned cousin. "It is the custom to give the guests the best pieces of meat. In Saudi

Arabia, they give them the sheep's eyeballs."

"What!"

"It's true!" said Françoise, laughing throatily. "They gave them to an American diplomat, who fainted."

"What if you can't eat them? I couldn't eat anything that stared at me!"

"You have to! You have no choice. It is a big honor to be offered the sheep's eyeballs. They contain the most nutrients in the sheep."

"And if you choke on them?"

"Everyone is terribly offended, although if you don't refuse them and manage to eat them, everyone is happy—even if you faint," chimed in Lassan as he delicately popped another handful of couscous into his mouth. "But here in Morocco, we consider that custom outdated. We no longer try to force anything on our guests."

Heaving a sigh of relief, I said, "Good! What's for dessert?"

We all laughed and continued stuffing ourselves with this delicious food, especially Pierre, whose nervous energy gave him a ravenous appetite. Of course, he never gained an ounce and remained thin and wiry.

Then the maids brought out more water to rinse our hands with and, to my surprise, a bowl for rinsing out our mouths and a toothbrush! I declined to use the toothbrush and the mouth-rinsing bowl, just the hand-rinsing bowl. Marc, Sifia, Marguerite, and Lassan brushed their teeth and spat into the same little bowl. When the maids saw the shocked look on my face, they giggled and took the bowls away.

Dessert consisted of a delicately heaped pile of couscous, like a pyramid, with cinnamon and raisins, sweet couscous.

Stomachs stuffed to the limit, Pierre and I exchanged looks and nodded our heads sleepily to show one another we wanted to rest.

"Lassan," said Pierre, clapping his cousin on the back, "that was a fantastic meal. Now, if you don't mind, I'm going to take a nap in your room."

"Sure!"

"Could I take a nap in here?" I asked, looking around me at the restful, cool, tiled living room. I had my eye on one sofa in particular in the back of the room.

"You are our guest. You may do whatever you like," said Marc, graciously. "We're going out to look at the orange groves."

Françoise stood up along with Sifia, Marc, and Tilman. Françoise laced her arm through Sifia's, smiled broadly with her slightly bucked teeth, and they began to talk like old friends as they ambled out toward the orange orchards. Pierre yawned widely, then walked upstairs to take his nap. I lay down on an overstuffed sofa covered with intricately woven, brightly threaded Moroccan cloth. I closed my eyes and listened to the clucking of the chickens in the adjacent barnyard, the whinnying of the horses, and other animal sounds. I fell into a peaceful sleep.

I don't know how long I slept, but I awoke to the strangest sensation. My lips...something was pulling at my lips. Was I dreaming? I shook my head and sat up quickly. To my surprise, a calico cat bounded away. Pierre's cousins, Lassan and Marguerite, stood in front of me, laughing gently.

"What's so funny?" I asked in broken French.

"You!" Lassan announced. Marguerite kept laughing.

"Why? What happened?"

"The cat was licking honey from your lips!"

"Really? How did it get there?"

"The cat or the honey?" Lassan teased me with a sparkle in his dark, flashing eyes. He was so good looking it made me nervous. I squirmed on the sofa. I didn't want to find Lassan attractive. I was going to marry Pierre and live comfortably ever after. *Point, finale.* My mind was made up.

"Um, both." I mumbled vaguely.

"Marguerite and I put honey on your lips so the cat would lick it off."

I looked stunned, so he continued to explain.

"It's an old Moroccan custom to do that to people who take naps. Or maybe it's just a family custom."

"Oh." Then I laughed, wiping the rest of the honey off my lips with my sleeve. "Well, it's the first time I...." I looked into their smiling eyes. "It's the first time I've encountered such a delightful custom. I like cats."

"Of course. They are very wise animals. The Egyptians knew that."

"You know Egyptian history?"

"Yes. I went to high school here."

"And they teach world history?"

"Yes."

"I wish I had studied more of it in the United States."

I surveyed this handsome youth standing in front of me with his very blond sister. His already manly chest showed slightly from under his loosely buttoned Moroccan shirt, open to the mid-chest, trimmed with the delicate embroidery. The midafternoon heat, combined with Lassan's beauty, caught me off guard. "Do you ever go to Europe?" I asked, stupidly.

"Of course. My father is from France—well, the Alsace-Lorraine. It became part of France after the war with Germany. He wants me to go to school there."

"Are you going to go?"

He sat down next to me and looked into my face with his grave, beautiful countenance. "I don't know. I love the farm. I love Ouezzane. All my friends are here. My mother is Moroccan. I was captain of the soccer team in high school!" He hesitated. "But my uncle says we should sell the farm and leave for Europe. He says the Moroccans are pushing us out."

"Is this true?"

"They are encouraging us to sell our land to Moroccans. The French businesses must take a Moroccan partner or leave."

He looked down at the mosaic tile floor ruefully.

"Why hasn't Pierre told me about this?" I asked, perturbed.

"It isn't official yet." He smiled his dazzling smile again.

"What do you think?"

"I don't know what to think. I'm only eighteen years old.

I'm Moroccan. I was born here. I love my country."

"So you should stay."

"Yes, besides my parents want to stay. My father plays tennis with the local *caid*, or mayor, and he thinks they'll let us keep the farm. My mother is Moroccan. So am I. It makes sense."

Such problems never existed in the United States except perhaps during our Civil War, but I now knew that in Europe and North Africa, people had lost everything, even their lives, in wars and revolutions too numerous to count.

"Everything makes sense and nothing makes sense," I said, lying back down on the comfortable sofa.

He laughed. "You are wise."

"No. Just a bit cynical."

Lassan looked pleasantly surprised. "Really? A cynical American. They say you love apple pie and your mothers."

"And what do you think?" I smiled.

"The only one I know is you, so I guess you love couscous too," he said, half humorous, half serious.

The cat came back to inspect my mouth. We started to laugh just as Pierre came downstairs, rubbing his sleepy eyes.

"I had a great nap!" he announced. "Let's go horseback riding, Lassan!"

Lassan jumped up immediately and they ran off to saddle the horses.

"Do you want to come, Geeny?" called Pierre to me over his shoulder.

I petted the cat, now content to curl up in my lap. "No, thanks. I've had enough horseback riding for a while." I stood up and walked slowly to the doorway with Marguerite to watch them laugh and joke as they saddled the horses. They jumped into the saddles and reared the horses up in front of me.

"Just like in the American westerns? Eh, Geeny?" said Pierre.

"Yes, just like in the movies," I answered drowsily. Pierre smiled and galloped off toward the green orange groves. "He's showing off for me," I thought, pleased.

I turned to Marguerite. "Will you live in France when you're married?"

"Yes, near the outskirts of Paris."

"Won't you miss the farm?"

"Yes," she said. She looked away, then smiled at me shyly. I started to say something, but she turned and darted out the door.

Instead of following Marguerite, I spotted one of the comfy-looking low sofas with plenty of cushions. I nestled down among them to continue my nap. The cat that had licked honey off my lips came over and joined me, curling up neatly on my tummy. We dozed off peacefully.

☼ THE DOWRY

GIBRALTAR LOOMED LARGE and implacable, just like in the insurance advertisements, as the ferry crossed the Strait of Gibraltar back to Algeciras, Spain. Pierre and I watched it pass in the clear, icy-blue waters of the Atlantic. Gibraltar has been a strategic piece of geography for hundreds of years. Whoever controlled Gibraltar, controlled the Mediterranean. I watched it go by. Pierre adjusted his brown leather jacket and scarf more tightly. A cold Atlantic wind raked the top deck.

"Were there lots of pirates and renegades in these waters a few hundred years ago?" I mused.

"The Phoenicians, the pirates of Carthage, the Moors, the English—just about everyone who pillaged the coasts of what are now Spain, France, and North Africa passed through the Strait of Gibraltar."

"Were there any noteworthy exceptions? Like us?"

Pierre smiled at me. We were almost the same height, so he always looked me directly in the face. It was a comfortable distance. "Not anyone as happy as us."

"Oh, good! I like to be different!"

We laughed. The ferry ploughed through the choppy waters, but I didn't feel the least bit seasick this time. I vowed I would never eat another oyster, at least not one that cost only ten cents a dozen. I loved seafood and would pay dearly for my gourmandism in the future.

The ferry docked amid eddies of deep-blue churning water and seagulls diving for the ship's garbage. Pierre drove his Austin Mini off the huge wooden plank that separated us from land and into the customs line. He had bought some antique Berber jewels in Morocco that he didn't want to pay duty on.

"There won't be any problem, Geeny. They never look through suitcases in Algeciras."

I looked at the customs official, and he looked at our huge suitcases in the back seat of the car.

"*Qué hay adentro?*" asked the customs official. "What's inside?"

"Clothes." answered Pierre, a bit impatiently. "*Ropa.*"

"Okay. Let's see," said the customs official.

"There's nothing in them," insisted Pierre, a bit more rudely.

"Put them over there!" insisted the official.

"You have a lot of nerve!" exploded Pierre. "I tell you, there's nothing in them!"

"Please, *señor*, take them out of the car." The official was stout, ruddy-complected and determined.

Pierre flung open the door and grabbed the suitcases. He hoisted them onto his shoulders and slammed them down on the table the official had pointed to. The official went over and poked through our clothes while Pierre fumed.

"What does he want, a bribe?"

"Pierre, I think he wants to look through our suitcases. It's his job." I looked at Pierre as he walked nervously around the customs depot. Small and wiry, he paced rapidly from one side of the enclosed area to another as the official took a good look at our suitcases. I stopped him when he walked by our car, where I waited.

"Pierre, you're going to make him more suspicious!"

"He's a bloody idiot!" Pierre stamped his foot impatiently, angrily. I thought he looked funny, and I started to laugh.

"What's so funny?"

"You!"

The official walked toward us. Pierre turned to him with his fists clenched by sides. I had never seen him this angry. He reminded me of a bantam rooster about to fight.

"You can go now," said the official calmly.

Pierre blinked his eyes. Then he walked quickly to the table where our suitcases lay open for inspection, closed them with a slam and hoisted them back onto his shoulders.

He crammed them into the back seat of the car and took off with a screech of tires. I had to bite my lips to keep from laughing. As we left the customs area, a sign appeared that said, "*Gracias por su amiabilidad en Algeciras.* Thank you for your amiability in Algeciras." I burst out laughing. I pointed at it and Pierre started to laugh too.

"*Gracias por su amiabilidad en Algeciras,* Pierre!" I chortled. Then I started to laugh so hard my sides hurt.

Pierre laughed, too, but not quite as hard as me.

Suddenly, while laughing, I felt a certain pressure in my lower colon, and, sure enough, I farted. I hoped that Pierre hadn't heard it. It didn't matter. The stench told volumes.

"Oh, my God! It must have been those oysters!" I gasped, still laughing from the customs incident.

"I'm going to have to ask your parents for a dowry!" said Pierre, rolling down the car window. "A big dowry!"

I looked at him to see if he was serious. He laughed, but Pierre rarely joked about money. A dowry! I hadn't heard that term except in literature. I didn't think it existed anymore. That he would even use the word surprised me.

"Um, I think that's an outdated custom, Pierre," I ventured, never too sure of myself on the subject of marriage.

"Well, my parents are much better off than yours."

"Well, yes, but...."

"Maybe we should have a marriage contract, just in case."

Now I was shocked. "Just in case what?"

"Oh, just in case some man talks you into divorcing me and then tries to get lots of my money."

"That's ridiculous!" I felt disillusion descending on me like a shroud. My husband-to-be talking about separating his wealth from mine. A written agreement. I couldn't imagine such a thing. Pierre sure was different when it came to money. I shut up and hoped he would change the subject. I had let him have the upper hand because his family's wealth intimidated me. Actually, he had taken the lead from the moment he made me speak English instead of Spanish, since the day I met him. I felt awed in the face of such...such an illustrious family, such wealth, chandeliers imported from

Venice....and I wanted to be part of it very badly. It was an enchanted world compared to what awaited me in the United States—a humdrum job as a secretary or in a laboratory working with rats....there was hardly anything I could do with a degree in psychology, just a bachelor's. Pierre provided just the easy out that I had been looking for. I much preferred marrying a rich man's son to going back to school for a master's in psychology. I wasn't interested in psychology any-more, I reasoned. I didn't even like being around mentally ill people. I had neatly stacked the cards against myself without realizing it, which was, unfortunately, my tendency. I lived for the moment, for the thrill—not for the long term. That re-minded me of my parents too much—their endless carping on security, my mother saying, "Now Ginny, get your teaching credential just in case your husband dies and can't take care of you." She would shake her finger at me as she talked. Anathema! My young mind instinctively felt the negativity, the death wish in her statement, and rebelled. She had pro-duced a magnificent rebel, but not a practical woman. We were both stuck with the results.

Pierre drove along the coast of Spain. He relaxed and started to look for a place to spend the night. He was my prince. In 1965, most women left things up to their husbands, and I was like most women in that respect.

"Do you think we should get married in the United States, Pierre?" I ventured.

"I've always wanted to see the United States, Geeny." He looked at me and grinned. Confident, relaxed, Pierre had no second thoughts.

Glad to hear that detail taken care of, I resumed my usual, easy-going personality. It felt good. I liked not worry-ing about anything.

"Let's stay at a *parador*, Pierre," I said.

The *paradores* were magnificent inns that Franco had con-structed throughout Spain. All of them had magnificent views of either historical landmarks or sites of natural beauty.

He smiled at me. "Sure. The one in Granada is great. Let's spend the night there."

I smiled back and forgot my anger. A resplendent night in a beautiful inn lay ahead of me, milking me of all my venom and vision.

☼ SANTA BARBARA

PIERRE, MY MOTHER, AND I sat in the living room that overlooked the patio of our exclusive Montecito home. Surrounded by the lush, green vegetation in our yard and our distant neighbor's, we could hear birds singing and the wind rustling through the branches of the eucalyptus trees. Montecito in 1966 was a woodsy suburb of Santa Barbara, renowned for its natural beauty and the number of great estates built by Hollywood celebrities.

My mother, ensconced in her favorite chair in the living room with the evening paper's crossword puzzle in her lap, looked up from under her glasses at Pierre.

"You must be very athletic," she said. Her attractive brow wrinkled as she scrutinized Pierre, trying to decide how he would fit into her bridge-playing social set in Montecito. She smiled a nice, but patronizing smile. Pierre could just as well have dropped in from Mars, as far as she was concerned.

Pierre smiled his big, toothy, infectious grin at her, then furrowed his brow.

"What do you mean, Mrs. Walters?"

My mother shifted her weight heavily on the chintz-covered easychair she spent most of her time in. It overlooked the gardens from our spacious living room.

Sharp and incisive, she wasted no time. "Ginny tells me that you do a lot of horseback riding, that you play a good game of tennis. Of course, Ginny has a degree in psychology."

"I am going to take over my father's antique store in Rabat, Mrs. Walters. I don't need a degree." Pierre stopped smiling for the first time since he arrived. His face hardened.

"Oh, well, that...a shop...yes, of course." My mother

104

laughed her shrill, supercilious laugh. Her bridge table laugh.

My father walked into the living room and began reading the evening newspaper.

Pierre stood up respectfully. My father buried his nose in the paper. Pierre cleared his throat. "Good evening, Mr. Walters," he said, loudly.

My father looked up briefly. "Hmmm? Oh, hello, Pierre." Then he continued reading the newspaper.

Pierre's face reddened. He clenched his fists, and his small, wiry frame shook visibly with anger.

"I have never felt so unwelcome in a place in my whole life!" he nearly shouted.

My father looked up. My mother raised an eyebrow. I raised both my eyebrows, pleasantly surprised.

"What?" said my father, nonplussed. His face remained impassive. His jowls drooped as always. He looked at Pierre as if he were a complete stranger.

"Ever since I have been here, no one has said one kind word to me. You have ignored me. I am going to marry your daughter, and you treat me like a villain!"

"Well...." My father didn't know how to respond to such an accusation. "What...ummm...marry Ginny?" His face remained immobile, expressionless. He did lower his newspaper.

"Yes, we're getting married, or didn't you know?" I inserted sardonically, used to my parents' callous treatment.

"Well, we had thought, hoped...ummm, well, of course, we appreciate you bringing Ginny back, Pierre, but...."

"But what?" I asked.

Pierre looked at me, then them. "Is there something wrong with you?" he asked. "We announced our intention to marry in Europe almost a year ago. I think it is quite clear that we plan to get married."

My father cleared his throat and then laughed feebly. "Yes, well, of course...."

"Mr. Walters, if you don't want me to marry your daughter, please say so." Pierre clenched and unclenched his fists, pacing nervously all the while. I had never seen him this angry. "Well, now, Pierre, I never said that," he countered weakly. His face remained blank and passive, as if he couldn't understand what was going on.

"I am going to visit my friend Oscar in Mexico. Then I will come back to see Geeny. I will not stay in such an inhospitable house," Pierre announced.

The atmosphere turned white-hot with anger. Personally, I was thrilled that someone finally had the guts to stand up to my parents.

"Now Pierre...." My mother stood up and came over to us.

"Yes, Mrs. Walters?" said Pierre openly, expecting an apology.

"It's just very hard for us, you know."

"What?"

"Well, you are a foreigner, and...."

"I'm French," asserted Pierre, angrily.

"And we're Americans," said my mother. "We gave you a lot of money after World War II that you never paid back. You foreigners expect us to give you everything, and you never appreciate it!"

"What does this have to do with Geeny and me?" asked Pierre.

"She's an American, and she should marry an American," announced my mother, her voice hitting a high C.

"I thought you had French blood in your family. Ginny told me you did." Pierre crossed his arms in front of him and stood his ground. I stood behind him, backing him up, thrilled to the core of my being. I loved Pierre for his frankness. And I hated them for their lack of warmth, lack of common humanity. I had always wondered what was wrong with my parents.

"Yes, but we've been in America for many years. My great aunt is president of the D.A.R. Our ancestors came over on the Mayflower. Besides, you don't look like us."

A lid on a pan rattled...something was cooking in the kitchen, something about to boil over...the Bird's Eye peas.

"Fine. I'm going to visit a friend in Mexico. I don't know when I'll be back," fumed Pierre, his face a deep red. My parents' rudeness deflated even his optimistic attitude. He turned on his heel, walked into his bedroom, and began to pack his things.

My father picked up the newspaper and tried to find his place. My mother stirred the peas.

Pierre left for Mexico City the next day.

Deeply grateful that someone had finally told my parents what he, and I, thought of them, I kissed him goodbye tenderly. "Be sure to write and let me know when you're coming back," I purred.

"Don't worry, Geeny. I will." He kissed me long and hard. Then he got into the waiting taxi cab. It drove out of our spacious Montecito driveway, surrounded by graceful eucalyptus trees and palms.

Now I knew why I had fought furiously with my parents since I was eleven. My fiancé was an intruder in my own home, an unwelcome guest—because he was a foreigner. And so was I. Pierre had voiced what I had always felt, that my parents merely tolerated my presence. My openness went against their mean-spirited British heritage. Years later I discovered we had a Hispanic forebear, someone named Pedro whom one of my Mormon aunts dug up in a genealogical quest. The British had been foreigners, too. I was mad as hell.

My mother stood between the cooking island, a space big enough for a chef to prepare a seven-course dinner, and the late-model stove in our kitchen. I could smell the Bird's Eye peas she had dumped into a pan to boil for our balanced dinner: a hamburger patty, a baked potato, and the infamous Bird's Eye peas. If we wanted something more, like dessert, there was toast and jelly. We lived among the rich and famous and ate like paupers. This, too, was my Anglo-Saxon heritage. Look good, but eat cheaply unless there are guests.

"Why does Pierre have to 'look like us'?" I raged, pacing back and forth in our kitchen. My mother was used to arguing with me and whirled around from the boiling peas with the scissors she had used to cut open the plastic bag still in her hand. "Ginny," she answered tartly, "Pierre is a nigger!"

"What?" I couldn't believe my ears. "Pierre is white!"

"I don't care. He doesn't look like us. And I'll bet he gets an awfully good suntan!" She scowled at me furiously.

"And so do I! Don't forget we have an Italian in the family tree! Daddy Judd told me so!" I hurled the words at her, hoping to shut her up forever.

"We don't have an Italian in the family!" Her eyes narrowed and her voice changed to a pitying sound. "Poor Ginny. You just can't seem to find a nice American like everyone else. So you go with the....dirty foreigners! And his mother is Spanish!"

"You are hopeless," I said in disgust and turned on my heel. I sat down in the living room, my head spinning. God, how that woman knows how to go for the jugular, I remembered, dully.

Memories of my mother and father sitting with Annie between them on the sofa many years ago, when we lived on Alexander Bell Drive in Arlington, Virginia, flooded my brain. They pointed an accusatory finger at me. I was twelve.

"You are corrupting your little sister, Ginny!"

"What are you talking about?" I asked, baffled.

"She is an angel and you are corrupting her."

"Annie, an angel?" I suppressed a laugh just thinking about it. Then I turned and stalked out of the room, just as I had done now. And Annie would forever be considered the "little angel" of the family, whereas I got a much juicier role, that of the "corrupting devil." I tried to ignore them as well as their attempts at unfavorable comparisons between me and my younger sister. Nonetheless, Annie's boyfriends would always be accepted regardless of race. Mine would always be rejected.

For a month Pierre sent me colorful postcards from Mexico City, then Acapulco, where he was having a huge bachelor's party with his friend from the University of Cambridge, Oscar Delgado.

My parents argued when my dad came home from his job

in Los Angeles. He had lost his engineering position in Santa Barbara, so he had found one in Los Angeles that required him to rent a tiny studio so he could stay there during the working week, as the commute from Santa Barbara was nearly two hours, too long for a man already in his fifties and whose morale had been shattered when he was passed over for captain in the U.S. Navy, an unprecedented occurrence for a Naval Academy graduate, an Annapolis graduate.

It must have been brutal, I reflected. He captained a destroyer at the time, and the twenty percent of his class, the first in the history of Annapolis to be passed over, was announced over the loudspeaker of his own ship. How could they be so cruel? I wondered, thinking of how painful public humiliation must be, especially in front of the hundreds of men he commanded on that ship, the U.S.S. Forrester.

He never told me anything about it, but my mother faithfully related the story to me and my sister. Indeed, after his disappointment, my father became a remote creature who only spoke to reprimand me and my sister.

"He could hardly face the world, he felt so put down," I imagined. I felt sorry for him.

After Pierre left, my mother told me curtly to get a job. The psychology laboratory where I started working required that I weigh urine specimens, among other unpalatable duties. After walking on a treadmill, the old ladies had to urinate in a little container. I had to weigh it so that their exact weight could be determined both before and after an endurance test. The point was to measure how well elderly people would survive in fallout shelters. The scientific method at its smelliest.

Mrs. Jones' urine was bright yellow, and she gave it to me with a shy giggle. I inhaled at the wrong time and felt a bit nauseated. Then I smiled at the human guinea pig and counted the days until Pierre's return, the odor of urine quickening my desire to get on with our trip, our marriage, anything but this. About a week after Pierre's abrupt departure, I got a postcard with pictures of the Acapulco cliff divers on it. The inscription read: "Dear Ginny, Hope to see you soon. I will stay in a hotel in Santa Barbara. Love, Pierre." My spirits soared. My prince charming was coming soon; soon Cinderella would be free of her awful parents and of weighing urine specimens in the psychology laboratory.

My parents, my younger sister, and I finished our dinner of the usual hamburger patty, Bird's Eye peas and a baked potato in stony silence. Annie had just let loose a diatribe on the superiority of communism to capitalism and, as usual, my father nearly went up in smoke.

"How...how can you say such, such...."

Then I burped.

My father turned on me. It was my turn.

"Ginny, how do you expect to find a husband with such unladylike...."

Annie burped.

"Neither of you girls is suitable for a proper...."

I burped again and smothered a giggle. My father's face turned crimson.

"I won't have this...."

Annie burped again. We both giggled. He started shouting incoherently, and we couldn't suppress our laughter.

"Another night at the Walter's respectable Montecito ...insane asylum...." I babbled through my laughter.

The phone rang. I ran to answer it just as my father turned to my mother for help. "Jane, can't you do something...."

"Geeny, it's me!"

"Where are you?"

"At the Santa Barbara Greyhound bus station. Can you come get me?"

"Of course! I'll be right there!" I hung up the phone. "Pierre's back! I'm going to pick him up," I yelled and dashed off. I ran out to the garage and jumped into my Karmann Ghia, speeding down our beautiful, tree-lined street with a high heart. A reprieve, a reprieve!

Pierre stood outside the Greyhound bus station with his suitcase. He was wearing his customary expensive British sweater over a white shirt and tie with gray slacks and an enormous smile, a sight for sore eyes.

I parked nearby and rushed to him. We embraced, and then he led me inside the bus station. We sat down at one of the formica tables in the makeshift cafeteria. He took my hand in his.

"Geeny, I think we can get married now."

"Great, Pierre! Let's do it!" I kissed him happily. Then I realized where we were. People stared at us politely, then turned their heads. A marriage proposal in the Greyhound bus station!

"Come on, I'll take you to my house."

"No, thank you. I'll stay in a hotel."

"Oh, okay. Which one?"

"There's one called the Virginia Hotel...."

"Named after me! Let's go there!"

He shouldered his suitcase and then tossed it in the back seat of my small car. I drove to the Virginia Hotel and he checked in. His room was not luxurious, but Pierre always liked a good bargain.

When I came back alone, my parents raised their eyebrows inquiringly.

"Where's Pierre?" my mother asked.

"He's staying at the Virginia Hotel until we get married," I said.

"When are you getting married?" asked my father, granite faced.

"Well, isn't that up to you?" I asked.

"Oh, no, Ginny. It doesn't matter to us. You can get married any time," said my mother in her best blasé bridge-table manner.

"Well, what about the wedding?" I frowned at these two people who had ignored me for most of my life. Who were they, anyway?

"What wedding?" blinked my father.

"Well, normally, people have a wedding when they get married."

"Oh, yes...well, we'll see...."

My sister walked by and I jumped up and down. "Annie, Pierre and I are getting married...soon!"

"That's fantastic, Ginny!" blurted Annie, seven years my junior but very grown up at seventeen. We jumped up and down happily, then ran off to play a game of badminton in our back yard, one of our favorite sports. My parents faded into the background, shadowy, murky figures that rarely came into full focus. There was too much fun in my life to be held back by those nay-sayers. As for the wedding, I didn't really care. I just wanted to keep traveling with Pierre.

☼ A CIVIL WEDDING

CHRISTMAS WAS TWO DAYS away. My parents' friends came and went. With a beaming face, I escorted them in and out of our elegant home in the woodsy hills of Santa Barbara. Talk of my marriage to Pierre was in the air.

"I'll make a wedding cake," beamed Darlene Jones, one of my mother's rich friends from Pacific Palisades. She smiled at Pierre. He smiled back at her, his eyes crinkling deeply in his impishly friendly face. "I think Ginny and Pierre will make a very good match." Pierre and I looked at my mother expectantly. My mother quickly changed the subject.

"How is Lynn Hosted? Are you still playing bridge?"

"I'll put ten tiers on it with frosted bells!" Darlene's words gushed out in a torrent of enthusiasm. She ignored my mother's reference to bridge. Her brown eyes glittered like a fox on the trail of a succulent dove as she talked of this incredible cake she was going to make for my wedding.

"Darlene, don't bother to go to all that trouble," my mother replied sharply, almost rebuking her. My father looked the other way.

"Carl, get some more drinks," ordered my mother. "Darlene likes martinis." My father obediently got up to fix some cocktails.

"I just want to do something for Ginny's wedding," announced Darlene. "You know I love to cook. Of course, I ordered a cake for my son's wedding." Darlene was filthy rich, at least my parents always said so because she had married a Jewish man the second time around.

"Yes, well, we're going to pay for her trip to the gynecologist," said my mother.

"A physical?" queried Darlene.

"To make sure...she is okay, um, down there." My mother laughed nervously. "You know what I mean." Darlene raised her eyebrows and pursed her lips, cutting whatever she might have said short.

I was used to my mother's morbid preoccupation with disease, death, and failure, particularly my father's.

"Jews know how to make money," my mother often said in his presence to make him feel guilty for having failed to attain the rank of captain in the navy.

Sometimes she simply said, "Carl is a failure." My mother knew how to hurt, how to go for the jugular. Sometimes it was hard to breathe when she was in the room. I instinctively held my breath because she might say something awful, hurtful, mean. For many years I thought my father really was a failure even though we lived in the best neighborhoods and I went to the university, considered a luxury for a girl in those days.

"Well, since I had to take this job at the library, we have to be careful," my mother said. "A wedding reception is expensive."

I hardly heard her. She always complained about money, or something that was ruining her life. Usually it was my father and his inability to assert himself, to get on in the world. Now it was a job she had to take because my father had lost his last engineering job and had been unemployed for nearly six months before he found another position as an engineer. She claimed that working at the public library made her so nervous that she often only slept four hours a night. I didn't see how writing numbers on the backs of books could make anyone that nervous, but my mother was always nervous.

Darlene uncrossed her legs and stood up. Still svelte and attractive at an age when many women looked like tired rag dolls, she paced confidently around the living room like a tigress on the prowl.

"Just let us know when the wedding is, and we'll be there," she said, and my mother nodded without enthusiasm. Pierre stepped forward and kissed Darlene's hand. She beamed at him.

"*Enchanté, madame,*" he said.

"You are marvelous!" she enthused. Then she looked at me. "He will make a very good husband, Ginny. Hang onto him! You must come to visit us in Los Angeles! You can spend the night, if you like."

"Thanks, Darlene, we may take you up on that! We want to visit Los Angeles," I said, smiling. "And we would enjoy staying with you and John."

They left and my mother went back to the kitchen to fix dinner. No more talk of wedding plans. Sally, another old friend of the family, discreetly mentioned she had a beautiful new lavender tulle dress she wanted to wear to the wedding. Hints abounded, but wedding plans were nonexistent.

I dug up all my old acquaintances from college. We went to some parties with them; but frankly, we found Santa Barbara quite dull apart from its beauty. We had only come here to get married and to see my family, mostly my sister. They had their world and we had ours. Theirs revolved around long-nurtured neuroses that I had worked very hard not to internalize. Whereas they were obsessed with caution, I was carefree and impulsive. Sometimes I claimed we weren't related except by blood. Only people with difficult parents understood my joke.

"We can continue traveling as soon as we're married, Geeny, then I can make some money to pay for our trip to Malaysia!" Pierre smiled his big Pierre smile, which wreathed his face in a sweet, jowly way.

I jiggled one of my crossed legs in excitement. "Yes, then we can visit Alex and take him up on his offer to serve us fifteen-course meals. I love Indonesian food!"

"But no oysters...."

"No more cheap oysters!"

"We'll drive to Mexico to visit Oscar and Molly, then continue our trip around the world!"

"That'll be great!" I beamed in happy anticipation. "They roll up the carpets here at ten o'clock," I sighed, crossing and uncrossing my legs in antsy exasperation. "There's nothing to do in this town at night!"

"Oscar will show us a great time! He took me to the best

parties when we were in England, Geeny!" Pierre's smile wreathed his face as he talked. "We can get married after Christmas and then go to Mexico!"

"Terrific!" More parties, more fun, I thought. A wedding? It didn't matter to me. Just a time-consuming formality.

"I don't want to get married in front of a lot of people, Geeny, it would make me nervous," confided Pierre.

"We can get a judge to marry us in the Santa Barbara courthouse!" I exclaimed.

"Let's do it the day after Christmas!"

"Okay! Now let's go see the Christmas carolers at the mission."

"Annie, do you want to hear the carolers?" I called out to my sister.

"Yes, Ginny! Wait for me!" The three of us jumped into my car and drove off into the pleasant night toward the beautiful Santa Barbara mission.

As we left, my mother gave me her usual dark look. She hated it when I took my sister places. She had long feared that Annie was under my evil spell, one that would make her independent like me.

My mother's neuroses were too numerous to contemplate, so I generally steered as clear from them as possible, fearing them and her. As for my sister, well, after all, she was my sister, my only sibling, and if she wanted to come with us, she was more than welcome. Basically, I didn't give much of a damn what my parents thought. If I had, I never could have gone to Europe, for they prophesied my immediate doom back there in the land of the dark ages.

Their sharp rebukes still rang in my ears, even though they had uttered them years ago. I could still remember them saying, "Don't you dare quit your good government job, Ginny! You'll get a good pension and...."

"I don't want a pension! I'm only twenty-three years old! I don't need a pension!"

"Well, you're wasting your money going to Europe. It's dirty and run down and terribly expensive!" intoned my father with growing anger.

"If you don't mind, I'll find out for myself," I replied curtly. I thought of the gorgeous young men Garcia Lorca described in his sensuous, striking poetry and smiled.

"You're only thinking of yourself!" wailed my mother.

I remember that I got up and left the room. No, no, I would not listen to them. I never had. My parents' negative thinking propelled me into a life of carefree abandon. In 1964 a lot of people thought I was crazy, but by the time the late sixties rolled around, it looked like I had simply been ahead of my time.

We drove to the Santa Barbara mission and got out of the car. The moonlight sparkled on the ocean, clearly visible from the mission's imposing facade. The night air, clear and cool, refreshed us. The carolers at the mission sang "Hark the Herald Angels Sing," "Oh, Little Town of Bethlehem," and other favorites. I bellowed right along with them, off key, as usual.

"Ginny, do you have to sing so loud?" asked Annie, impudently.

"I can't help myself, Annie," I protested. My mother had told me to mouth the words when I was six years old. But I just can't help but sing Christmas carols.

"Oh, come all ye faithful...."

"Not so loud!"

"I can't help myself!"

"Shhhh...."

Pierre smiled at us. He found my sister sweet, except for her backtalk to my dad about communism and hippies. He didn't approve of children who were disrespectful to their elders.

A few days earlier, Annie had assembled a rag-tag group of her high school friends, the beginnings of the hippie movement, dressed in patched and flared blue jeans, barefoot, on our living room floor. My father stumbled across the gathering and then retreated to the den. He said nothing. But Pierre took me aside.

"Why didn't they stand up and greet him? How dare they just sit there in his living room and not even say hello!"

"My father lives in his own world, Pierre," I explained as I surveyed the group of high-school-aged children seated around our living room floor. They chatted and laughed, then listened to Annie's boyfriend, who I later learned sold drugs, talk about the new "hip" culture and how cool it was. Pierre scowled at them and left the living room. He could not comprehend my father's acquiescence to the rudeness of strangers.

"That's the way my father is, Pierre," I explained. We passed by the den. Daddy, as Annie and I called my father, had his nose in a *Scientific American*. Little else seemed to interest him.

"Besides, this is America, not Europe. Children aren't brought up as strictly as...."

"They're a bloody bunch of spoiled brats!" ranted Pierre with his English-French accent. "If this were my house, they'd have to stand up and shake my hand or get out!" Pierre bristled with annoyance at this lack of respect. I had to be taught to stand up and shake hands with people older than myself in Europe because no one did so here. I found myself thinking like Pierre. We Americans were spoiled brats! But then children in Europe were brought up differently, more strictly, and their parents had good manners, too.

"Oh, little town of Bethlehem...." my sister sang sweetly. Her long blond hair illuminated by a street lamp, she looked quite angelic.

Pierre put his arm around my waist and hugged me close. I could feel his warm breath on my neck as he tried to sing "Jingle Bells" in English. "Jeengle bells, jeengle bells, jeengle aalll the way." Then he turned to me, his prematurely lined face sweetly serious. "Geeny, let's get married right after Christmas. The day after."

His impatience pleased me.

"Yes, let's!" I whispered.

"Shhhh!" Annie shushed me again.

"Pierre and I are getting married!"

"I know!"

"The day after Christmas!"

"No kidding? Oh, little town of Bethlehem...."

As we drove up the winding road to our house, I looked out at the ocean. The moon cast a golden carpet of serene beauty on it. My life will be like that, I thought. Then I smiled at Pierre. He stared intently at the road ahead.

Christmas day dawned bright and clear. I ran into Annie's room and woke her.

"Pin!" I shouted. "Pinned to the bone!" This was an unusual expression that we had invented to mean more or less "Gotcha!"

"Oh, Ginny," she cried in dismay, "you woke up first again!" She rubbed her eyes and pushed the covers away.

"And you told me you would be the first! Come on! Let's open our presents! I'll wake up Pierre."

We tumbled into the living room, where the lights on the tree twinkled, left on from the night before. Gaily wrapped Christmas presents lay underneath. The family dog wagged his tail in anticipation as we all tore through the wrappings.

"Oh, Ginny, a Moroccan dress! Cornflower blue. I can wear it to the party tonight; it's the in thing to wear Moroccan style clothes." Annie stood up and put it on over her pajamas and twirled around to model it. Her face radiated happiness. At seventeen, she was lovely.

"You look great in it," I laughed. "Especially with those accessories!" Annie sat down and tore open some more gifts.

I opened Pierre's present, knowing he had bought something for me in Mexico. He watched me with a big smile as I unwrapped a silver and turquoise necklace and matching bracelet.

"They're magnificent!" I exclaimed, holding them up for Annie to see. My mother walked into the room just as I held it to the light.

"Oh, isn't that a pretty trinket," she said, her voice laced with its usual sarcasm.

"That's real silver inlaid with real turquoise, Mrs. Walters," said Pierre.

"Really?" cooed my mother, her face remaining impassive.

"Here's something for you, Mrs. Walters." Pierre handed my mother an oblong box wrapped in shiny silver paper. She unwrapped it and took out another solid silver bracelet, an exquisite piece of undeniable value.

"How unusual!" she exclaimed. "Pierre, you shouldn't have."

"What about me?" rumbled my father as he walked into the room, fastening the belt of his silk bathrobe.

"This is for you, Mr. Walters," said Pierre, dutifully handing my father a square gift wrapped in sparkling gold. My father tore the wrapping paper off and took out a nicely worked leather wallet from Mexico.

"Why, thank you, Pierre," said my dad, quite sincerely. He smiled at Pierre, and I thought how smooth his face looked for a man his age when he smiled.

"This is for you, Pierre," chirped my mother, handing him an oblong box that looked like it contained a tie. It did. A red tie.

"A Christmas tie, a very nice Christmas tie," said Pierre, holding it up for the rest of us to see. "I'll wear it today. Thank you very much, Mr. and Mrs. Walters."

I received my usual pair of flannel pajamas, as did my sister. My parents were hopelessly practical when it came to gift giving.

"Thank you," we chorused and then went in to prepare breakfast as my mother and father tried their best to figure out what to do with my exotic gifts from Spain and Morocco: a leather drinking gourd for their coffee table, caftans, reproductions of an early Goya from the Prado that looked almost like the original oil. They looked uneasy. All these foreign things!

Then came our favorite gift—Grandma's! Grandma always sent us a huge package that she shopped for throughout the year in bargain basement sales. She was renowned for her frugality when it came to herself and unstinting generosity to all others. She didn't have a mean bone in her body. We had lived with her for many years of my childhood, and she was truly a second mother to me.

My father was away at war when I was born. Just out of Annapolis, he helped command ships to fight the Japanese during World War II, and I didn't see him until I was three years old. This was not unusual for "war babies," as we were called.

I had two mothers during those three years: my own, and my grandmother, who adored her first grandchild. I would always be her "little Ginny," her pet name for me.

"I get to open it," yelled Annie, and we both ripped off the wrappings, laughing and hooting. Out came an incredible amount of gifts, almost all of which we couldn't wear. The dresses and blouses were two sizes too big and completely out of style; but it didn't matter. They were from our beloved Grandma, the eccentric of the family who sang in church and on buses, and loved every creature who ever crawled the earth, especially her four grandchildren.

An off-red sleeveless dress looked almost wearable and I dashed off to try it on. It was a bit big, but with a blouse underneath it looked pretty good. I ran out to show it to Annie and Pierre.

"What do you think?" I asked, wiggling my hips and swiveling around, making fun of fashion models.

"A steal, a steal," yelped Annie, always ready to join in the revelry.

"I'll wear it tomorrow, when we get married!"

Annie laughed. "Something old, something new, something borrowed, something...red!"

We howled with merriment. There was no quenching our high spirits.

"And then Pierre can work here and then we can go to Mexico and on around the world..."

"And live happily ever after."

"In Madrid," I added.

"But first I must learn my father's business in Morocco, Geeny," Pierre added, always practical underneath his exterior verve.

"Morocco," I thought. "Yes, and then start an antique shop in Madrid, where all our friends are!" I couldn't imagine a life without wonderful friends.

Pierre and I had already agreed on one thing: no children. "They would get in the way of our travels," said Pierre, and I wholeheartedly concurred. Marriage was one thing, children quite another. I would get married to appease the beasts of convention, but I didn't want to have children. Not yet, anyway.

Our wedding day dawned bright and clear, another perfect day in Lotusland, as Santa Barbara is often called. I jumped up and ran to the kitchen. My mother was already there, scrambling eggs and frying bacon.

Annie came in drowsily, wiping the sleep from her eyes. She was still in her pajamas.

"Let's have breakfast on the patio," I said. "It's so beautiful out!"

"Okay, Geeny," said Pierre, rounding the corner from his bedroom.

We grabbed some plates and silverware, piled our plates high with eggs and bacon, and headed for the patio.

"We're getting married today, mother," I said. My mother continued to scramble eggs.

"Whatever you say, Ginny," she mumbled, morosely.

The sun warmed us as we drank coffee and gobbled the eggs, bacon, and toast.

"Pass the marmalade," said Pierre.

"Do you want more coffee?"

"I have to do some shopping before we get married, Pierre."

"Yes, I want to get some things, too."

We had already picked out a delicate gold wedding band, so we were ready. I felt heady and excited, like I had when I was in Madrid during the year of the free spirits.

Pierre and I jumped into my car and drove downtown to the Santa Barbara County Courthouse, a Cinderella fairy tale of a building, one of the many local landmarks.

We ran to the judge's office.

"We want to get married, sir," said Pierre respectfully.

The judge, old and wrinkled, looked up from under his horn-rimmed glasses at us. "Do you have a marriage license?"

"Yes, sir. We got one the day before Christmas," said Pierre, smiling enthusiastically.

The judge continued to stare at us. I wore my grandmother's gift, the off-red jumper dress, with a white blouse underneath. Pierre wore his usual sweater, tie, and slacks outfit. I smiled and laughed, wondering what he was waiting for.

"Well," I said, fidgeting impatiently.

"Very well," muttered the judge. "I will be free at two o'clock this afternoon." He looked up at us sternly.

A dour old man, indeed, I thought.

"That should be just fine," I sang out merrily. "I have some shopping to do, and then we can get married."

Pierre grinned his contagious grin, but to no avail. This judge apparently lacked a sense of humor altogether.

Pierre and I skipped off gaily to do our errands, forgetting about the judge, who was, after all, of no consequence to us except that he would perform the ceremony.

How dull, I thought. I had always hated boring formalities. I'd been to two weddings and avoided funerals altogether. I never wanted to see anyone I liked in a casket. Cardigan sweaters were on sale at the Hughes department store. I got two for the price of one. Like my mother and grandmother, I loved a bargain.

"You look very pretty in them, Geeny," said Pierre while I modeled one of them in the store for his approval. He looked at his watch. "Now it is almost two o'clock. We have to go back to the courthouse."

The courthouse loomed large and solid, made of white adobe and adorned with beautiful colored tiles and a red tile roof. We ducked in and went to the judge's office.

He looked up at us, his eyes slightly dazed.

"Could you wait outside?" he asked. "I'm not quite ready."

"Sure!" I bubbled, anxious to get on with the day, to go home and get dressed up for dinner and then dancing. We had to celebrate!

"Could you tell me where the men's room is?" asked Pierre.

The judge narrowed his eyes to a barely perceptible squint. He looked like he had a migraine headache. "Down the hall and to your right," he said and stood up abruptly. He ushered us out of his office and closed the door behind him. It banged shut and the sound resonated through the silent hallway.

Sterile and boring, the hall offered nothing of interest to me, so I started rummaging through my bag of newly acquired sweaters to admire them. Suddenly a police officer stepped into the hallway and gave me a furious look. "Can't you see that court is in session? Be quiet!" Then he stomped back into the courtroom.

I hadn't noticed the "Court in Session" light.

Pierre came back from the bathroom.

"You'll never guess what just happened!" I whispered quietly, still laughing.

"What?" said Pierre.

"A policeman got mad at me for making too much noise in the hallway."

"Really?" Pierre started to laugh with me. Everything struck us as hysterically funny.

Just then the judge opened the door to his office.

"You may come in now," he said sternly.

I gulped some air and forced myself to stop laughing. Pierre stopped, too. After all, we were about to be married.

We stood before the judge, who peered out through his thick glasses at me in my grandmother's red bargain basement dress and Pierre in his casual sweater and slacks. I still held my shopping bag.

"Where is your witness?" he asked, impatiently.

"Witness? I didn't know we had to have one!" I exclaimed.

"We just want to get married!"

The judge cleared his throat a few times and then said, "Very well, I'll ask someone if they will stand in for you." He pushed the heavy chair back from his oversized desk littered with legal documents and left the room in search of a witness.

"Pierre," I gasped, "He's going to get that policeman who told me to shut up!" I covered my mouth and then burst out laughing.

Pierre started to howl with laughter. We looked at each other, our eyes crinkled in merriment, unable to control our mirth. I had visions of the portly policeman stepping into the room with the dour judge.

"I can't stop laughing!" I said to Pierre, who seemed to be having a hard time himself. By the time the judge came back with an elderly secretary, we were doubled over with uncontrollable laughter.

When I saw a woman instead of the policeman, I was relieved, but I couldn't stop giggling. Every time I giggled, Pierre would catch his breath and giggle too. The judge frowned at us.

"Please stand up and repeat after me," he admonished. We stood in front of him and tried our best to control our laughter.

"I promise to have and to hold," said the judge.

"I promise to have and to..." I giggled. "And to hold..."

The judge frowned sternly at me. "In sickness and health..." he continued, scowling at us.

"Een seekness and health..." repeated Pierre. Then I burst out laughing at his accent.

The judge gave us a look that reflected the hopelessness of the situation. Then he continued staunchly. "For better or for worse...."

I took a deep breath and hit a high C. "For better..." then I gasped for lack of air, "or for worse!" Both Pierre and I held our breath and chortled, trying to contain our laughter by keeping our mouths shut. The resultant puffed-up cheeks and laughter seeping out of them made us even more hysterical.

"I pronounce you man and wife," the judge said, curtly, cutting the ceremony short.

Pierre and I took a collective sigh of relief. He put the

band of gold on my finger and kissed me. I gulped and then laughed gaily. We were married!

We looked at each other in delight and started to run out of the judge's office.

"And I think you are very foolish to give up your citizenship, young lady!" the judge called to me as we ran out.

I spun around in surprise. "I'm not giving my citizenship up!" I retorted angrily and then looked at Pierre. He hunched his shoulders in perplexity, and we ran out to go back home and tell everyone. Life was too much fun to be bothered by stuffy judges.

It was already dark by the time we swung my car into our Montecito driveway. The trees formed a familiar, graceful pattern which I had grown to love. I inhaled the night air deeply and felt Pierre's hand in mine. We looked at each other and laughed.

"We're married!" I laughed. "I'm your wife!"

Pierre smiled broadly, happily.

"You're my little husband!"

I pulled him toward our house and we dashed into the living room. My father sat there, his nose in the evening paper.

"Daddy," I squealed in delight, "Pierre and I got married today!"

My father looked dully up at me from the evening newspaper. "Oh, well, what about dinner? Aren't you going to fix dinner?"

Fix dinner? On my wedding night? I thought giddily. "No, daddy, we thought you'd take us out to dinner to celebrate!"

My father continued to stare at us sullenly. Perhaps he was tired. "Your mother's at a bridge party. I suppose...."

"Let's go out to dinner, Mr. Walters," interceded Pierre politely. He stood in front of my father. "I invite you." This meant he was going to pay. That was how the French said the dinner's on me. *Je vous invite.*

My father put down the newspaper and looked up at us. His facial expression remained immobile.

"Where do you want to go?"

"To the Philadelphia House!" I squealed. "The roast beef is delicious there!"

So off we went to a nice old British-style restaurant where we had some excellent roast beef with horseradish. Very spicy, very good. No one said much. Pierre quickly drove my father home, and I put on a deep magenta dress and my European suede heels to go dancing at the Santa Barbara Inn. Mostly older people would be there, but Pierre and I didn't care. We had done it! We were married! The international playboy and the crazy American adventuress, married! And happy!

I looked at Pierre in a new light. Tenderness welled up in my breast for my new husband. His face had premature lines. It was not the typical Anglo-Saxon face. There were deep creases around his mouth. His face revealed a strong yet gentle character. What I liked best was that Pierre had natural self-confidence. He never let anyone take advantage of him or me. I felt so secure in my happiness that I couldn't stop smiling at him. He smiled back, took my hand and kissed me. Then we drove gaily off to the Santa Barbara Inn to dance and drink Bloody Marys.

After a few drinks and dancing some fast and slow ones, I asked Pierre, "Where do you want to spend the night?"

"Why not at your house? It's as nice as any hotel."

"Well...I guess so." I hesitated. Spend our wedding night in my own bedroom? Something was wrong here, but I couldn't put my finger on it. I remembered something my grandmother had told me, "Keep your eyes wide open before marriage, honey, and half shut afterwards."

I could almost picture Grandma smiling at me with her peculiar little squint that came from nearsightedness. I could see her, so caring, so time-worn. Suddenly I remembered her playing her old piano in the living room, leaning back and singing at the top of her lungs, "Holy, holy, holy, Lord God almighty...."

"Why are you so quiet, Geeny?" Pierre squeezed my hand as we drove into our spacious, curving driveway under the eucalyptus trees and got out just like on any other night.

"I was thinking of my grandmother," I smiled at him happily.

"On your wedding night? What about...."

"Oh, don't worry! I know you're right here! Besides, nothing has really changed."

Nothing had changed, except now Pierre had the legal right to sleep in my room. We went in, undressed, and made love. Nothing special happened between us.

I woke up the next morning and rolled over drowsily. Pierre was still asleep next to me. It was still very quiet in the house. Suddenly my sister's light footsteps dashed over the carpet as she ran down the hallway past our bedroom. I heard her yell, "No!"

Then my father shouted "Yes!" loudly, and she yelled a defiant "No!" again. I rolled over and stretched. Annie and I had always fought with our parents. This was nothing new, except it was earlier than usual.

There was a brief silence. Then I heard thuds of flesh on flesh. My sister started to scream hysterically. I couldn't believe my ears.

I jumped out of bed.

"Pierre, my father's beating Annie!"

Pierre got up and just looked at me, unmoved.

I ran into her bedroom in my nightgown. Annie cowered in the doorway. Her hands were in front of her face, trying to ward off the blows. She looked so fragile, like a slender stalk of grain waving in a storm. My father struck her hard and fast, again and again in the face and on her body.

"Stop it!" I shrieked.

The hitting went on. I jumped on my father, who was enraged beyond recognition, and pried him off of her. Tears streamed down Annie's bruised face. His was red with fury.

"Are you all right?" I asked her anxiously.

"Yes, I think so," she quavered.

My father stood there, panting heavily, then turned and stalked off to the living room. I don't know where my mother was.

Pierre just stood there.

"What happened?" I asked her, incredulous. My father had never laid a hand on her in her life that I knew of.

"I just said 'no' and he kept on hitting me...." she sniffled, wiping her nose.

I put my arm around her to comfort her as best I knew how. Pierre didn't say anything. My mother came into the room.

"What happened?" she asked.

"Daddy just beat up Annie!" I shrieked, my face filled with incomprehension. My father had never laid a finger on us during our childhood. He had been the passive member of the family, my mother the disciplinarian. She had given me a hair brush spanking once I'll never forget. Nothing made sense.

My mother looked at my seventeen-year-old sister's face, red, puffy, turning dark blue in places. Her eyelids swelled shut. There were black-and-blue rings underneath her eyes.

My mother turned and walked into the living room, where my father was. I have no idea what she said to him. The rest of the day was a blur. No one thought of calling a doctor, much less the police.

By evening my father had apologized, and we all went down to a seafood restaurant in Santa Barbara to have dinner together. It was the first time my father had ever taken the family out to eat that I could remember. Annie sported two huge shiners and some bruises on her face, but she was smiling. She seemed to be taking it well. She sat next to my father. I sat opposite them next to Pierre. My mother sat at the end of the table and moaned about the price of the dinner. Her most maddening trait was to harp on how much everything cost. Tonight it seemed particularly distasteful.

With order restored, I assumed everything was back to normal. But, then, I never could understand my family and their penchant for treating life like an affliction. Perhaps they make it into an affliction, I thought with some detachment. I had never really talked freely to anyone in my family other than my grandmother in Florida and my sister.

We shared the same blood line, yet had little else in common. Perhaps it was my openly passionate quest for adventure, my optimistic nature of the *bon vivant* that alienated us. I accepted life as readily as they rejected it. Treated as an outsider since I could remember, I remained aloof, never asking for or giving any sign of affection.

"I think she deserved it," Pierre remarked.

My mind snapped back to the present. "What!" I couldn't believe my ears. My reverie ceased.

"For being disrespectful to your father," continued Pierre.

"But he beat her like an animal. If I hadn't intervened he might have killed her!"

"You should respect your parents." Pierre nodded his curly head in approbation. I began to wonder if European child-rearing methods weren't a bit too strict.

I shook my head and turned to Pierre, who busied himself with a road map of the United States.

Years later I wondered if Annie hadn't taken blows intended for me. I was the one who had married a foreigner against my parents' wishes. Perhaps it was our presence that had made my father snap. Especially our presence in the bedroom, on our honeymoon night. It was something I never fully comprehended, except that a girl could be beaten for crossing a man, possibly even killed. I remembered reading about prostitutes being stoned to death in ancient times and adulterous women murdered by their husbands quite recently with no legal repercussions. "A crime of passion, the man has been found innocent on the grounds of temporary insanity." Yeah, sure.

Annie's horrible beating became a taboo subject overnight, although I never forgot how close she came to being beaten to death by a mild-mannered father turned murderous. Why? I was never sure. Who could say why someone suddenly turns into a rogue elephant and tramples innocent people? My sister and I defied social convention, and my parents tried to beat the defiance out of us, or, at least, her.

Annie went to a counselor at a free counseling center for four years following her beating. To this day she swears by her counselor and she adores my father. She has become a convention-respecting woman, and she and my father are quite close. She forgave him for her peace of mind as well as his. Back in Santa Barbara, it was business as usual. The most pressing issue at the moment was a small piece of paper called a "green card," which would allow Pierre to work in the United States.

A purplish-faced government employee leaned unctuously over the counter at City Hall. He smiled at us. Then he said to Pierre, "You will have to wait at least nine months before you can work here."

"But we're married!" I cried out angrily. "I'm an American citizen!"

"But he still must have a green card to work," the employee continued in the same, nauseous tone of voice.

Pierre and I exchanged furious looks.

"Let's go to Salt Lake City where your grandparents live, Geeny," Pierre said. "I'll bet I can work there."

"Why?"

"Because the Mormons convert foreigners to their religion and bring them back to the U.S."

"And put them right to work," I nodded in agreement.

My eyes sparkled at the thought of those magnificent slopes for skiing, my favorite sport. "And we can go skiing at Park City and Alta!"

"We can see your grandparents again!" exuded Pierre.

It was settled. Pierre and I would go to Salt Lake City to find work and then continue our trip around the world.

Annie came into my room that night as I packed my bags. She sat on my bed and watched me. I turned and looked at her. Her bruises had disappeared, but her face looked wan and sad. Her light blond hair fell limply on her slight shoulders.

"Ginny, I'm going to miss you," she said simply.

"Annie, I'm going to miss you, too!" I said, hugging her warmly. "You'll be all right won't you?" I thought she would. The episode with my father had passed like so many bad dreams.

"I think so. I'm going to get some counseling."

I looked into her eyes and my face softened. Here I was going off on a gay adventure, and she was left behind to finish high school—to live alone with my mother and father.

"You'll see your friends, won't you?" I wasn't sure what I should say. There was so much happiness in my life, so little in hers. She nodded vaguely. "Once we're settled in Morocco, you have to come to visit us! We can travel in Europe together, too," I smiled at her encouragingly. "Promise!"

"That would be fun," she agreed.

"You can get a cheap student flight over, and I'll take care of the rest!"

My enthusiasm cheered her up a bit. "As soon as I graduate from high school," she promised.

I hugged her to me, and we said goodbye. I watched her walk out of my room, pushing a wisp of hair out of her eye. A spasm of regret seized me, but what could I do? I was married to Pierre.

✸ MARRIED IN MOROCCO

I SMILED CONSTANTLY when Pierre and I returned to Rabat, after our year-long honeymoon spent traveling through the United States, Mexico, and Europe. Married to someone as free-spirited and independently wealthy as Pierre made life feel like an ongoing party, as if the parties we had in Madrid had never and would never stop. But I wondered why people rarely returned my smile here. Was something wrong?

Then there was Tilman, Pierre's father, his huge hulk parked on a Louis XVI armchair in the middle of his antique store, beaming at me, telling me how much he loved living. The chandeliers glittered approvingly, their reflected light dancing merrily on his almost totally bald head. I smiled as he tried to tell me about his life.

"I've never worked a day in my life," he intoned with Pierre translating.

"Really?" I replied, nodding enthusiastically.

"I've loved everything I've done." He swept his large hand in the air, indicating the multitude of antiques and original paintings in Art et Style.

"First I built a farm in Ouezzane with my brother, Marc. We have one thousand hectares, you know." His eyes twinkled. I knew one thousand hectares was roughly five hundred acres, just as I knew and loved the story he was telling me.

"Then I met Françoise at the University of Algiers. When she got tired of living at the farm, we sold one of the apartment buildings her father left her in Algiers to buy this antique store. I've built many houses, the beach house in Alicante, all without a contractor."

Tilman puffed his chest up proudly and would have gone

133

on, but Pierre interrupted him.

"Papa, we have to go to the *medina* to eat shish kabobs with my friends now."

Tilman frowned at his son. "Always off somewhere with your friends. When will you learn that discipline is necessary in life?"

I laughed as the two of them got their backs up, like friendly cats. Then Tilman guffawed and let Pierre go.

As we drove toward the *medina*, Pierre suddenly stopped the car to watch some Moroccan police leading a man away in handcuffs.

"*Merde alors!* That's Mr. Leblanc! He's a client of my father, and bought the villa in Agdhal from him!"

Pierre jumped out of the car. I watched, intimidated by the police.

"Mr. Leblanc, Mr. Leblanc! What happened?"

"My Moroccan partner accused me of embezzlement! Now he has everything I own, including the villa! My wife and children have nowhere to stay!"

"But this is impossible! You are a rich man!"

"I *was* a rich man," rejoined Mr. Leblanc, sadly.

One of the policemen moved angrily toward Pierre. Pierre shook his fist at him and jumped back into the car.

He drove swiftly to the *medina*, explaining all the way.

"Mr. Leblanc is one of the wealthiest men in Rabat. He had to take a Moroccan as a partner in his business or lose everything. So he tried, and look what it brought him!"

"Why did he have to take a Moroccan partner?"

"It is the new law that requires that everything belong to the Moroccans. That's why the French are leaving. That's why we have to move to Spain."

"We still have enough time to get out, don't we?" Fright ran through my brain like a freight train, neatly derailing all my other thoughts of merriment and pleasure.

"We think so," muttered Pierre.

"You're not sure?"

"Nothing is sure in these countries."

Pierre drove through a magnificent horseshoe-shaped

archway in the wall that surrounded most of Rabat, a thousand-year-old wall, as thick as it was majestic. My eyes darted to the rugged contours of the adobe bricks that had held firm such a long time. How could this wall withstand the onslaught of all the armies of ancient Europe and the Turks, yet everything within be so unstable? I found it hard to be rational.

Pierre parked next to some street vendors skewering and barbecuing shish kabobs near a table full of people. On closer inspection, these turned out to be Pierre's friends, eating heartily already.

We joined them and soon the spicy shish kabobs, barbecued to a turn, erased the memory of Mr. Leblanc and the police. I regained my composure and smiled brilliantly at the friends at the table. None of them seemed disposed to smile back, but Bernard Simon, Pierre's Jewish-Moroccan friend who had married Christine, a French woman, returned my smile.

"You are from the United States," he said with an incredibly thick accent.

"Yes," I replied, smiling.

"I spent only a year there when I was in college, preparatory for accounting," he continued in fractured English.

"But you still remember your English," I inserted tactfully.

Bernard smiled, a glint in his eye. His even white teeth lit up his very round, very jovial face and somewhat overweight countenance. He was eating with gusto, so I had to wait as he downed another shish kabob.

"Yes, it was great!"

"Why didn't you stay?"

"It never occurred to me. Everything I have—my family...everything—is in Morocco."

"That's a good reason for coming back." I crinkled my eyes at him agreeably. I liked this large, outgoing man.

"But perhaps Christine and I should go to France."

"Why?"

"I am Jewish-Moroccan, and they refuse to advance me in my job because I'm not Muslim."

"Oh," I nodded my head, thinking of the man being led

away in handcuffs earlier. I looked over at a beggar sitting numbly in front of his begging bowl nearby, at the poor, shabby people in the street. I had never seen anything like this in the prosperous sixties in the United States. Suddenly I felt uneasy. I looked at Pierre's other friends, none of whom spoke any English. One of the women, Michelle, spoke Spanish, for her parents had been immigrants to Morocco from Spain. But she was at the far side of the table. When I finally managed to say something to her in Spanish, she answered politely, then continued talking in French.

Pierre, my only life raft in this sea of French shur-shuring—for French sounded sort of like snakes slithering through grass—talked to another friend, Jean Marc. I was stranded.

I turned back to Bernard. Suddenly an announcement was made over a loudspeaker. Everyone except Pierre and Jean Marc stopped eating to listen.

"Pierre, what are they saying?" I managed to disengage Pierre from the animated conversation he was having with Jean Marc about spending the night at the beach.

Pierre looked at me with a trace of irritation. The others listened with surprise, then started talking all at once.

"Pierre, what did they say?"

The loudspeaker blared on in Arabic. Pierre looked at me and condescendingly translated.

"Geeny, the Egyptians have declared war on Israel."

"What?"

"The radio says they are ten kilometers from Tel Aviv."

"But isn't Jordan ten kilometers from Tel Aviv?"

Pierre explained carefully. "Yes, but the Jordanians will give the Egyptians access to Israel."

"What's going to happen?"

"We don't have to worry. We're in Morocco. Israel is thousands of kilometers from here."

I turned to Bernard, who talked nervously to his wife, Christine.

"Bernard, are you worried?" I asked.

He turned to me and smiled quickly. "No, not really, but

you never know," he answered. Then he continued talking to his wife.

Christine stood up and excused herself, a worried look on her normally pleasant face. Bernard nodded briefly and they left.

Pierre resumed his conversation with Jean Marc, laughing a bit to show that he wasn't worried.

The loudspeaker continued to blare away. Eating charcoal-cooked meat on a stick no longer appealed to me. I had to know what was going on. I interrupted Pierre again.

"What are they saying, Pierre?"

"They say they will wash the Jews into the Mediterranean on a carpet of blood." Pierre smiled so I wouldn't get too alarmed.

"What?"

"That's just the Arabic way of saying things, Geeny. You don't have to worry. Just eat your dinner and don't worry."

"You didn't tell me there was going to be a war when I came here!"

"It's in the Middle East, thousands of kilometers from here. Really, we are safe. King Hassan is pro-Western. He was educated in France and accepts millions of dollars in foreign aid from the U.S. We don't have to worry." Pierre smiled broadly, his toothy grin and tousled hair contrasting sharply with this dramatic statement.

"But Pierre...wash the Jews into the Mediterranean Sea on a bloody carpet!" With a frightened look I implored him to explain this bloody rhetoric to me. "Do they mean it?"

He patted my knee under the table and then continued talking to Jean Marc. In consternation, I continued eating, albeit with a certain loss of appetite.

The next morning dawned clear and crisp, with sun streaming in through the big glass doors that opened onto our balcony. I rubbed my eyes and yawned lazily. Pierre turned over and we smiled at each other.

Breakfast was as delicious as usual, with huge cups of *cafe au lait*, marmalade Tilman had made that oozed onto the white tablecloth when I tried to put too much on my toast, and Amina drifting in and out to make sure we had enough to eat. Françoise murmured in her seductive voice to Tilman and then to Pierre, and I couldn't understand a thing.

I spoke to Françoise in Spanish, asking her about the announcement over the loudspeaker last night.

Her eyes sparkled as she smiled at me and explained in Spanish. "The Arabs always exaggerate. It's just their way of speaking. They don't have a trained army. I'm sure this so-called attack is badly organized and can't damage the Jews' position. They are well prepared."

"What about the Jews here? What about Bernard and his wife? They left right after the announcement…"

"They just went to get their little boy, Didier," inserted Pierre while downing another buttered *tartine*. "They are upset, of course, but no one bothers the Jews here."

"They don't?"

"No…well, on a rare occasion…they are shipping all of the poorer Jews to Israel so there will be no problems."

"How many Jews is that?"

Françoise looked at me, her eyes full of understanding. "Virginie, these things don't concern us. The worst has already happened. And that was the fault of deGaulle…in Algeria."

At the sound of the name deGaulle, my usually placid father-in-law erupted like a volcano, albeit a French volcano. I couldn't understand a word he said, but judging by the color his face had turned, beet red, he was not pleased.

"What's he saying, Pierre?" I begged my husband to translate.

"That deGaulle was a son of a bitch to abandon the French in Algeria. Look, Geeny, the history of North Africa is very complicated. Maybe I can give you a book to read that will help."

"A book to read.…" I accidentally spilled more gooseberry jam onto the pearly white tablecloth. Amina came in from the kitchen and I tried to apologize. She smiled and Françoise said not to worry about the tablecloth. "Amina will wash it," she laughed blithely. I knew she would have to "wash it" on a scrub board in the laundry room next to the kitchen.

Pierre popped out of his Louis XV dining room chair and returned with a thin, well-worn volume titled *The Lords of the Atlas* by Gavin Maxwell.

"This book will explain everything," Pierre assured me.

Taking the book, I pushed my Louis XV chair back to leave the table. Everyone winced.

"What's the matter?"

"Geeny, you make so much noise when you push your chair. Try to lift it so it doesn't scrape against the marble floor."

"Noise? I didn't notice. Sorry. I'll try to be more careful." They looked reassured as I left the table to read this magical book that would explain this country I was having a harder and harder time comprehending. With typical American confidence, I nonetheless assumed everything would be back to normal soon enough, and Pierre and I could continue our carefree life. It was all I had ever known.

The glittering chandelier, whose tulip-shaped candle holders defined the elegance that surrounded me, cast a pretty pattern on the page as I immersed myself in the history of Morocco. All the extremes of courtesy and cruelty passed before my eyes. I was just reading about the custom of throwing a huge party in the courtyard of the palace of Marrakesh for the poorest people in town as the old-fashioned way of raising an army, a very hung-over one at that, for the men were drugged, then forced at gunpoint to maraud the outlying villages for "taxes" for the sultan of Marrakesh. The I.R.S. seemed much less daunting after this particular passage. Then the Jews from the Mellah, or the Jewish section of town, got to salt the heads of those who didn't want to pay their taxes. I'd heard of death and taxes, but this was extreme! After the heads were properly salted, they were stuck on the spikes on the ramparts to cast an evil eye at all who would threaten the security of the fabled city of Marrakesh, the jewel of Morocco.

The clicking footsteps of Pierre's brisk walk announced his arrival, so I smiled and put the book down.

"We have to make a trip to Alicante, Geeny," he announced.

"Why?"

"My father wants me to take some things there."

"Like what?"

"Furniture, Berber jewelry…"

"Berber jewelry?! I didn't know you sold that."

"We're going to try to start selling it in Spain."

"You mean when we open our antique shop in Madrid?"

"I'm not so sure about Madrid anymore."

"What?"

"It's very hard to make a living in Madrid, Geeny. You have to sell a lot of antiques to stay in business."

"But you promised me we'd stay here a year so I could learn to speak French, and then move to Madrid!"

"Things change, Geeny."

I could hardly believe my ears. "What do you mean? You love Madrid as much as I do!"

"It's too expensive, Geeny. In Alicante we can live at the farm and I can start an antique shop there much cheaper."

"Alicante! I'll die of boredom! There's nothing there!"

"We have to be practical, Geeny."

"Not that practical!" I threw my hands in the air in a gesture of disillusionment, something completely new to me. Live in Alicante at the farm—never!

Just then the loudspeakers blared another message. The Moulets' apartment was around the corner from King Hassan's État Major, or military headquarters, so we could hear the announcements of the progress of the war between Egypt and Israel.

Pierre listened for a minute, then started to hunt for something in the bedroom.

"What did they say?" I demanded.

"Now they are six kilometers from Tel Aviv," he remarked casually.

"They're almost there!"

"They're at the Jordanian border. It's six kilometers from Tel Aviv," laughed Pierre. He looked at me. "Don't be frightened, Geeny. This is just the way they talk. The Jews can take care of themselves. You Americans can't understand these things."

Heaving a sigh of frustration, I turned my back to him. The chandelier sparkled brightly on my mounting anger.

"Geeny, don't worry. Everything is going to be all right." Pierre scratched his head and turned around. "Now, where did I put the keys to the farm."

"Keys to the farm?" I was incredulous. How could he talk about the farm when the Egyptians were six kilometers from Tel Aviv?

"Yes, we're going to take some things to Alicante in a few days. I don't know where I hid the key to the farm. You should see it! It is huge, a two-hundred-year-old key."

"I can hardly wait," I replied, tartly.

Amina, the Moulet's maid, tiptoed into the house holding *Le Petit Marocain*, the four-page daily newspaper. She placed it carefully on the Moulets' Louis XIV dining room table, a magnificent piece of furniture with a thick, round, beveled slab of marble for a tabletop. This was a piece of furniture made to last forever. There were wormholes in the thick, hand-carved base shaped like the capital of an Ionian column, which only added to its value.

Once in the kitchen, she peeled off her long black gloves and then took off her veil, folding them carefully and putting them in a kitchen drawer. Then she took off the heavy *jallabah*, a thick outer garment made of densely-woven grey cotton, which covered her caftan, a shimmering robe made of a multicolored transparent rayon. Several undergarments came between this and Amina's final layer of underwear. Everything was held together by a silver belt.

I walked into the kitchen as she hung up her *jallabah*.

"*Bonjour,* Amina," I said, practicing the only French I knew at this point.

"*Bonjour, madame,*" she replied, lowering her eyes in deference. "*Le journal, il est à la salle à manger.*"

"What?" I was at a complete loss. I turned on my heel

and got Pierre, who was still rummaging around our bedroom trying to find the damned key to the farm in Alicante.

"I can't understand what Amina said! Come interpret for
me." I stood before him, my eyes full of urgency.

"Of course, you can't, Geeny. You don't speak French yet."

"So interpret for me!"

"She's just the maid, Geeny."

"I don't care! I want to know what she said!" I started to
tug him by the arm.

"Geeny, I have to find the keys to the farm!"

"Pierre, you are obsessed with these keys! Forget them for
a minute and tell me what your maid said!"

Françoise walked into the room, pushing her tousled
black hair out of her eyes in a haphazard attempt to form an
early morning hairdo.

"Mama, I can't find the keys to the farm," announced
Pierre.

"*Eh, bien,* where do you think you put them?" inquired
Françoise, always solicitous of Pierre's least ennui.

"I thought I hid them in the locked case in the dresser
drawers, but they aren't there."

Pierre and Françoise exchanged looks of amused concern. "Did you look in the armoire, *mon cheri*?" she asked.

I left the room and went into the living room, which ad-
joined the dining room. I picked up the newspaper Amina
had placed on the dining room table and couldn't understand a word. It was written in French.

Brandishing the newspaper, I returned to our bedroom,
hoping to get some information out of Pierre. He held several keys in his hand by the time I got there, and Françoise
clasped her hands in front of her, making suggestions regarding the whereabouts of the other keys. She smiled radiantly,
happy to be of help to her darling only son.

They looked at me holding the newspaper.

"*Merci bien,* Virginie," remarked Françoise. Then she
chortled a guttural laugh and said in Spanish, "My son has so
many keys he needs a locksmith."

I laughed politely, then pointed at the newspaper. "What

does it say?"

"Oh, *Le Petit Marocain?* Nothing," laughed Françoise, who seemed to find humor in everything.

"Nothing, *nada?* It must say something."

Françoise took me by the hand and led me aside for one of her confidential remarks.

"This newspaper never tells anything of value. The real events are never reported to us, although we get glimpses of them from time to time."

"What do you mean, 'the real events'?" I blurted, hoping to get a hint about what to expect in this country.

"I found it!" announced a jubilant Pierre, holding up an enormous, wrought-iron key that looked like it must have been forged by Hercules.

"Thank God," breathed a relieved Françoise, taking Pierre affectionately by the arm. "My son has all his keys."

"Now I can take the jewelry and furniture to Alicante," said Pierre.

"Now, in the middle of a war? Shouldn't we wait to see what happens?" I asked.

Françoise looked at me as if I were a child. She took me by the hand again.

"Virginie, so much has already happened in North Africa that these events hardly phase us. We are used to such things."

"What things?" I demanded. Pierre turned to face me.

"Geeny, I was on the road to Casablanca the day Mohammed V died under anesthesia during a routine tooth extraction. People swarmed down the hillside and blocked all of the cars. I feared we would be torn limb from limb like Christine's father."

"Christine's father was torn limb from limb?! Bernard's wife's father?"

"Yes, during the Independence Movement in 1954."

"Why?"

"He was driving through the farmlands near the Rif Mountains, very near our farm in Ouezzane, when a crowd of people descended from the hills and tore him and the other

Frenchman in the car to pieces. No one ever knew why."

"Were they soldiers?" I asked, wide-eyed with horror.

"Yes, but there was no evidence of anything unusual. They were just driving along a country road."

"When was the Independence Movement?"

"The Moroccans got their independence in 1956." Pierre looked at my ashen face. "It was not a bloody movement."

"Except for the beheadings at the king's palace!" interjected Françoise, always fond of supplying ghastly details.

"But this bloodbath was between El Glaoui, the pasha of Marrakesh, and the loyalists," argued Pierre.

"Good Lord!" I exclaimed and sat down on one of the Louis XV chairs in front of the settee.

"Virginie, we have tried to explain this country to you, but you wouldn't listen. You are American. It is a different world there." Françoise went off like a firecracker. "We have to take a Moroccan partner in our business or get out of Morocco. You saw Mr. Leblanc being led away in handcuffs. His Moroccan partner accused him of cheating him."

"Yes," I nodded my head somewhat numbly. I was beginning to forget about partying forever. It was dawning on me that life was not exactly a beer bust in Morocco. Actually they didn't drink alcohol; it was forbidden by the Koran. However blood letting seemed quite acceptable—if it was in the name of Allah.

I nodded numbly at my hosts. I was their captive audience. I only wanted to understand what was going on in this country, and they were my only interpreters for the moment.

"How long will we stay in Alicante?" I asked Pierre, opening the suitcase I had just unpacked.

"Only a couple of weeks, Geeny. Just long enough to leave these things at the farm and for me to buy some tires and things at Andorra."

"Where's Andorra?"

"It's a duty-free port between Spain and France." Pierre spoke as if I were a complete ignoramus, and indeed, I was beginning to feel like one. The days of *"arriba la fiesta"* evaporated like so many Saharan mirages. I began to pack.

☼ ALMOST TO ALICANTE

PIERRE ALWAYS PACKED THE CAR tightly, but this time we had an additional load, a huge Louis XVI sofa and matching armchair. Pierre fussed around the car with one of the workers from the shop, scrambling and shouting orders in Arabic that I couldn't understand. The sofa swayed like a giant whale for a moment, then went up and onto the top of our Simca. The chair fit into the back of the car. They finished quickly, and I opened the door. A suitcase jutted between the driver's seat and mine, but I could squeeze in.

Pierre jumped into the driver's seat, and we sped off to Tangier through the semi-arid countryside, past sturdily built homes with blue with white paint framing the doors in the small, roadside towns. Cacti jutted out of the ground haphazardly. Occasional eucalyptus trees dotted the horizon.

"It reminds me of Mexico," I commented.

"The dry part of Mexico," rejoined Pierre. "Would you pass me the water?"

I unscrewed the cap of the Evian water. He took it and guzzled while he drove, never slackening his pace.

A car appeared just in front of us. We almost sideswiped it.

"Pierre, be careful!" I admonished.

"Geeny, I know how to drive!" he shot back, accelerating as I gripped the arm rest next to me.

Pierre always drove like we were on the Indianapolis Speedway. Speed was his thrill, his drug. He knew no other way to travel. I inhaled, forcing myself to relax.

Soon enough, Tangier sparkled on the hillside that led to the harbor where we would catch the ferry to Algeciras, Spain. Pierre gunned the car into the customs line and impatiently waited his turn. The customs agent approached, his floppy blue hat shielding his sweating face from the sun. He took out a pencil and paper when he saw us. From a distance, a radio blared news in Arabic about the war with Israel.

Pierre held out his passport with the traditional ten *dirham* bill, worth two dollars, clearly visible.

Pointing at the sofa atop our car, the custom's agent started to babble excitedly. "That cost a lot. I know that's expensive. I've been to Casablanca. I know that's expensive."

Pierre frowned and reached for his wallet. The customs agent continued to talk excitedly about the value of the furniture we were taking out of the country. Pierre slapped another ten *dirham* note in his passport. The man continued to rave on, so Pierre looked even more disgusted and put another ten dirham note in his passport, a total of six dollars in American money. Suddenly the man motioned us to the head of a long line of cars waiting to board the ferry.

."*Allez-y!* Go ahead!" he shouted, and we rolled past the other waiting vehicles. Pierre started to laugh.

"He missed the Berber jewelry," he turned and smiled at me. I smiled naively back, happy that he was happy.

As he drove the car onto the lower deck of the ferry, I noticed another boat, a cargo boat, pulling out of the harbor in front of us. People milled around on the decks.

"What's on that boat?" I asked.

"Probably Jews."

"You mean Jewish people?"

Pierre glanced quickly at me. "Yes, Geeny. They're taking the poor Jews to Israel."

"Really? Because of the war?"

"Because there is a place for them now."

"What about Morocco? I thought this was their home."

"Morocco has been their home for hundreds of years, but they are better off in Israel."

"Why?" I was beginning to feel a bit stupid, but I wanted to get some straight answers. The truth seemed so elusive in this country.

"They were never allowed to be really equal here unless they had a lot of money. They were still Jewish and had to stay away from the Moroccan society."

"Why?"

"They are not Muslims." Pierre frowned at me in vexation.

"The Muslims and the Jews have lived here like brothers for many centuries, but the Jew could never ride a horse, only a donkey."

"So the Muslims were the big brother?" I ventured, trying to understand the complex situation.

"Don't worry about it. We are leaving the country in a year."

"So they were inferior to the Muslims?"

"Not exactly. The Jews are Jews, and the Muslims are Muslims. They control the country." He sighed and went on. "Do not expect to understand everything about this country—don't worry about it. It has nothing to do with us."

Pierre turned and squinted at the ocean. I squinted at the boatload of people as it pulled away. They looked cramped but not unhappy. I couldn't tell. My stomach felt queasy.

The trip across the Strait of Gibraltar took an hour. Then we had to go through customs again, this time on the Spanish side. Things went smoothly enough until Pierre couldn't find my passport. Then he started to search his papers, the car and me.

"Pierre, you had it with you in Tangier!"

"I know," he muttered, frustrated. Sweat started to bead on his brow as he ransacked our suitcase.

"Geeny, you're going to have to go back on the train."

"But I can only speak a few words of French, much less Arabic!" I couldn't picture myself fielding all the questions in customs, much less everything else involved in getting back to Rabat alone, without Pierre.

"Don't worry," he smiled and kissed me. "I'll write a note to the ambassador to say it's okay." Then he added, "I can't go back to Morocco with everything I have in the car."

"The ambassador?" I asked unhappily.

"The French ambassador. We know him. He will help you if you need help."

"Pierre, are you out of your mind?"

"It will be O.K., Geeny. You are a smart girl. You will get home safely."

I stared into his sparkling eyes. He grinned his big Pierre smile and then warmly reassured me everything would be all right. Heaving a sigh, I nodded my head in acquiescence.

Pierre floored the accelerator as he left me, Berber jewels hidden under the floorboards of the car, with the huge Louis XVI sofa swaying in the wind.

"Don't go so fast! The sofa is going to fall off!" My eyes widened as Pierre gunned the car into the beginning of a curve.

"Geeny, this is the way I drive! I have to go fast or I will get bored. Don't worry about the sofa. It is strapped on very securely. I watched Rafael do it!" He waved a confident hand at me and disappeared into the distance.

I thought of burly Rafael, the Moulets' cabinetmaker, tying the huge sofa onto the car. Slow, sure, an excellent craftsman, he had worked for the Moulets in their *atelier*, or workshop, for twenty years. He would do almost anything they asked.

Then I followed the line of people waiting to take the ferry back to Morocco. News blared over the radio in Arabic. It sounded ominous. I nervously moved forward in the line.

Two men in their early twenties turned to me. One was slender with a blond, frank face. The other looked even younger. He smiled an even smile and said something to me in French.

"I don't speak French," I faltered. "*Pero hablo español.*"

That opened the magical door. He spoke Spanish, his parents had been immigrants from Spain to Morocco. Where was I going?

"To Rabat," I answered, smiling.

"My father is coming to pick us up in Tangier. He can give you a ride. My name is José Ornelas."

He put out his right hand and I shook it firmly.

"*Gracias, muchas gracias. Me llamo Ginny…eh, Virginia Moulet.*"

I figured I'd better translate my first name into Spanish. They nodded their approval. I beamed and followed them onto the ferry, not daring to let them out of my sight. I couldn't believe my good luck. Or my bad luck with my passport. It didn't matter now. I instinctively knew I was in good hands.

The sun was setting, a crimson orb sinking into the horizon, when we arrived in Tangier.

"When is your father arriving?" I asked José politely.

"Tomorrow morning."

"Tomorrow morning?" I echoed, surprised.

"Yes, we're going to spend the night in Tangier."

"Oh."

"Don't worry. We'll take care of you. A woman should never be alone after nightfall in a Muslim town."

I nodded my head dumbly as we walked over the cobblestone streets past the flat facades of the hotels near the wharf.

"We'll make sure your room adjoins ours. Just in case you have to call out during the night." They smiled sweetly at me and I smiled sweetly back.

We entered a few hotels, only to be told they didn't have two vacant rooms next to each other. Finally we found one with two adjoining rooms.

I entered my room, observing the traditional mosaic tile that covered the floor and went halfway up the walls. A single light bulb suspended from the ceiling lit the room. And the lock? I tried to lock the door with the key they had given me, but it didn't fit. I jangled it in and out several times, then went next door to see my friends.

"My door doesn't lock," I told them.

José looked up from his suitcase. "Those idiots! What do they think?" Jean, the French-speaking friend, talked rapidly in French, gesturing toward my room.

"We can move your bed into our room and you will be

safe," José announced gravely. I nodded numbly, thinking of Pierre speeding wildly along the narrow road to Alicante with the huge sofa lurching back and forth. What choice did I have?

Jean and José gallantly moved the bed from my room into theirs, placing it between their two beds. Then we all sat down and chatted in Spanish and French with a couple of English words occasionally popping out of my mouth, as my Spanish was still far from perfect.

Their fathers had immigrated to Casablanca, just forty miles south of Rabat, and had prospered. It was a good thing I had run into them, because they would take care of me. Jean opened his suitcase and took out a silver-hilted dagger. I ran an approving finger along the blade and he smiled.

Then José opened his suitcase and took a bottle of wine out of it.

"We thought it would calm your nerves if we had a glass of wine before bedtime," said José.

I looked at our opened suitcases, the bottle of red wine and the two young faces looking earnestly at mine. I trusted them.

"Let's get some glasses," I suggested.

Jean went down to the front desk and reappeared with three wine glasses. José poured the wine with an elegant flourish. We took a small sip to test it and then smiled broadly at one another. It was a very good wine.

I raised my glass high and said, "Here's to a good night's sleep!" Jean and José clicked the rims of their glasses against mine. I smiled at their boyish faces, so young yet responsible. Then we sat down on our respective beds, mine nestled securely between theirs. They looked at me and we laughed at the unconventionality of our improvised bedroom arrangement. A one-night stand, if there ever was one.

I raised my glass again and said, "Here's to a good night's sleep!"

We laughed gaily, then snuggled down under the covers and fell fast asleep.

The morning light streamed in through the tiny slats of

the wooden *volets*, or ceiling-to-floor shutters, that darkened our room. Having slept deeply, I stretched and uttered a sigh of contentment. Opening an eye, I surveyed my surroundings. The high ceilings, the shuttered windows, the opened suitcases on the floor. Then I turned toward José and remembered where I was.

Jean moaned and rubbed his eyes. I jumped out of bed and ran into the bathroom, knowing they would want to use it, too. I splashed water on my face and smiled at my reflection in the mirror. Then I laughed at myself for my nerve, a married woman spending the night with two men barely twenty years old, maybe younger. My princes in shining armor! I wondered where Pierre might be—probably at the farm in Alicante by now.

Smoothing out the wrinkles in the dress I had slept in, I ventured back into the bedroom. Jean nodded politely at me, murmured *"Bonjour,"* then shot into the bathroom. José still slept.

I opened the shutters and stared out at the town of Tangier, gracefully sloping down toward the harbor, where men loaded crates of oranges onto a tanker. The sunlight sparkled on the minarets of a mosque painted an iridescent blue and gold. A profound quiet engulfed the town; even the distant harbor looked peaceful. I wondered if it were a holiday.

"My father will be here at nine o'clock."

I turned to find José up and dressed. Jean came out of the bathroom.

"We must eat breakfast and meet him at my uncle's."

"Your uncle lives here?"

"He has lived here for forty years." José stared at me, unblinking. "Of course, he has plans to leave."

I nodded my mute understanding, then listened to the unusual quiet of the morning.

"Why is it so quiet?"

They exchanged uneasy looks.

"I don't know. We'll find out from my uncle."

Carrying our suitcases, we went down the mosaic staircase, each pattern dedicated to Allah, and José and Jean paid the hotel bill.

"Let me pay my part," I protested.

"No," they both said resolutely. "You are our guest."

I nodded my head slightly and tried to protest, but they wouldn't hear of it.

José's stout uncle squatted in front of his tannery table, working on a leather wallet. His balding head glistened with perspiration. He smiled broadly and stood up to greet us, wiping his hands on his tanner's apron.

First he hugged his nephew, then he shook hands with Jean and me.

"Please, come into the living room," he gestured toward a room with a huge brass tray in the center with a samovar on it.

"You must want some coffee. Have you eaten anything yet?"

José shook his head. His uncle clapped his hands together, and a Moroccan woman came out of the kitchen.

"Prepare some food, Fatima," he said, and she quickly ducked back into the kitchen.

As he poured coffee for us, his bald head bobbing as he and José talked enthusiastically, I ventured a question.

"Why is it so quiet today?"

"Don't you know?" responded the uncle, surprised. "The war with Israel is over."

"It is?"

"Yes. Yesterday. It lasted just six days."

"Just six days?" I had never heard of a war that lasted only six days.

"Yes, they're calling it the Six-Day War."

"Who won?"

"The Jews, of course," boomed the uncle's powerful voice.

Jean and José smiled their approval.

"The Jews now occupy some of the Arab's land, and they are madder than a wet hen. That's why it is so quiet. This is a day of mourning."

"Did many people get killed?"

Not many. But their pride has suffered an enormous blow. Losing to the Jews is *hashuma*...uh...shame."

Just then José's father drove up in his Simca, a small, compact European car. We quickly finished our coffees and ran to greet him.

After shaking hands and bussing cheeks, as is the French and Spanish custom, we got in the car and took off. José's father was in a hurry. I settled back to watch the countryside. The stately palms that lined the exit from Tangier seemed to shimmer, mirage-like, as the sun rose higher in the sky. Was this all a mirage? I mused, looking back at Tangier as it receded in the distance.

Jean and José spoke in French to José's father, and I grew drowsy. The heat of the day grew more and more oppressive. My eyes closed. I slumped between the arm rest and the car door in the back seat and fell asleep.

Images of strange ships and people whirled through my mind when suddenly a loud thump awakened me.

"What was that?" I asked in Spanish.

"A bird," replied José.

"A bird?" I thought maybe I was still dreaming.

"Sometimes they die in mid-flight, then fall straight to the ground. This one hit the windshield and bounced off."

"Is it that hot?" I asked, refreshed from my nap.

"Very hot, not too unusual for this time of year," he replied.

I shifted my view to the semi-arid countryside. Scrub bushes and occasional palm trees dotted the slight hill we were climbing. Suddenly, without warning, a large band of people swarmed down from the hillside. There were both men and women, and they were completely covered by the heavy *jallabahs* that protected them from the sun. A cloud of dust hung in the air behind them. I could hear them shouting in Arabic.

"What are they saying?" I asked, the pit of my stomach churning like a cement mixer.

"Don't worry, we can get away!" shouted José's father as

he floored the accelerator. The car lurched ahead and I turned to watch the crowd fade into the distance.

"What's going on?!" I demanded.

"We'll find out when we get to Rabat," answered José, who then conferred in a low voice with his father.

I looked at Jean sitting next to me, but he only shook his head. *"Je regrette,* Virginie," he said. I wished I could speak French so I could understand him. I would learn, I vowed, gripping the arm rest tightly.

We arrived in Rabat to find Pierre's father standing in front of Art et Style. Shaking his fist angrily, he shouted at a crowd of silent onlookers. A broken window told the rest of the story. Françoise stood next to him, wringing her hands in front of her in her inimitable way. Occasionally she said something to placate him, but he was too angry to listen.

When I got out of a car driven by strangers, Françoise ran up to me, her eyes wide with fear.

"Where's Pierre?" she quavered.

"In Alicante by now, I'm sure!" I shot back.

"What?"

"He couldn't find my passport, so I had to come back alone...well, these gentlemen offered to accompany me." I gestured toward Jean, José, and his father, who had gotten out of the car to see if they could help. Just then a policeman ran up and blew his whistle, pushing the passersby away from the store and cordoning off the broken window with a sturdy rope. As he twisted it tight between the door handle of the store's entrance and the broken window, more people gathered and started to shout.

Tilman started to shout back at them, and the policeman joined in. A mixture of French and Arabic curses ensued. Suddenly, José's father intervened and said something that made the crowd shrink back.

The policeman waved his baton at them, for he was un-armed, as was the custom in Morocco in 1967. Then he turned and with a huge smile shook Tilman's hand, talking rapidly in either French or Arabic, or a mixture of the two. Two other policemen arrived on foot and positioned themselves in front of the store. Tilman looked at them with a mixture of relief and anger. Meanwhile, Françoise chattered nervously and held onto her husband's arm.

"What happened?" I begged her in Spanish.

"Someone threw a rock through the store window. They took some things before we could get here. The Arabs always take advantage of the situation. This bloody war."

"But nothing of value!" boomed Tilman. "They have no taste."

Suddenly they all laughed.

"*¡No tienen buen gusto!*" translated José, and I started laughing, too. After all, good taste was all that mattered in France.

José's father went up to my in-laws and introduced himself. They shook hands, laughing all the while.

I wondered what Pierre would have done in such a situation. I kept laughing with the others.

Then I turned to José. "*¿Qué dijo tu padre?* What did your father say?"

"He said something in Arabic that meant the evil eye will get them if they don't leave immediately."

I looked into his eyes to see if this was true, and he beamed merrily at me, nodding his curly head, laughing at my astonishment.

"They are very superstitious. They believe that everyone here is a potential murderer and that they themselves are potential murderers."

Before I could register the meaning of this last rejoinder, my mother-in-law walked over to me, pushing her black hair back to cover the bald spot on top of her head. She wore her gold dress, with expensive pearls around her neck. I knew, however, that perspiration and dirt marked the collar of that dress, for Françoise seldom had Amina wash her best clothes.

"Virginie, who are these men?" she asked, staring coldly into my eyes.

"This is José, and that is his father and his best friend, Jean. They helped me get back here after Pierre lost... um...couldn't find my passport at the border. They even spent the night with me to protect me from the...." I faltered, unable to finish the sentence and realizing I had probably said the wrong thing.

Instead, Françoise took me by the hand. "You should never be without your husband in this country. People may not understand your reasons, however innocent they may be." She gave me an imperious look down the beaked spine of her nose. "And you need to help Pierre with passports and other details. He can't do everything."

"Yes, of course," I mumbled humbly out of respect for her age. "But I could have been hurt on the trip back." My eyes filled with anger and I averted my head so she would not see my true feelings.

"We are glad you got back safely," she added, hugging me. I sighed with relief and hugged her back, realizing that my mother-in-law would probably uphold the centuries-old reputation of mothers-in-law. But, then, I was no saint, either.

The next morning dawned hot and humid with heat rising in waves. The dreaded *sherghi*, or hot desert winds, were upon us. During these heat spells few people ventured outside for fear of sunstrokes. The clammy heat made my clothes stick to my skin. And the radios had quit blaring news about the war. Lethargy reigned for all except Françoise, who wrung her hands and walked in anxious little circles, her heels clicking on the mosaic surface of the dining room.

"When will Pierre get back?" she worried.

"I'm sure he will return as soon as possible, Françoise," I reassured her. "Unless he forgets his passport."

She spun around and watched me stifle a giggle.

"This is *très grave, Virginie!*" she insisted.

"Yes, I know, Françoise," I said more somberly.

"The last time Tilman and I went through the Moroccan customs, they had the *culot* to make us submit to a body cavity search! You Americans can't imagine what they are capable of!" she fumed.

"A body cavity search?"

"Yes!" she glared at me.

"They made you take your clothes off?"

"Just to humiliate us!"

"Oh. I'm sorry." I couldn't imagine my refined in-laws naked in front of a bunch of sweaty officials. I had never heard of a body cavity search in my life. Françoise's eyes bored into mine, so I turned my face to the wall and studied the figure of Neptune on one of their magnificent gold-plated clocks.

"Wealth does not protect you from everything," she continued, a bit shrilly. "Sometimes it even invites disaster." I nodded my head gravely. She gave me a steely-eyed look to make sure I had grasped the importance of what she had said, then turned and strode nervously into the bedroom to talk to Tilman.

Pierre returned in a few days. He clenched his fists in bright anger when he heard that the store had almost been looted.

"Did they get any of the jewelry, *maman*?" he asked plaintively.

"*Non, mon cheri*, only things of little value. *Des chinoiseries.* Chinese things." Françoise held him tightly for a minute to reassure herself that he was all right. Amina entered the room with coffee and piping-hot milk for our breakfast. When she saw Françoise clutching Pierre she looked a bit surprised. I laughed and winked at Amina, so she smiled discreetly, then put the coffee and milk on the tablecloth that always covered the huge, round dining room table when we ate.

Tilman joined us and we had a good laugh at the poor taste of the people who had tried to rob us. Then I asked about the war with Israel and they laughed even harder.

"Why are you laughing?" I asked Pierre.

"Because the war was over yesterday."

"Yes, I know that! But how did they win?" I exclaimed, suddenly feeling angry and left out.

"Don't worry, Virginie," said Françoise, putting her hand on mine to make me feel better. I thought of the war the United States was fighting in Vietnam and wondered when it would be over.

"All they left behind were their sandals," Françoise told me in Spanish, so I could understand. "That's all that was left of the Egyptian army." She chuckled at her sally, and I smiled to show I appreciated her wit. I later learned that the Israelis had counterattacked the Egyptian air force while the planes were still on the ground, destroying their capacity for air strikes in one fell swoop. The war had really ended at this point, although the foot soldiers were still near Tel Aviv. They eventually ran for it, taking refuge in Palestine, and they did leave a sea of sandals behind which *Paris Match* pictured on the front cover of the magazine the next month.

When Françoise and Tilman had left the table, Pierre showed me a new record he had bought in Spain.

"Look, Geeny, it's American! 'Feeling Groovy.'"

He went over to the small record player and put it on, a single 45 r.p.m. disc. The lyrics filled the room with a happy melody. Pierre took me by the hand. We began to dance on the smooth mosaic floor in the dining room. Pierre took me by the waist and smiled into my eyes. I was delighted. The rhythm picked up and he swung me into an easy swing dance as Amina opened the door to collect the plates from the table.

She watched us shyly. Pierre said something to her in French, and she smiled and bowed her head. I heard her respond "*Oui, monsieur,*" as I spun under Pierre's outstretched arm to the mellow beat of the song.

Amina cleared the table as Pierre and I swung around the dining room, careful not to run into her. My confidence in Pierre was restored, as well as in the future. I could not believe anything really bad could ever happen to us.

Later in the day I curled up in one of the brocade-covered armchairs and listened to the Assimil records Pierre had bought me to help me learn French, something I wanted to do as quickly as possible. Amina dusted the furniture as the voices on the record repeated, "*C'est un homme. C'est une femme. Ce sont des enfants.*" I repeated these sentences, and Amina began to laugh at me. I caught her eye and started to laugh with her, for it must have been comical to see me talking into the thin air. I thought of what Pierre had told me about her, that she was the daughter of the youngest wife of a wealthy sultan's harem in the south of Morocco, near Marrakesh. Her mother had been too young to know how to fight for her share of the inheritance when the rich old man died, and she and Amina had only a small grocery store to support them. Then Amina married at age fifteen and had her only son. But her husband left her for another woman. She had no money for herself or her son, so she remarried a humbler man and worked for Europeans. But she seemed to know she was a cut above the rest because she always wore long, black gloves under her burnoose to work and carried herself with great dignity.

"*Ca va bien?*" I asked her. "How are you doing?"

"*Très bien, merci, madame,*" she replied with a slight inclination of her head and a wry smile.

I smiled back, hardly believing this woman could be my maid, and that I was living in the lap of luxury in Morocco. I never felt perfectly at ease in this country. I was glad we would only stay a year, long enough for me to learn French and for Pierre to reestablish his father's antique store in Madrid, where I felt we rightfully belonged, with our friends from the university, from the year of the free spirits. How distant that seemed now.

I sighed and repeated, "*Le chat est beau. Le chien est gentil.*"

✸ HIGH SOCIETY IN RABAT

PIERRE PARKED HIS CAR in front of Club Equestre, which was lit up and filled with its members. Many were Pierre's childhood friends. They had belonged to this club most of their lives, founded by their parents, who loved horseback riding. Housed in a low, ramshackle building with little pretension, the club served as a meeting place for many of the old colonists. Wealthy Moroccans married to American and European women also joined and were dressed with careful elegance for the *soirée* thrown by the club's president, Monsieur Petit, a man reputed to own half the apartment buildings in Paris.

Pierre jauntily opened the car door for me, and I got out, walking up the path that led to the club in my best silk dress. Bernard's wife, Christine, was there with their four-year-old son, Didier. He was their only child, and they insisted on taking him everywhere with them. Tonight they had dressed him in a velvet suit that would have put Little Lord Fauntleroy to shame. Christine smiled graciously and shook my hand, saying *"Enchantée."* I did the same, frustrated that my knowledge of French was still too limited to converse freely.

I knew that Christine's father had been torn to pieces by an angry crowd during the independence movement back in 1954, and I always felt a bit awed by this horrible event. I treated her with special consideration as, I suspect, did the rest of us, although her warmth and friendliness would have merited special treatment in any case. She never made any reference in my presence to her father's tragic demise. She seemed very well adjusted, content to be the wife of Bernard, her Jewish-Moroccan husband, and the mother of Didier, a little boy with an unusually serious demeanor and perfect manners. He came up to me and offered his small hand. I took it and smiled, echoing his charming *"Enchantée."* Then he rejoined his mother, content to stay in her beaming presence for the rest of the evening.

Macloud and Michelle, childhood friends of Pierre's and married to two of his best friends, also shook hands with me. I managed an awkward *"Je suis heuruese d'être ici"* that I had practiced with Pierre. They nodded their heads and then went their own way, talking and laughing with the crowd of people they knew so well.

Something must be wrong, I decided. Not that I expected the whole world to bow down to me because I had mastered one French sentence. That it had taken me an entire afternoon in the antique shop with Pierre to master it made no difference. Determined to be sociable, I walked over to Michelle, who I knew spoke Spanish, and tried to strike up a conversation with her. She said a few sentences in Spanish, then quickly resumed speaking French with another woman.

"What's going on, Pierre?" I asked my husband, balancing a drink in one hand and caviar in the other as he laughed with Jean Michel and Alain. "These women won't speak to me...not even in Spanish." He looked a bit vexed, then excused himself and took me aside.

"Geeny, Michelle comes from a family of poor Spanish immigrants. She's married to Alain. She doesn't want people to think of her humble roots."

"The Spaniards I know aren't particularly humble," I retorted.

"It's different here, Geeny." Pierre's big, limpid, brown eyes begged me to understand. "The French colonized this part of Morocco, and they consider their culture superior."

"But you're half Spanish," I shot back, wondering if this class and race thing was worse in Rabat than in the United States.

"Yes, but my family has been wealthy for over two hundred years," explained Pierre as if he were talking to an ignoramus.

"Are you saying that your friends are class-conscious

snobs?"

"Look, Geeny, you must understand that this is not the United States of America. The people here, even from good families, have not had the money to enable them to travel and experience other ways of life and cultures like you and I. They just want to live a simple life."

"Simple and exclusive!" I commented sourly.

"Look, Geeny, we're only going to be here for one year so I can learn the antique business from my father and so you can learn French. I told you that before we were married, remember?"

"I know, Pierre, but I don't think I can stand spending even a year in a town where no one will talk to me."

He gave me a dark look.

"Perhaps things will improve with my French. It is getting better, don't you think?" I ventured.

Pierre didn't comment on my French. Someone had caught his eye from across the crowded room, and he signaled to them with his champagne glass. He looked quickly back at me as he made his way through the crowd and said, "And you have Amina for your maid. Life will be easy for you here, Geeny."

"She'll probably tell me more interesting stories than anyone else," I yelled, suddenly conscious of several heads turned in my direction.

Pierre disappeared into the crowd, and I drank considerably more than my share of the champagne that night. As it turned out, Amina had more to say than the whole lot put together.

☼ AMINA

AMINA WATCHED ME out of the corner of her eye as she dusted the Empire mantel with the Neptune clock on it. The luminous chandelier sparkled overhead, reflecting more light than I felt, for having lived with great wealth for over two years now, I found it beautiful to look at but certainly not worth what people were willing to go through to attain it. Like marrying someone you did not completely love. Perhaps it was because Pierre so carefully referred to everything as his and not mine that I had come to feel so indifferent.

Amina moved gracefully, her diaphanous caftan covering a loose, formless dress underneath. Now able to speak French with greater agility, I listened to her small comments about the weather and her family. I knew that she had one son from her first marriage and had married again, someone she didn't love, out of necessity.

"*Madame,*" said Amina as she polished some silver candlesticks, "the silver tarnishes very quickly in this moist climate."

"Amina, silver is not the only thing that tarnishes in this climate."

Amina understood my oblique reference to my own marriage. She began to tell me the story of her first marriage.

"*Madame,* you are my only friend. I used to have many friends when I was married to my first husband and my baby was still breast feeding. I invited them to our house all the time and let them share everything I had. That lasted for one year. Then my husband left me to marry my best friend." She turned to face me unhappily. "He has never given me anything. Not even a sucker for my baby. Not even a piece of candy." She grimaced with pain and clicked her thumbnail under her front tooth to show how little her husband had

163

given them.

"At least he let you keep your child," I commiserated, commenting on the Muslim custom of allowing the husband to take the children if he wished. Indeed, divorce was very informal in this country. All a man had to do was clap his hands three times, saying "I repudiate thee" each time. Then the wife was put out on the street with a basket of belongings to return to her family. And the husband often requested her bride price, whether he had paid for her in actual money or in sheep and other presents. "A woman should never marry into such a religion," I thought, sadly. Many European and American women were virtual prisoners of their husbands and their families, unless they wanted to leave without their children.

"I was only fifteen years old, *madame*," continued Amina. "I came from a good family. We are Berbers, not Arabs. We are honorable people." I nodded. The Berbers, the original inhabitants of North Africa before the Mohammedans, or newly converted Muslims who invaded North Africa over a thousand years ago, were generally considered more trust-worthy than Arabs. They had put up a fierce resistance to the Arab invasion. Some still maintained their nomadic indepen-dence in the mountainous regions of Morocco.

"My father was a sultan and had many herds of sheep," continued Amina, "but my mother was the youngest of all of my father's wives. She didn't know how to fight for our por-tion of the inheritance. All she has is a grocery store in Salé, and I'm afraid she is going to give that to one of her boy-friends. *Madame*, my mother is twice my age, yet she acts like a child."

Bit by bit, Amina told me how she had taken jobs as a maid and married a man who worked for the king, who had a good job and housing as well, but whom she did not love. Her story moved me, and I began to let her go at one o'clock every day, much to the consternation of Pierre's friends' wives, so that she could take care of her child, now twelve years old.

I was criticized by the other wives in Pierre's group of

friends for being too lenient with my maid. Somehow that really upset them, perhaps because the French are so concerned with order and cleanliness. A fanatically clean house, the way the French like theirs kept, never interested me that much. I never cared what Pierre's friends or their wives thought of me, anyway. I had a stubborn individualistic streak that went back for generations.

I often wondered how my female ancestors had fared, because my life could have been very difficult without an indulgent, wealthy husband to allow me to do as I wished.

Then Amina confided that her husband might take a vacation to attend a celebration. One of his brothers planned to marry a second, younger wife. Muslims can have four legal wives, and as many concubines as they can afford. Although this custom had changed somewhat during the French colonization, the men who could afford it often took a second wife. The king could have countless wives. Mohammed V had had twelve, and his son had two legally, but he was reputed to have loved many women.

When Ahmed had left, Amina told me rather pointedly, *"Madame,* I am going to the steam baths to get all of the dirt off of me. I want to cleanse myself."

I knew Amina had remarried out of necessity, for a woman with a child can barely survive in a country where the minimum wage is officially one dollar a day, and even that meager amount was rarely honored.

She seemed pleased with herself that week, singing little chants in her native Berber language. Amina was proud of her Berber heritage, as her people considered themselves better than the Arabs—more honest, harder working, cleaner in spirit.

She had told me many times of the Berbers' superior qualities as well as her ancestors' hatred for the Arabs who had conquered them when Islamism swept the world with Mohammed's new vision and fierce armies.

The next week Amina came to me with a downcast look on her face.

"What's wrong, Amina?"

"*Madame,* do you think you could get the pharmacist to give me some of those pills you take when you are unhappy with *monsieur?*" She cast her eyes downward, not daring look me in the face for fear I would say no.

"What pills, Amina?" She surprised me. I didn't know she observed my moods so closely. As I didn't take valium or mood-altering pills, I guessed she had surmised that European and American women just did this as a matter of course.

"Amina, if there were such a pill I could take that would make me happy, then I would buy them not only for me but for all my friends as well. There are no such pills."

"*Madame,* I need something from the pharmacy. I can't stand it today." Her eyes beseeched mine.

"What is wrong today?"

"It is my husband. He is back from his brother's wedding celebration. He is an Arab, Madame. He does not understand me. I was so happy while he was gone. Now I am miserable again. Please get me some of those pills. I will pay you for them."

I thought for a moment. I knew they sold all manner of drugs over the counter at the pharmacies in Rabat. I could probably get her some valium. Then I thought better of it.

"Amina, we always blame others for our troubles, but I have learned that mine come from within. The same is true of my happiness. If your husband were to leave you forever, you would be miserable because you could not support your child, send him to school, and allow him to get a decent education."

Amina sighed impatiently. "*Oui, madame.* Now, would you get me the pills. I can't stand it today. The contrast is too sharp. I can see too much today."

"The contrast is too sharp...." I looked at Amina, my maid who came to work wearing long black evening gloves under her burnoose. I realized how much she must have sacrificed to work as a maid, marry beneath her into a race she hated, all because she had once been young, trusting, and happy.

"Yes, Amina. I'll get the pills for you. I can see you need them today and maybe again tomorrow until you get used to being with your husband again."

Amina took my hand and kissed it. Although this was the customary way of showing gratitude, it always made me uncomfortable, especially when a woman kissed my hand. A man was a different story.

I realized how closely Amina observed me and my mood changes, for her well-being depended to a large degree on pleasing me. "Perhaps she knows me better than I know myself," I mused. "I just hope I never become that dependent on someone for my well-being."

I thought of how separate Pierre and I had become this year, except at bedtime, of course. I had to pay my dues every night, but my treasury was running low.

Speaking of the devil, he burst into the living room brandishing a tennis racket.

"Come on, Geeny, let's go to the king's new golf course!"

I turned and looked at him. He was exhilarated from his tennis match and ready to propel himself into the next event. Pierre had more energy than anyone I had ever met.

"Okay! Let's go!" I replied with enthusiasm.

The king's latest golf course was reputed to be a masterpiece that had cost nearly a billion dollars. Most of the money had come from American foreign aid, I was told. I knew that Morocco was one of the seven most favored countries on the United States' list of countries to give money to.

"General Znaidi has invited us!"

"Who's that?"

"Geeny, he's a very important officer in the king's army."

"Oh. Should I wear something special?"

"No, just get ready quickly, because we're all meeting him there."

"We're all…"

"Jean Michel and Macloud are invited too. Jean Pierre got us the invitation because Macloud is such an expert horseback rider."

Macloud gave horseback riding lessons at the Club

Equestre and had won many prizes in horse-jumping contests. She was also pretty neurotic about her husband, often calling me to try to get me to spy on him and Pierre when they were out playing Ping-Pong, Pierre's favorite pastime in Rabat. I always declined, saying I was trying to read Camus or Proust or some other French author.

I dressed quickly, putting on a jaunty mini-dress I had made myself. The French women made fun of me, but I still liked to sew and often did.

Off we drove in Pierre's faithful Simca, and soon the poplars that lined the two-lane highway leading to the king's new golf course whizzed by. Pierre drove fast, as usual. We soon pulled up to a fortress-like establishment, all in granite and stone with the latest modern sculpted look. An impressive sign at the entrance read "The People's Golf Course."

Laughing out loud, I pointed to the sign. "The people wouldn't even have a car to get here in, much less the time or inclination to play golf!"

"Now, Geeny, don't be sarcastic," laughed Pierre. "The king does whatever he likes with his money."

"Yes, of course." I thought of his last birthday celebration and the huge poster portrait of him that had been erected in the center of Rabat. He wore golf clothes. There was not a trace of anything Moroccan about him except his face, which was light brown with soft yet distinguished features. But golf clothes? While his people worked for under a dollar a day and lived on mostly garbanzo beans and mint tea?

"This guy doesn't worry about his image, does he?" I commented.

"He doesn't have to; he's the king."

I wiggled my nose at Pierre to show what I thought of the king.

"He rules by divine right, Geeny. He's a descendant of the Alouites, of Mohammed."

Pierre swung the car into a parking lot full of expensive Mercedes Benzes.

"Remember the story Bernard told us about the guy the king had named Minister of Education, who bugged him every day about when his Mercedes would get there...what color it would be, would it have air conditioning, radio..." I chortled.

Pierre was already out of the car, striding confidently toward an impressive bulwark of a clubhouse encased in huge, artistically arranged slabs of granite.

"The king could stay here and play golf with no worries even if all hell broke out," I mumbled to myself.

"Hurry up, Geeny! They're already here!"

I ran to catch up with Pierre. He offered me his arm, and we walked in as regally as possible. Pierre spotted a group of Moroccan men dressed in military uniforms seated with some of the members of Club Equestre, namely Jean Michel and Macloud and Jean Pierre Rivière, the king's horse trainer.

I smiled and offered my hand to the men, kissed Macloud on the cheek, and sat in a chair that an obsequious servant offered me. One of the generals' wives sat with him, unusual in Moroccan society, but this was an unusual gathering. Usually the French and the Moroccans kept to themselves. This woman sparkled like a jewel from her beautiful almond-shaped eyes to her gold-encased toes, for she wore gold rings on two of them. She smiled at me. Her skin was flawless, like silk. Her beauty stunned the eye, and I found it hard to look at her without staring. She smiled at me. I smiled back, then averted my eyes, trying to hide my curiosity.

"They emasculated him," repeated Jean Michel, somewhat reassuringly.

"*Que-ce que ca veut dire?*" I inquired. Emasculated sounded strange in French.

"They cut his balls off," Pierre whispered loudly in my ear.

"Oh!" My eyes opened wide. "A horse?"

"No," said General Znaidi without pausing. "The lover of General Alaoui's wife."

"I see!" I said, and shut up. My eyes however continued to bulge out of my head. "That will fix him!" I laughed in spite of myself. Everyone looked at me; then they all laughed.

"Would you like a drink?" asked Pierre, frowning at me.

"Um, sure," I faltered, fearing worse things might pop out of my mouth if I drank. Pierre should have known better. But everyone kept laughing and talking about this extraordinary event. The king's right-hand man and childhood friend, General Alaoui, had caught his wife *en flagrante* with one of his soldiers, and they had taken the poor man into the forest and emasculated him. I winced involuntarily.

After a couple of drinks, I asked Pierre, "What about the king's birthday party?"

"It's been postponed."

"Why? I thought we were invited."

"No reason. Maybe he decided to have a quieter party this year."

"I see." I had another slug of whisky. My head reeled.

"Do you want to play some golf, Geeny?" asked Pierre.

"Love to." My words slurred together.

Everyone stood up and either prepared to leave or to play golf. I was prepared for most anything after three whiskeys.

"Be careful," whispered Pierre.

"Don't worry," I whispered back, teetering onto the golf green.

Immaculately tended grass interspersed with elegant woodsy areas and miniature lakes greeted my eyes. The sky was a clear blue without a hint of a cloud.

Someone handed me a golf club. I took a wild swing and my golf ball stayed on the ground while some dirt flew into the air.

"*Merde!*" I swore under my breath.

Pierre teed off beautifully. His golf ball arced high and straight down the middle of the green.

"Good stroke, Pierre!" exclaimed Jean Marc.

Pierre laughed diffidently. "Natural abilities," he bantered.

"Like the time you fell off the horse...."

"I was riding it backwards...."

I looked off into the horizon as Jean Marc and Pierre exchanged sallies, something they had done since childhood.

Then I saw the king. His retinue consisted of several servants and soldiers. They held a canopy above his head when he walked, and stood deferentially out of his way when he hit the ball.

Everyone stopped playing to watch the king. Once he hit a ball into a sand trap. Another was placed immediately in front of him and this time it arced gracefully toward the putting green.

"I'll bet he always shoots below par," I said, somewhere between snide and drunk. I never could drink more than one drink at a time without getting inebriated. The others ignored me. I stared at the gold braid on General Znaidi's uniform. Pierre squeezed my arm and I stopped. "It could be dangerous to be a free spirit in this country," I murmured in his ear.

He put his finger to his mouth, begging me to be quiet. I nodded my head. Then I started to laugh. And laugh. The exquisite general's wife turned to look at me. Pierre suddenly took me by the arm and propelled me back to the clubhouse.

"Too much whisky!" he announced. The others nodded briefly, and I ended up sitting in the clubhouse for the duration of the golf game. Pierre had to sit with me to keep me under control.

"Geeny, you can't behave like this here!"

"I'm drunk!" I said loudly.

Pierre looked around, then escorted me out of the club and to the car.

"I can't help it! You kept offering me more drinks."

We drove home in silence, the People's Golf Course receding in the background.

☼ CHRISTMAS IN SPAIN

THE STREETS OF RABAT hummed busily with the usual assortment of traffic, from Mercedes Benzes to horse- or human-drawn carts. I stood on our balcony and surveyed the neatly trimmed orange trees that lined our street and led to Allal ben Abdullah, the street Art et Style was on. The air was crisp, but not cold. It was December. It was Christmastime, but in a Muslim land no Christmas trees or holiday fervor surfaced. The holy man called the faithful to worship in the mosque at sunrise. Life ran according to the Muslim traditions. Pierre and I had decided to spend Christmas in Madrid, our favorite city, which would be aglow with Christmas lights.

A huge overstuffed armchair swayed on top of the car precariously. Pierre had attached it as securely as possible with the help of his workers. The legs of a marble-topped table jutted out of the back of the car, a hatchback. More furniture for the Moulets' new house currently under construction at the farm in Alicante. Pierre and I always took furniture with us when we traveled, to help his parents furnish their "castle in Spain," a veritable mansion they were having built so they could leave Morocco and still live in the *grande style*.

"Pierre, it's going to fall off!" I yelled.

"*Merde*," swore Pierre, as he slammed on the brakes and jumped out of the car.

He fastened the heavy armchair more securely and then jumped back in, flooring the accelerator again.

We whizzed through a small Spanish village on the narrow road just above the Mediterranean Sea. Chickens squawked, old women grabbed small children, and I flinched. The sea sparkled like maple sugar in the distance, so I tried to focus on the azure blue water and ignore Pierre's manic driving.

Before I could say "shish kabob" Pierre was driving into the familiar dirt road that led to La Cruz, the family farm. On a piece of nearby land, I could see men pouring cement.

"That is where my parents are going to live," announced Pierre proudly.

"I'm sure it will be magnificent," I murmured. "But where are we going to spend the night? At the beach house?"

"No, Geeny, here, at the farm," admonished Pierre as he produced the enormous wrought-iron key he and Françoise had once hunted for so ardently.

A thick wooden door creaked open, and Pierre turned on a switch. A feeble light bulb hung from the ceiling, illuminating furniture piled upon furniture—almost a second antique store.

"This is where my parents store things for their new house."

Pierre pointed to a single bed. "We can sleep there tonight."

"Isn't it going to be a bit uncomfortable?" I looked at the eerie shadows cast by the dubious light bulb suspended from the ceiling.

"It is a very comfortable bed, Geeny! It was made by Mohammed at our workshop."

I sighed and watched him unload the sofa with the help of one of the farmhands.

"Don't worry. Everything is all right."

"What about dinner?"

"We are invited to Bernarda's house for dinner on Christmas Eve."

"The communist?"

Pierre gave me an imploring look. "Bernarda is very nice, Geeny. She helped me when I was in England. She gave me money when no one else would. She is just a communist because she suffered so much during the civil war."

"Bernarda suffered?"

"She was very hungry when Franco cut off the food supply to Barcelona."

I burst out laughing, thinking of how obese Bernarda was.

"She's certainly made up for lost time!"

"Geeny, don't make fun of her. She can't help it."

Stories of Bernarda flashed through my mind: the time she refused to shake hands with Paul, a friend of the family, who had made a wonderful meal for Pierre and his numerous aunts and uncles, a man who lost everything after the Battle of Algiers.

She held her pudgy hand brimming with rings inlaid with precious stones and said, "I refuse to shake the hand of a capitalist who exploited the Arabs."

The poor man's face fell. Emilia grabbed Bernarda and pushed her aside, rushing to the poor man's rescue.

"You don't know what it is like to lose everything!" She raised her hand as if to slap Bernarda in the face, but her husband, Michel, caught her hand in midair and restrained her.

"Emilia, ignore her. She is not worth it." Then he turned to their friend.

"Please accept our apologies."

Sebastian stuck out his hand, and Paul clasped it warmly. Everyone except Bernarda and her husband shook Paul's hand, kissed him on both cheeks, and thanked him for the lovely meal. Bernarda pouted in the background.

"So we will leave for Madrid tomorrow?" I asked, shaking myself from my reverie.

Pierre nodded his head, then motioned for me to help him move a solid mahogany dining room table with a marble top. I stood on one side, he on the other. The table refused to budge.

"This is like our marriage," Pierre sighed.

"An antique with cold marble on top?" I laughed.

"And you are as stubborn as this table."

"Me? I'm the one who follows you!" I put my hands on

my hips, outraged. "You said we would be out of Morocco in one year, and it's already been three."

Pierre stood opposite me, unblinking.

"It isn't easy to start an antique store in Madrid, Geeny."

"So are we going to stay here? With your parents?"

"Why not? Life will be easy for you in Alicante."

"Easy? Is that all you want out of life, Pierre?"

"Geeny, you Americans are too demanding." Pierre arched his eyebrows imploringly. I stared into his large, soft brown eyes, then walked over to him and put my arm around him.

"I'm sorry, Pierre."

He kissed me. I kissed him back. The tension poured out of us like water from a burst hydrant. We started to make the bed that stood amid the clutter, lighting the candle in the antique brass candle holder next to it. I got under the covers with him and snuggled into the hollow of his armpit.

We lay side by side for a moment, then he extinguished the candle and kissed me again.

✹ THE GIFT

Madrid glittered brightly as we drove through its streets aglow with Christmas lights. The air was so cold I could see my breath in front of me. Although it almost never snowed in Madrid, it felt like Christmas. Pierre and I stayed in our old apartment with Manolito. It was like old times, laughing, eating, visiting places together. Then Bernarda called to remind us of our Christmas Eve dinner invitation. I winced at the thought.

Juan's marriage to Bernarda, the self-proclaimed communist from Barcelona, alienated most of the family from him as well as from Aurelia and Don Celin, his wealthy parents. Juan had become Pierre's least-favored cousin after he beat Pierre up when they were teenagers. But when it came to Bernarda, Pierre was all heart. I remember her now, sitting on our sofa at our apartment in Madrid, talking a mile a minute. Juan looked out the window at some unknown object.

Bernarda wore a tight-fitting red dress, defying anyone to comment on her weight, which we didn't. She crossed and uncrossed her plump legs repeatedly while twisting a huge diamond ring.

"Yes, I have married into a bourgeois family." She fluffed her blond hair impatiently. "Even though I am a communist. So what? I can't help it if Juan is a stock broker and his parents own such a large company. Don't forget that I nearly starved to death during the Spanish Civil War." She shifted her weight and I held my breath as I heard a loud tearing noise. Bernarda looked down and sneered at our sofa. "What cheap material. It ripped."

"Don't worry, Bernarda! I'll have it fixed at our workshop," reassured Pierre, always anxious to defend her.

I sighed with resignation. Pierre always said he'd have things repaired at our shop. After three years of marriage, I knew this wasn't true. He overlooked the furniture in his own home. And me. We were permanent fixtures he took for granted. Besides, he'd rather water ski or sit in the shop and joke with Jean and Fredy, his old school chums who played chess with him there in the afternoon.

"Have it fixed in your shop?" asked Bernarda with a raised eyebrow.

"Yes, don't worry about it, Bernarda," placated Pierre.

"By the cheap Moroccan labor you exploit, no doubt," she continued, a steady rat-ta-tat-tat of noise issuing from her mouth.

"If I didn't give them work, they would be paid even less by the Moroccans," parried Pierre. "Or they'd have no work at all."

Bernarda stood up. "Oh, you colonists are all the same. 'If I didn't exploit them, someone else would.'" Her voice shrilled into a high, sarcastic nasal whine.

I flinched, then smiled benignly at her. I'm the hostess, I have to be polite, I thought with irritation. I really felt like slapping her in the face. I counted to ten to calm my temper.

"At any rate, you're invited to have Christmas Eve dinner with us. I'm going to fix mussels." She turned, her fat rump waving like a red flag.

"Thank you, Bernarda!" purred Pierre, smiling in-gratiatingly. "We'd love to come!"

"Will Aurelia and Don Celin be there?" I asked hopefully. After all, they were her in-laws.

"I suppose I'll have to invite them, won't I, Juan," pouted Bernarda. Juan's face remained a white cloud of passivity. He never said much. Maybe she was his mouthpiece. Like the rest of Pierre's family, I didn't like Bernarda. She acted like a defiant, spoiled child who grabbed everyone's attention by misbehaving.

That she was now fat and married to a rich man did not appease this insatiable woman's appetite for revenge. "They" were to blame for her hunger during the civil war because "they" had not suffered from it. She wanted everyone to know that she, Bernarda, had gone hungry while "they" had lived a life of ease in Algeria.

That the tables were now turned, that the Bonmari family and all the other colonists had been forced to leave Algeria, as well as their possessions, for a much more difficult existence, made no difference to Bernarda. Emilia and her husband had never made any foreign investments and "they," therefore, had lost everything when DeGaulle pulled the French troops out. I wondered if Bernarda knew how much Emilia suffered.

Bernarda now led a life of material wealth and ease replete with servants, but in her mind this didn't make up for what she had suffered during the Spanish Civil War. Hunger. I could understand hunger leading to anger...but for the rest of one's life? No, it was pointless to carry on about something once it was clearly over. Yet Bernarda took especial pride in arrogantly turning the knife in the wound if anything smacked of capitalism. "How could she marry a stock broker? The head of one of the biggest firms in Madrid?" I wondered.

She adored Pierre and always commented on his generosity. They had a mutual admiration society. He always reminded me of the time she had lent him money in England when he was in a tight spot. Pierre was considered the soul of generosity by almost everyone, yet when it came to me, he was a hopeless cheapskate.

Something reminded me of the time Pierre had caught me selling some old books and clothes to the rag merchant in Rabat. One glimpse of Pierre's furious frown, and the old man vanished with a quick *inshallah*. If Allah wills it. I looked up at Pierre.

"What's the matter?" I asked.

"What are you doing selling things to a rag merchant?"

"Why not? They were just old books and clothes. We have to leave this country soon...."

Pierre turned purple and started to sputter. "Geeny, Geeny, I told you...." It reminded me of the time I had asked him to open a bank account in my name. In Morocco you had to have three hundred dollars to open a bank account. As Pierre took all of my paychecks, I couldn't open one on my own.

"Geeny, you can't have a bank account! The shop is not making much money this month."

"But Pierre, I make over three hundred dollars a month teaching English, which is a lot in Morocco!

Pierre's face turned purplish and his wiry frame stiffened. "I know, Geeny, but we spend that money on vacations that we could not afford otherwise."

"Then where do you find the money to buy so many antique Moroccan jewels?"

"I use my father's money for that because we can take the jewels out of Morocco; but you know we aren't allowed to take any cash." Pierre's face turned redder. I feared he might be on the verge of a mild stroke.

"I thought you could get your friends to deposit money for you in their accounts in France."

"Yes, but it is very risky and I lose twenty percent on the black market, Geeny. Don't you see my position?" His voice hit a twangy note halfway between vexation and pleading every time he said my name. "Geeny...."

"Pierre, I want a bank account in my own name!"

"I won't sign for it! It's out of the question. Can't you see that we can't afford it? Besides, you should consider yourself lucky to live at the level we do. Without my family or background, you could not enjoy our prestige or friends. In the United States you could never have the lifestyle we have here."

Strutting back and forth nervously, hands clenched, Pierre broke out in a sweat. I hated to see him like this. I meekly tried one more time. "Pierre, my mother always had a bank account and a fistful of credit cards."

"In France it is illegal for a woman to have a bank account unless her husband gives his written permission!"

"What? Illegal?" I couldn't believe my ears. But I didn't want to make Pierre too angry. He was my husband. He was all I had. Little did I know that the women's movement was in full bloom back in the United States in 1967, while I lived in a veiled world where women couldn't even have their own bank accounts without their husbands' written permission.

So I sighed and shut up at this point rather than press for petty needs. I could live without a bank account.

"Oh, Pierre, simmer down," I said coldly. I turned to walk away, but he caught me and spun me around. I saw the raised hand and yelled, "Hit me and we're divorced!" He lowered his hand as I walked into the living room, cool as a cucumber. No man would ever lay a hand on me. Money was one thing. Violence was another.

Our lives had become more and more separate once we had finished traveling and settled in Rabat. Pierre was either at work at the antique shop or off playing golf or Ping-Pong with his friends. He and Alain Sauves even won the Ping-Pong championship of Rabat. Tac, tac, tac, tac. I could still hear that hollow little ball bouncing from one side of the table to the other. Pierre jumped like a gazelle with great prowess, smiling his huge smile, rarely missing a shot. He was famous for his Ping-Pong game and good nature. I was the infamous grouch, nose in book, never completely happy in this foreign land except when I taught my English classes. Or went to the farm in Ouezzane. I loved the farm. So green, so peaceful. Marc and Sifia were so hospitable. Pierre's cousins, Marguerite and Lassan, always touched me with their playful kindness.

That tonight was the night of Bernarda's Christmas Eve dinner party was ironic. Here Pierre and I were in Madrid, at the apartment on Felipe II where we had spent the year of the free spirits, attending the University of Madrid and partying, laughing at everything and everyone, thinking life was always going to be festive and gay.

I put my comb down on the dresser and looked at Pierre as he fastened his cufflinks. His scrawny legs stuck out from under an enormous cotton dress shirt that he was going to tuck into his dress pants in a moment.

"Will Aurelia and Don Celin be there tonight?" I asked, trying to find something to look forward to.

"Of course they will, Geeny. Bernarda is very close to them. She always invites them." He pulled on his pants and looked through his ties. He picked the dark blue one with a paisley print that he always wore.

"You always wear that tie," I laughed. "Why don't you wear a red one...for Christmas?"

Pierre cocked his head and looked at me, then looked back at his ties.

"The red one doesn't match my suit, Geeny," he said.

"Just a suggestion." I finished combing my hair and put on a black crepe evening dress. I fastened a gold brooch to it that I had had since I was in college. College seemed a long way away now. Had I really gone to Berkeley and been outrageous, left my sorority with friends who got kicked out, my best friends, I mused silently. The fun years were over. Respectability had set in like a mold, and I felt rotten, tainted by it.

Then I rummaged through the closet and pulled out a red-white-and-black poncho Pierre and I had bought while on our honeymoon in Taxco, Mexico. We had searched through every store in town until we came upon this stunning piece of craftsmanship. The wool was soft and pure white. By far, it was the most beautiful poncho we had ever seen. Pierre bought it immediately and gave it to me.

"I think I'll wear the poncho you gave me during our honeymoon in Mexico. It has red in it. Maybe I'll look more like a member of the proletariat in it."

"Geeny," Pierre scowled at me, "Bernarda gave me money in England when I really needed it. She is a good and generous person." His French accent whined in my ears, grated on my nerves tonight. I think it had always annoyed me, at least subliminally.

"Yes, I know, I know. She's a saint. And I'm an American. You know she's going to toss some anti-capitalist remarks my way tonight. Not that I really care that much."

"She's invited Sebastian," remarked Pierre casually.

"Good! That should liven up the evening!" I smiled at Pierre, remembering the good times the three of us had shared last summer at the beach house. Pierre smiled back. He's not all that bad, I thought. I just am not really attracted. But a good marriage is more important than....

"Ready, Geeny?" asked Pierre with his plaintive whine.

I stood up. He held out my coat and I wrapped it around me. We were ready.

Everything was in motion at Bernarda and Juan's when we arrived. Bernarda busied herself with the caviar hors d'oeuvres and Juan opened bottles of white wine. Pierre's Aunt Aurelia and Uncle Don Celin sat on the white sofa and smiled at us as we walked in the door.

Bernarda wore a tight pink dress, and her rump jiggled like jelly when she walked. She spun around to buss Pierre on the cheek when we stepped into the living room. I shook hands with her and bussed Aurelia and Don Celin. Suddenly, Sebastian came out of another room. We smiled at each other happily, glad to see one another. He walked over to Pierre.

"*Comment ca va, mon vieux?*" he laughed, shaking hands with Pierre and slapping him on the back. "How's it going, old man?"

"I'm not so old," chuckled Pierre. "I can whip you at wrestling any day."

"I've gotten better," murmured Sebastian, staring at me all the while. My black crepe dress suddenly seemed elegant. I felt beautiful; I felt appreciated.

"*Bon soir, Virginie,*" he said and we bussed each other on both cheeks slowly, smiling happily. "Your red-and-white poncho matches your dress perfectly." We laughed.

"*Bon soir, Sebastian.* How are your studies at the Sorbonne?"

"Not bad, but I like my vacations in Spain better!"

Everyone was excited to see one another. I smiled at Aurelia as I sat down next to her. She chatted animatedly about how happy she was to see all of us.

"I only get to speak French when my relatives visit," she

beamed at me. "So I've joined a French club just to be able to take part in the family conversations. One forgets a language, you know."

"That's so true, Aurelia. I find it harder to speak English lately." I smiled sympathetically at her.

I looked at Sebastian, who inclined his superbly sculpted head in our direction. He had lustrous skin, the kind I had always envied, the kind the young men in Lorca's poetry had. Smooth as silk. He seemed older, more sophisticated, different from when I had first met him. He was only sixteen then. He kept smiling at me. He still seemed very sweet and young. I thought I detected some uncertainty in his smile, some vulnerability, something very appealing.

The maid passed the hors d'oeuvres and I squeezed some lemon on the caviar. It was delectable.

I turned my head to Aurelia and Don Celin. "And how is your business?" I asked, trying to rekindle our conversation.

"Very good, thank you, Virginie." Aurelia smiled brightly at me. She wore a plain blue dress with her bun pulled tightly back from her head. She always dressed simply and elegantly. How cruel of Claudine to compare her to a nun, I thought. Bernarda entered the room talking loudly. A saint would have been a better description for anyone with a daughter-in-law like this.

"Isn't Sebastian turning into the pretty boy?" commented Bernarda, intercepting a baffled look we exchanged. "You must have lots of girlfriends in Paris, Sebastian," she continued. He looked at me and shifted his weight uncomfortably. "Or perhaps boyfriends," she added. "Well, in Morocco, you know...." Bernarda's shrill laugh rang out discordantly among her guests.

"At least they're not members of the Communist Party!" he shot back. "But then, are stock brokers' wives allowed to keep their cards?"

Bernarda grinned grotesquely. Everyone stared at her, cringing in fear of her retort. "You know perfectly well...."

"This is Christmas Eve, Bernarda," Don Celin said quietly. "Let's not talk about politics now."

Bernarda furrowed her brow and started to get red in the face. "I nearly starved to death because of that fascist Franco during the Spanish Civil War!"

Everyone caught his breath. Don Celin was so gentle, so old—how could she make a scene? She scowled furiously at all of us.

She looked so much like a silly harlequin, standing there like a pampered child, that I burst out laughing. I stopped almost as soon as I had started, but it was too late. I had laughed at Queen Bernarda.

"What are you laughing at?" she demanded.

"Nothing, nothing at all, Bernarda," I said. Everyone looked at me expectantly. "I just can't imagine you hungry!" I ducked my head in case she decided to throw something, and I caught Pierre's angry glare.

"Virginie!" he intervened. "Bernarda is a warm-hearted, generous person. What does it matter if she is a bit round?"

Bernarda gave him an imperious sneer and then turned her back on me. I looked askance and found Sebastian smiling broadly at me. A sympathizer!

Pierre cleared his throat and corrected himself quickly. "That is, round...but more on the voluptuous side of round." He gave her a wink. She relaxed and smiled at him. Then she frowned at me.

"What does an American know about communism, anyway?" She stood up and adjusted her low-cut gown, which left little to the imagination. She pulled her tight sheath skirt over her fat buttocks and huffed back into the kitchen. I gave Pierre a dark look and then stood up to straighten my dress. Sebastian came over and maneuvered me into a corner where no one could overhear us.

"I don't know why I came here," he said, his eyes downcast.

"You don't like Bernarda," I said while staring at the sensual curve of his lips.

"No," he continued, his voice lowered to a hush. "She is disgusting. She flaunts her communism, and her respect for deGaulle, who abandoned us in Algeria and reserved a nice jail cell for anyone who protested." He grimaced at the painful memory.

"Are you still taking karate lessons?" I changed the subject as tactfully as possible.

"Yes." Sebastian relaxed and smiled at me. "I love sports."

"Just sports?"

"No, not just sports." He looked at me and smiled playfully, showing the two dimples in his cheeks. "Why are you wearing that poncho?"

"Oh, because it has red in it—for Christmas, you know—and because I hardly ever get to wear it. It's so beautiful, I hate to see it just hang in my closet." Sebastian nodded. "Pierre gave it to me in Mexico for a wedding present."

"He has good taste!" He grinned at me and I felt like the compliment extended to Pierre's taste in other things—women, for example. Not that we were to be tasted....I looked back at Sebastian and lost my train of thought. This worldly young man made me feel dizzy.

"Excuse me, Sebastian," I sat down next to Aurelia again. She smiled brightly at me and fingered my poncho.

"What a beautiful poncho," she commented.

"Yes," I smiled into her exquisite face, lines running through it like fine porcelain. She is like fine porcelain, I thought. Fragile, yet durable.

We fell into a lively conversation about the family, politics, and Madrid. Finally she talked of her favorite nephew, Pierre. She told me what a good, generous man he was, how she had taken care of him as if he were her own son when he spent his summer vacation with his parents at the Bonmari family farm in Alicante, on the coast of Spain.

I nodded my head in gentle agreement, although the word "generous" stuck out like a sore thumb. Our recent scene over my nonexistent bank account ran through my mind. Nonetheless, I smiled at her and said, "Yes, Aurelia, Pierre is a kind, generous man." The words slipped out with startling ease. I didn't know I could lie so well, and wondered how much of myself I could give up so gracefully.

I changed the subject to Juan and Bernarda. Aurelia

talked of their work and minor achievements with maternal pride. She beamed intelligently at me while talking of Juan's recent promotion at the stock exchange. The rest of the family called her a martyr, yet I failed to see what they meant. She was an intelligent woman who accepted without complaint that which she couldn't change, and with a dignity I admired intensely. What else could she do at her advanced age? She was nearly eighty.

Bernarda reentered the room. She had added some more bright red lipstick to her puffy face. She played the role of the gauche harlequin well, strutting like a peacock over to where Aurelia and I sat.

"Well, Virginie, how do you like my new sofa? Juan and I bought it at the Galeria del Sol for only 20,000 *pesetas.*"

"It's very comfortable, Bernarda." I looked at Aurelia and tried to include her in the conversation. "Aurelia tells me you are helping Juan do the accounting at Don Celin's bookstore."

"Oh, that," she grimaced. "It is really a waste of time. But I do it to save money for Aurelia and Celin, who don't want to hire a bookkeeper. These capitalists are all the same, you know. Money, money, money!" She laughed grotesquely.

Aurelia continued smiling. She didn't even flinch, and Don Celin was impassive as always. I wondered if he had even heard what Bernarda had said. The men of the Bonmari family had a maddening knack for ignoring what their wives suffered most from.

"Come into the kitchen with me and help prepare dinner, Virginie," commanded Bernarda in a voice that was not used to being countered.

Sorry to give up my place at Aurelia's side, I followed Bernarda into the kitchen without enthusiasm.

An elegant display of hors d'oeuvres had been set out on the counter by the maid, who busily removed mussels from their shells. Bernarda did not acknowledge her presence, but went to the stove to fry some bacon. When she finished, she had no place to let the bacon grease drain.

"Give me a hand towel, Maria," she said to her maid.

The woman handed Bernarda a fine linen towel without looking either of us in the eye.

Some paper towels lay nearby. I grabbed them and handed them to Bernarda. "Here, this will keep the linen clean."

"Virginie, what do you think I keep Maria for?" announced Bernarda, snatching the paper towels from me. She motioned toward the maid, who quickly averted her eyes. "She can wash the grease out in the morning. Besides, we pay her too much. Do you know she refused to come here tonight unless I paid her extra?" Bernarda scowled at the maid, who looked away. "What a woman!"

The aggressive irritation in Bernarda's voice was unmistakable. I could hardly believe my ears, but I knew one thing for certain: Bernarda's communist prattle was the biggest lie I'd ever heard.

"Have I told you about our new car?" asked Bernarda proudly.

"Excuse me, Bernarda, but I think I'll join the others in the living room." I smiled at the poor maid. "It was nice meeting you," I said and made a quick exit.

I eagerly resumed my seat next to Aurelia. We chatted happily as she fingered my poncho, commenting on the excellent quality of the wool and the workmanship.

Bernarda entered the room again and loudly agreed with her mother-in-law.

"What a gorgeous poncho!" she nearly shouted to make sure she had everyone's attention.

"Thank you, Bernarda," I said, curtly. She could have noticed it earlier when I was in the kitchen, I thought with mounting vexation. How could Pierre possibly like this woman? Bernarda looked at Pierre, who had been talking quietly with Juan and Celin. She added, "I wish I had one like it."

Pierre smiled broadly at her and looked at the rest of us to make sure he had our attention as well.

With a magnanimous flick of his wrist he said, "You may have it, Bernarda. It's Christmas Eve, and I wanted to give

you something to thank you for your generosity in England."
He looked at me, frozen like a rabbit against the snow.
"Geeny, give it to her."

I couldn't believe Pierre's words. I was too stunned to react. Then I realized he wanted to impress Aurelia and Leon
with his legendary generosity. That it was at my expense, that
I loved this poncho, his wedding gift, had not occurred to
him.

I sat glued to the sofa, hoping my beautiful poncho was
going to remain on my shoulders. Too late. Pierre walked
over to me and started to pull it over my head. I struggled
for a moment to keep it, then gave up. It would have ruined
the party for everyone. I wanted to shout "No, that fat, self-
indulgent pig who wipes grease on hand towels for her maid
to wash while calling the rest of the family capitalists who exploit cheap labor...no, that grotesque buffoon cannot have
my poncho that we bought on *our* honeymoon!" Instead, a
sick smile froze across my face. I looked to Aurelia for support, thinking that through her own suffering she would understand what I was going through. I saw a glint of sympathy
in her eye, even though she was smiling just like me, pre-
tending everything was just fine. Sebastian gave me a look
that penetrated me to the core. He, of all people, felt my
pain.

Pierre pulled the poncho off my shoulders and over my
head. I smoothed my rumpled dress and hair, but nothing
could smooth my feelings of betrayal. Bernarda nearly had
the poncho, flying like a red-white-and-black emblem over
her fat shoulders, when Sebastian stood up and took it away
from her.

"Pierre, why don't you repay your debt to Bernarda in
another way? Virginie is clearly upset." He smiled respectfully
at his cousin and handed me the poncho. "Besides, it looks
better on her."

Bernarda trembled visibly. "You little capitalist rat!" She
yelled. "How dare you come in here and..."

"It's Christmas Eve, Bernarda," said Sebastian, quietly,
and took out a cigarette from a pack of Gitanes. He struck a

match to light it. Everyone held their breath.

Bernarda exploded. "How dare you!" She stomped furiously out of the room. I heard her yell, "*Salope*," which means whore in French, at her maid in the kitchen.

Aurelia looked at me briefly, and just briefly I thought I saw a gleam of satisfaction in her eye. Pierre ran after Bernarda. Juan just continued talking to his father. Sebastian lit his cigarette.

I tried to check my laughter, but it welled up in me like a geyser. About to burst out laughing, I hastily excused myself.

"I have to go to…to the bathroom," I said and ran into the hallway. I held my sides and tried to muffle my laughter. Then someone put his hands over my eyes. I turned quickly to find Sebastian smiling broadly at me. We exchanged mirthful looks, and chortled with stifled laughter.

I looked into his eyes. He squinted gleefully at me and giggled. It sounded so cute, so childlike, so refreshing. I straightened up and tried to regain my composure. "I have to go back in the living room now. I don't want them to think," I giggled again and so did he "…there's anything wrong."

Sebastian and I walked into the living room to find Pierre standing there with his usual broad grin spread across his face. He looked almost as grotesque as Bernarda. For a brief instant our eyes met. I quickly looked away, lest I follow my instincts and belt him right in the middle of the Christmas Eve party. Aurelia smiled crisply, her porcelain skin untouched by the fracas. I returned her smile, but with a kind of twisted smile, not a real smile.

The maid came out and announced that dinner was ready. We all stood up and walked into the dining room and proceeded to eat mussels and drink white wine as if nothing had happened. We laughed, smiled, and tried to forget where our lives had gone wrong. After all, it was Christmas Eve.

☼ SUMMER LOVE

THAT SUMMER I could hardly wait to get to the beach house, the *chalet* where Pierre and I had fallen in love, where I had had the best times of my life. I loved it like an old, trusted friend. The high, curved ceilings of the living room gave my mind space to relax. An archway divided the room into two parts, one larger than the other. An unpainted earthen water jug decorated one of the corners. A few beach chairs were scattered around. The small, plain table sat pushed over to the side. There was no special furnishing plan. This was a beach house with no special design or purpose save that of simplicity, the simple life, the serene life. Sitting in it alone, I never failed to notice the quiet of the place. It was always cool indoors in contrast to the heat of the August day. I listened to the hum of the locusts outside, a steady, mesmerizing drone that often put me into a deep mid-afternoon sleep. If anyone approached the beach house by car, I would be forewarned by the sound of the engine, since there were no other cars around. The rocky, rutted road that led to the beach house protected us from most of the intrusions of modern civilization. The beach house was perched on the edge of the Mediterranean with only the sea and clear, blue sky as far as the eye could see.

Sebastian entered from the kitchen coughing, and I had to smile at his boyish form, his sweet face. Pierre's younger cousin—his second cousin of whom we were both very fond.

"Why are you coughing?" I asked, grinning at his tousled mop of hair. His skin was toasted a golden tan by the sun, and it contrasted beautifully with his dark brown hair.

"I spent the night on the beach when I was in Malaga, and I have coughed ever since," he explained.

"Then you should take vitamin C. Here, I have some capsules in the kitchen." My maternal instincts surged forth, and I was sweetness and light as I dissolved an effervescent vitamin C tablet in a glass of water. Sebastian drank it up like mother's milk.

He smiled at me. "My mother has abandoned me this summer."

I laughed at him. "Mia has abandoned you for a whole summer. Poor baby!"

He smiled appreciatively at me and then offered to help me cook dinner. As I looked at his perfect teeth and flawless skin, his strong yet perfectly contoured face, down to the small blue bikini bathing suit he was wearing, something gave in me. I think it was my resolve.

Sebastian and I became inseparable. He was never more than a few steps behind me when we shopped in the village market; he sat next to me at meals, and was unable to unglue his love-smitten stare from mine. I became his surrogate mother that August and something more.

He arrived on a motorbike the next day, carrying his things from the farmhouse to our beach house so he could spend nights as well as days with us. I sucked in my breath. Pierre was his jovial self, happy to see his younger cousin joining us. They had played together in Rabat when they were younger, although Pierre was ten years his senior.

"Hit me in the stomach," Sebastian demanded every evening, usually before dinner.

Pierre would grin good naturedly and take aim. Pow!

"Again!" demanded Sebastian.

Pow!

"I'm going to be the karate champion of France!" Pow!

"You're going to win the *pederaste* championship of France," laughed Pierre, socking him in the gut again.

I watched as long as I could stand it, then went to my room where I read some more of *La Porte Etroite*, the book by Gide that Sebastian had recommended to me.

More and more I found myself turning to him for advice regarding marketing, food preparation, and finally, literature.

He astonished me with his mature observations and profound interest in literature. Pierre only read history, or about
"things that really happened."

I could picture Pierre and me lying in bed together, our
shoulders touching, reading our separate books, immersed in
our separate worlds. He could only read history books; fic-
tion did not mean anything to him. I read Proust while
Pierre read *The Third Reich*, parts of which I read over his
shoulder. But I always returned to Proust, who was infinitely
more charming than Hitler.

Then at ten o'clock we began our bedtime ritual. It always ended the same way, without variation.

"Hurry up, Geeny, you are keeping me waiting."

"Yes, Pierre, I'm coming," I would answer as I hurriedly
gave my hair the last of the hundred strokes I had been told
were so good for it.

Pierre often stood in the middle of our bedroom with his
shirt and tie still on, but nothing else. The business transac-
tion of the evening was about to take place. I had told Pierre
I no longer enjoyed having sex with him every night, and he
had responded that he could not go to sleep without it. I was
his sleeping pill, his tranquilizer. We anesthetized each other,
only in different ways.

At first he had been hurt when I told him, after three
years of marriage, that I didn't enjoy sex with him every
night. I was afraid to tell him that I couldn't remember when
I had enjoyed it with him.

He bought some books printed in Sweden with pictures
of couples copulating in seven different positions. It was
called *The Seven Positions*. Pierre decided that something was
technically wrong with our marital relations. After I loudly
protested being put into numerous uncomfortable positions,
he closed the books and stopped trying. He would make light
of our predicament and chuckle.

Pierre ran around in a fervor all day, brandishing his
Ping-Pong racquet or looking for a golf club or getting ready
to do something with his boyhood chums, while I languished,
reading the French classics I loved. As for the shop, it didn't

take much looking after since there were practically no customers save a hardened old colonist who intended to stick it out, but all the rest had long ago departed for France or Spain.

Both sports and Pierre's friends bored me, so I read, which fascinated me. I read in French because Françoise had left a repository of books in the bathroom, of all places, which was huge and had two large closets where she stored all her books after she read them. Being a writer herself, she had amassed a collection of paperback books that would do a bookseller shame. It was a shame that Pierre had not inherited her penchant for the intellectual, the acerbic wit, the worldly wisdom, contained in all those books. But they were not history. Little did he know, but many of them were at least partially autobiographical, especially Proust, my favorite. And now his delightful young cousin shared my tastes. If ever there was a formula for divorce, this had to be it. Yet I was loathe to relinquish Pierre, our love, or what was left of it, and above all the security of such a distinguished family. So Sebastian and I stared, but we did not touch, which made our relationship all the more titillating.

Living with Pierre in Madrid had been like living on a merry-go-round of friends, parties, ski trips, trips to Toledo, Segovia, the Prado with our art teacher and the other students—every day was a surprise package. I had never met anyone with as much vitality and enthusiasm for life, *joie de vivre*. A bit insensitive in bed and behind the driver's wheel, like the time he made his small Austin Mini careen wildly, zig-zagging it down the street to prove how well it could take curves to impress his friends who stood watching the spectacle on the side of the road while I sat in the car, petrified. Wham! In my fear and anger I slapped him full in the face to make him stop. It was the only way I knew how to do it, for he ignored my terrified pleas. He slapped me back, stopping the car to do so, thank God. Then he made me get out of the car and walk home, he was so furious.

Once at home I found myself locked out. Miserable, I waited for him, thinking all the fun would be over, and that I would have to forget about Pierre's world of glamor and money and crazy driving. But that part no longer mattered.

What mattered was that I was scared, afraid of being rejected. I had always wanted to be accepted. I blamed myself if someone didn't like me. I had no detachment, no sense of self that I would be just as well off without someone else, and perhaps better. Such an insecure little girl, trying to be pretty for Pierre; hadn't I been routinely tortured for years in an orthodontist's iron chair and carefully watched my complexion, used special soaps, and curled my hair for this very goal—a man, a man at all costs.

My parents had only exacerbated my worst fears by telling me I would never be pretty or popular, but that they would spend money straightening my teeth just the same because they would like me to have friends—friends, friends, you must have friends, I remember them telling me as they sat together, their arms crossed, in our living room. They themselves had been insecure, and they projected their fears onto me. I fought their feelings of inadequacy and always established myself by rebelling, doing crazy things, and convincing myself I wasn't like them through acts of bravado. But I never backed down. I was not a coward.

With Pierre I had my chance to definitely prove, once and for all, that I was worth something, that I could be pretty and popular and even marry a rich man—hit the jackpot and catapult myself out of my parents' petty realm of control. But there is always a price if one buys one's independence with another's help, which is indebtedness to the second party. I thought I was making a smart move by putting up with second-rate sex, dangerous driving, humiliation, domination, anything if he would marry me and establish me as…as what? I didn't even know. But I wanted so many things that he could offer, I had to prove so many things to my mother and myself before I could even begin to wonder what I wanted to do, really, with my life, that I had stuck it out for three years. And now here was his beautiful cousin smiling with an intensity I had never felt, like the sun. I radiated the same intense warmth for him. I was lit up like a hundred watt light bulb.

Then Pierre's best friend from Rabat, Alain, arrived at the beach house. There was a flurry of activity. Alain whipped around the isolated beach house at a frenzied tempo and Pierre easily fell into step with him. Like two race horses, they egged each other on; after all, weren't they the Ping-Pong champions of Rabat?

Sebastian and I exchanged disapproving looks as Alain mounted a huge, incandescent bunsen burner to light the main room. Antique kerosene lamps or candles were the usual sources of light after sunset, as the beach house had no electricity. This suited the mood of rustic, ocean-washed tranquility of the beach house perfectly. But Alain was all efficiency, a modern man, even on his vacation. Pierre never countered any of Alain's actions, and as I was just his wife and Sebastian the younger cousin, we voiced no dissent. Our complicity against these modern freaks was tacit. When Alain belched loudly at the dinner table, we stifled our laughter after exchanging bug-eyed looks.

Pierre ignored our reactions to his friend. As a rule, he never noticed anything that might be in disharmony with his world. Self-deception had always been his strong suit, I realized. Or perhaps he pretended to ignore things which he felt were beyond his control.

I woke up the next morning next to Pierre and walked into the living room of the beach house. Sebastian rounded the corner and smiled at me. Dazzled by his beauty, I smiled back.

"Would you like to have some breakfast?" I asked, sweetly.

"*Bien sur*," he replied. "Can I help you fix it?"

"Sure! You make the coffee, and I'll fix the toast."

We moved the light wooden table onto the terrace so we could look out over the Mediterranean as we ate. We sat down, poured ourselves some coffee, and started buttering the toast. Pierre and Alain joined us in a few minutes.

"We're going to Andorra to buy some tires and new tennis rackets," announced Pierre.

"Really?" I said, surprised.

"Yes, we're going to make the trip in three days," chimed

in Alain. "Pierre can drive while I sleep, and vice versa."

Sebastian and I exchanged furtive looks.

"Can't I go with you?" I dutifully replied.

"Geeny," Pierre replied in his high-pitched, whining British accent, "you are not well enough to endure such a trip."

I had expected him to say this, as I had been under the weather with a case of dysentery for a long time, but I had learned to live with it. I was thin but fit. His next remark caught me off guard.

"You must stay at the farm with Aurelia and Don Celin."

"No way!" I reacted angrily. "I refuse." I crossed my arms over my bikini top and stood my ground.

Pierre knew when I was determined to do something my way, and it usually upset him, especially when it interfered with his plans. After all, he led a life of perpetual motion, a style which fit his temperament perfectly, and anything that countered his desires posed a threat to his well-being.

I rarely interfered with his plans, so Pierre knitted his brow and looked at me so beseechingly that he reminded me of a clown. I started to laugh.

"I'll stay at the beach house, but not at the farm with Aurelia. I have to stay here and rest." I crossed my arms even more tightly over my chest. My mind was made up.

"But," implored Pierre, his eyebrows arching comically, "please be reasonable, Geeny. The beach house is isolated. You can't stay here alone."

"I can take care of myself. No one ever comes here, anyway, because it is so inaccessible." I squared my shoulders and stuck out my chin. "If anyone ever tried to hurt me, they'd be very sorry."

"I haven't been well lately, either," interjected Sebastian to our surprise. "I can stay in the beach house with Virginie and make sure no one bothers her." He stuck his right arm straight out, karate style.

This comically gallant gesture broke the tension between us. Pierre and I started to laugh.

Pierre hesitated for a moment, God only knows what crossed his mind, but only for a moment. His face cleared.

His eyebrows resumed a normal, relaxed position on his face. He was relieved. The last obstacle to his trip had been eliminated. I wondered if it had occurred to him that he was leaving me with my true love.

Sebastian and I looked at each other, then averted our eyes to the dusty ground we were standing on. The intensity of my feelings made it hard for me to exchange casual glances with him. I think he felt the same.

I forced myself to assume my usual relaxed attitude while my mind and emotions raced ahead. Thinking of spending three days and nights in the most romantic place in the world alone with Sebastian made me feel giddy.

Sebastian nudged me. I jumped. "Now we can take down that ugly bunsen burner," he said, smiling, always smiling. I thought he had the most beautiful smile in the world.

Picking up on my excitement at the prospect of spending three sun-blessed days together, he laughed and added quietly, "We know how to decorate the beach house because we appreciate it and all the beauty around it." He motioned toward the sea and my eyes followed his gesture.

"And people who don't appreciate it will be forbidden," I continued. "I'll put up a sign that says 'No desecration allowed.'"

"And no belching during dinner," laughed Sebastian.

I started to laugh, but remembered that Pierre and Alain were still standing there, so I stifled my giggles.

Instead, I turned toward the panoramic view of the Mediterranean that gracefully curved along the perimeter of the sea. Alicante was visible six kilometers away, and even further was Benidorm. One of the adobe archways that enclosed the beach house terrace framed this view.

How wonderful to share it with someone that loves staying here for the same reasons that I do. Although these thoughts still ran through my mind, like a servant making sure that the gas was turned off and the electricity out before departing for a voyage, I assured Pierre that I would miss him and that he should make his trip as quickly as possible without driving too recklessly, as he was prone to do, for he could have an accident…an accident…my mind wandered, then snapped back to reality. I was shocked at my own hypocrisy.

How selfish we all are, flitted through my mind.

I pictured Pierre and Alain together, always laughing, playing Ping-Pong, water skiing or planning some future adventure together that I would learn of once all the details had been worked out. I realized that Pierre was much closer to his best friend than he was to me at this point, and that part of my attraction to Sebastian came out of loneliness. Maybe things are just taking their natural course, I mused.

With these thoughts fresh in my mind, I stood next to Sebastian and waved a cheerful goodbye to Pierre and Alain as they left for Andorra. They left a huge cloud of dust in their wake, disturbing the quiet serenity of the late-afternoon scene. I looked over at Sebastian and felt happy. The sun beat down on my bikini-clad body. An even more intense warmth projected itself by my side. Sebastian was smiling delightedly at me, a smile which I couldn't help but return in equal measure and intensity.

We had three days. All malevolent thoughts fell from my mind like venom milked from a viper. The beauty of the sky and the azure blue sea made me heady with pleasure. I felt like I was dreaming; but I knew I wasn't, because it was all here right in front of me.

Sebastian and I could tear off our bathing suits and make love if we wanted to, then and there. He stood very close to me, right in front of me, wearing only a low-cut French bikini bathing suit that hugged his strong, bronzed torso. I couldn't avoid his gaze. It was as deep and penetrating as if we were really touching each other. I had to take a step backward. I felt stripped of my will, naked and embarrassed.

After all, he is seven years younger than me, a mere child, not yet twenty, ran through my mind. People still mistook me for a teenager, but I was twenty-six, and I knew how to count.

My passion confused me. Maybe this is one-sided. Maybe I'm just imagining that he is in love with me. Lost in a complicated forest of doubt, I looked at the ground. Not wanting to corrupt him or take advantage of our unusual situation, I decided to let him make the next move.

Perhaps noting my confusion, Sebastian asked me if I would like to take a walk on the beach. I quickly consented, no longer sure what I was supposed to do.

We walked slowly along the soft sand without speaking, not wishing to violate the beauty of the sunset-streaked water and sky with words.

I began to feel drunk from the sensations inspired by the beauty around me. As we approached some sand dunes I looked over at Sebastian and inquired, "Would you like to sit and look at the moonlight on the water?"

"*Mais oui!*" responded Sebastian.

We sat mutely on the sand and stared at the water for a few minutes. Sebastian turned to me and I to him.

"Would you like to roll in the dunes?" When I looked surprised, he explained, "We used to do it when we were children. Only there were more dunes then. It was like a small, private desert."

"What happened to them?"

"Trucks came and took the sand away to make better beach fronts for hotels."

"Raping nature," I said quietly, feeling my way with my words.

"Don't say that!" laughed Sebastian, and he started to roll me down the face of the sand dune.

My body turned to jelly at his touch, so I must have been easy to roll. Exhilarated, I jumped up and cried, "I bet I can leap farther than you in the sand!"

"Three chapters of Gide say you can't!" laughed Sebastian merrily, jumping almost to the bottom of the dune.

"The dinner dishes say I can!" I chimed in.

"Whoever jumps the farthest doesn't have to do them!" yelled Sebastian as he hurled himself down the dune with abandon.

"Whoever cooks doesn't have to do them!" I shouted, egging him on to greater feats of leaping until we were both panting and laughing from exhaustion. We found ourselves leaning against one another at the bottom of a sand dune with the moonlight reflecting our giddy happiness.

"Let's go back to the beach house now," said Sebastian.

"Why?" I countered. I wanted to go on playing in the dunes and walking on the beach forever. "I want to walk some more."

"We can walk to the beach house," said Sebastian softly.

"Why the beach house?" I insisted headily, still drunk with the rapture of the night.

"Because it is a destination."

Sebastian's existentialist remark caught me off guard. I had forgotten how sophisticated he and his family were. I realized he was right: we needed a destination, a focus of interest to keep our minds from degenerating into childlike narcissism. Still, the beauty of the night captivated me. The moonlight laid a golden carpet at our feet as we walked back to the beach house. When we reached the terrace I had to stop and suck in my breath. My heart beat wild rhythms and I was unusually agitated. Sebastian turned to face me. Our eyes met and we couldn't take them off one another. Again, I stepped away from him to keep from impulsively kissing him.

"Why don't we make dinner?" suggested Sebastian.

I nodded my head, went into the kitchen, and opened the tiny ice box.

"It looks like we'll have to have eggs for dinner," I said with apprehension, for it was such a meager bill of fare, especially to offer a Frenchman.

"Okay. Let's eat! I'm hungry!" replied Sebastian with enthusiasm.

"After all, I have to keep you well fed if we're going to romp on the beach like two kids," I rejoined while deftly beating eggs for an omelette.

Sebastian ate eagerly, declaring, "These eggs are delicious, Virginie. I didn't know American women could cook! I thought you were just beautiful!"

I could hardly believe my ears. I hadn't received a compliment from Pierre in three years, and he had never called me beautiful. "Pierre hates the way I fix eggs. He'll only eat them if the maid fixes them."

Sebastian smiled ruefully at me, as if he knew all too well what indignities I suffered with Pierre. He had always sympathized with me for being stuck in Rabat, a city with little to offer other than cheap labor.

He looked up at me. Our eyes interlocked once again. He said softly, sensually, "Virginie, you are too refined and sensitive to be happy in a place like Morocco."

I beamed at him for understanding my dislike of Pierre's choice of residence.

"Whatever you do," he continued with downcast eyes, his long lashes adding mysterious depth to the chestnut brown irises of his eyes, "don't have any children there."

I was caught off guard. "Why not?"

Sebastian raised his eyes and looked at me intently. He smiled sweetly, but said nothing.

"I don't want to have Pierre's children anyway! I'm afraid they might look like him," I jested.

A silence fell between us.

We carried our plates and silverware out to the table on the terrace. We ate our omelettes quietly, only pausing to glance at the sea that arced gracefully toward Alicante, lit up with dimly glowing lights. I glanced at Sebastian as he ate slowly with his eyes lowered. Burnished by the sun, his smooth, fine skin, his dark, chestnut-highlighted hair that framed the firm contours of his face made me almost wince. His delicate features coupled with the masculine self-assurance of his reflective, dry, and often very sarcastic observations echoed my own point of view. Why does he have to be so young...and my husband's second cousin? It was maddening.

Some self-destructive tendency in me made me want to realize my fantasy of finding my perfect lover, my perfect match, a fantasy I usually repressed because it seemed so unlikely. No one was perfect. It was the impossible Cinderella dream. I instinctively resisted being completely absorbed by anyone, no matter how attractive that person might be. Yet, like the proverbial moth attracted to the flame, I was tanta-

lized by just the kind of relationship I most feared and de-
sired.

I finished my dinner quickly, determined to find
Sebastian less attractive.

"I cooked; you get to do the dishes," I announced dryly.
Then I turned and walked into my room to get ready for
bed. I slipped into a light cotton nightgown, then stretched
out on one of the peasant-style, straw-stuffed beds to read by
the light of the antique kerosene lamp. But Sebastian's sweet
image kept thrusting itself onto the pages of my book. I had
finally met someone in real life who captivated my imagination to the point that I didn't even want to read Gide. I got
up, put on a light robe, and walked into the kitchen.

Sebastian stood next to our indoor well, vainly trying to
hoist a bucket of water up. The pulley was broken so that we
had to throw the bucket face down so it hit the water
squarely, filling with water that we could then pull up by
hand. You had to hit the water just right with the bucket,
something Sebastian had never quite mastered. He looked
down at the bucket floating on the surface of the water.

"Let me do it." I hoisted up the bucket and tossed it
down with perfect aim. As I hauled the bucket back up, hand
over fist, I teased Sebastian. "You may be the future karate
champion of Europe, but I'll still be the best bucket tosser."

He tried to take it from me, but I struggled to maintain
control, and the bucket won. It hurtled back down into the
well, spilling its contents.

"*Alors!*" swore Sebastian. "At this rate I won't even qualify
in the *pederaste* karate matches."

I laughed heartily, for *pederaste* means "gay" in French,
and Sebastian took infinite pride in his masculinity.

"Okay. I'll give you a chance to redeem yourself. If you
can fill the bucket with water two times out of three, I won't
even mention to Pierre or anyone else that you considered
entering the gay karate matches."

Sebastian assumed an air of comical concern to amuse
me. He began to heave the bucket down the well as if his life
depended on it, just to make me laugh. He hurled the

bucket again and again until I had to hold my sides, which were sore from laughter.

"Sebastian, are you going to let an American woman outdo you? Watch!" I took the bucket and threw it down the well. A splash and gurgle let us know I had made a direct hit, that the bucket was filling with water. As I hauled it back up with all my tiny strength—for I was not very strong— Sebastian smiled broadly at me. The candlelit kitchen leant a disconcerting beauty to his face. I dropped the bucket back into the well.

"You even spill water gracefully," remarked Sebastian.

I looked at him and froze. Insults I could handle, but compliments...and from Sebastian.... I wanted to take him in my arms and caress his smooth skin, feel his hard muscles, kiss him all over. Instead, I took a deep breath to gain control of myself.

"*Sebastian, je te dis bonsoir*...goodnight. Sleep well and dream...have pleasant dreams."

He just kept smiling at me. No matter what I did, it seemed to please him. It scared me a bit. As I closed my bedroom door he whispered, "And may you dream, too, Virginie."

My thoughts were a thousand miles from Pierre as I lay down to sleep with just a sheet thrown over me. The warm night air caressed me into a deep slumber with as much finesse as any hand, even Sebastian's.

☼ A SURPRISE VISIT

I WAS AWAKENED from a deep and peaceful sleep by a car horn beeping incessantly. I didn't know what time it was, only that I had been awakened from a sound sleep and that it was pitch black outside. I doubted that it was Pierre and Alain. They hadn't even had time to reach Andorra, much less return. But it had to be someone who knew how to make their way over the winding dirt road full of rocks and potholes which led to the beach house.

I panicked. It might be Josine, Alain's wife, twice as loud and obnoxious as he was. I always avoided her in Rabat, and the last place I wanted to see her was here, in the beautiful Mediterranean beach house, when I had three days to spend alone with Sebastian.

But it must be her, I reasoned as well as I could at whatever hour it might be. Josine had informed Pierre and Alain that she would join them at the beach house it if fit into her vacation plans, even though she and Alain no longer shared their vacations.

She's making an exception to drive me crazy, I thought, furious. Josine always took my hospitality for granted. After all, I was just the young American wife of Pierre, the one who owned the beach house, the one who really counted. I boiled inside. Then I heard footsteps scurrying around the beach house and voices calling, "Alain, Josine, we're here! Let us in!"

Relief flooded my brain. It wasn't Josine, just friends looking for her and Alain. It occurred to me to not let them in. But years of training to be a good hostess got me out of bed. I lit a candle and went to one of the wooden shuttered windows. "Who's there?" I shouted through the wooden slats.

"Marie and Daniel!" was the reply.

"Who are you?" I shouted back, incredulous. I had never heard of any friends named Marie and Daniel.

"This is the Cassière residence, I presume," was the stern answer.

I couldn't believe my ears. "No," I said, my indignation mounting with each beat of my accelerating heart. "This is the Moulet residence."

A very subdued "Oh" penetrated the slatted shutters this time.

Then they explained. Josine had drawn them a map to the beach house, and they had just spent three hours trying to find it. It was three o'clock in the morning and they were very tired. Josine was supposed to meet them here. Somehow she had told them the place belonged to her.

It almost does if you consider squatter's rights, I thought, thinking of one summer when she had come with her children and maid.

Marie and Daniel shouted that Josine should be there any minute, which I considered improbable given the late hour, but I knew Josine was crazy enough to drive all night. I decided it wasn't humane to leave them standing out there in the middle of nowhere with no place to go when there were two vacant bedrooms in the beach house.

"Come around to the front door and I'll let you in," I said curtly, not thrilled at the prospect of sharing my cozy situation with two intruders. Nevertheless, I let them in and led them to one of the larger bedrooms, showing them how to light the kerosene lamp by the bed. They thanked me and I returned to my room. Sebastian awakened for an instant as I walked past his room, a candle in my hand.

"*Qu'est-ce que se passe?* What's happening?" He mumbled groggily.

"You'll find out tomorrow morning," I answered. "Go back to sleep." And he did, instantly.

Great help he would have been in an emergency, I thought as I curled back into bed, hoping that the gods of mercy would prevent Josine from coming tonight.

My humor was not the best when I awoke the next morning, but at least Josine had not arrived yet. I put on a facial mask so I wouldn't have to communicate with the new arrivals, and started eating breakfast wordlessly with Sebastian.

Halfway through my second marmalade-coated piece of toast, a very tall man emerged from the bedroom I had shown him to at three in the morning. Accompanying him was a petite, bleached-blond woman of about forty. He looked about ten years younger than her.

I glanced up from my piece of marmalade-dripping toast without the least hint of friendliness. Indeed, it would have been difficult to say *"bonjour"* because my facial mask was beginning to harden.

I guess it had never occurred to Daniel that he might be unwelcome anywhere in the world, for he held out his hand immediately and introduced himself and his wife, Marie, with aplomb and a huge grin that told me he considered himself a very likable person. I was not so easily convinced this morning as I sat next to my true love, Sebastian.

We introduced ourselves as the wife of Pierre Moulet and his second cousin who was watching out for me while Pierre and Alain bought duty-free goods in Andorra. Suddenly I felt like the cat caught with its paw in the goldfish bowl, sitting at the breakfast table in my semi-sheer nightgown with my husband's good-looking younger cousin.

This didn't seem to faze Daniel and Marie. They continued smiling, talking about themselves, their vacation (which was marvelous), the Ivory Coast where they lived, which had wonderful tropical weather year round. They loved to water ski in the harbor there. At this point Sebastian inserted that we had a boat and water skis and could all go skiing in the nearby fishing port of Santa Paula if Daniel would help him drive Pierre's boat. I blanched at the possibility of them wrecking Pierre's boat, but no one else seemed to consider that aspect, and they agreed that they would do it that very morning.

"By the way, Virginie, would you mind if we cleaned out the bathroom we're using?" asked Daniel.

I couldn't have reflected the amount of surprise I registered to hear a Frenchman, used to having servants as they all did in the ex-colonies, asking if he could clean one of my bathrooms. I nodded my mute assent.

"Could we do some shopping for you, too?" added Marie. "Perhaps make you dinner?"

That broke the ice as well as cracked my facial mask, because I smiled so hard while offering to show them the nearby fishing village where they could buy enormous prawns very cheaply, tour Alicante by night and go water skiing…the works. This was the most congenial couple I had ever met. I was so used to having my hospitality taken for granted that I was truly delighted to have some guests who appreciated it, even it they weren't invited and arrived at three in the morning.

Furthermore, Marie and Daniel turned out to be a timely diversion, for now Sebastian and I had the perfect excuse to spend every minute of our two remaining days together. We were their hosts.

Sebastian found Daniel amusing, for he had a humorous, wry manner of talking. Whenever he said something he considered particularly witty, he would cup his hand to the side of his mouth, and addressing someone who seemed to be under the table, would add, "I'm a tease."

Sebastian would imitate this idiosyncrasy to make me laugh. Whenever Marie and Daniel were out of earshot, he would cup his hand as if talking to someone under the table and mimic Daniel. While I was still laughing, he remarked that Marie had a high, nervous laugh which annoyed him.

He confided, "I think she laughs that way because she has never had any children and is nearly forty. A childless woman is usually abnormal."

"Wait a minute!" I exclaimed. "I don't have any kids and I don't feel the least bit abnormal. On the contrary, I feel free and happy."

"Oh, you're too young to have any problems yet," replied Sebastian with blasé confidence.

"Maybe you are, too," I laughed. At the same time I examined the smooth-skinned man-boy sitting in front of me. Behind that angelic Rubenesque smile were undoubtedly many firm convictions about what people and life were supposed to be like, I mused.

When he made sweeping generalizations about women bearing children, I realized that these beliefs had been passed from generation to generation, like the farm, that they were part of his cultural heritage as well as his macho intellectual outlook. He would judge me as he did Marie if I didn't have children.

I quickly swept this inopportune awareness aside. My strength as well as weakness lay in my willingness to understand and accept the shortcomings of those I loved. That was my ancestral heritage as a woman.

Within an hour after offering to show Marie and Daniel the nearby port of Santa Paula, we were off to see the sights, now a happy foursome, laughing and joking, not unlike double-daters. We waterskied in the port, dodging ancient fishing boats nearly one hundred years old. Our spirits sparkled like the sun on the waves.

Afterwards we sauntered along the jetty as fresh and carefree as four teenagers. Sebastian and I always walked side by side, touching shoulders whenever we got a chance. Our intimacy grew bolder in the face of newcomers, for Marie and Daniel did not know if our relationship was platonic or if it had been consummated. Daniel kept trying to force the secret out of me.

"How thoughtful of your husband to leave you in such good company," he said with a wink to let me know he was just teasing me again, and that I didn't have to take him seriously unless I wanted to.

I looked at Sebastian's innocent face for a moment and then answered, "Sebastian is my cousin." I smiled demurely, catching his eye. Sebastian was delighted by my explanation, and from then on he referred to me as *"ma cousinne,"* feminine for cousin in French. And he became *"mon cousin."* Now our intimacy was valid and acceptable, for we were members of the same family and could love one another as such. But the desire I felt in my groin would have made the relationship closer to incest if I had been Sebastian's blood cousin.

Daniel continued to make teasing remarks about husbands who left their wives alone for three days in isolated beach houses with cousins, but we paid no attention to him. His constant stream of banter made us draw even closer together, as if to form an invulnerable unit, focusing only on one another's words and looks. I consulted Sebastian about what kind of seafood to buy, when to take the boat out and when to bring it back...just as I would have consulted Pierre. Sebastian swelled with pride, for my confidence in his ability to help make decisions inflated his status to that of an adult, something that had rarely happened to this charming nineteen-year-old. He replaced Pierre with very little trouble and enjoyed his newfound status.

As we walked past an ancient, grizzled fisherman mending his nets, which were spread out like huge doubled-over cobwebs all around him, I touched Sebastian's arm so he would notice. Sebastian almost embraced me while complying with my wishes. We stood facing each other for an instant, almost in one another's arms. Then I turned adroitly to admire the old man's handiwork.

"Your nets are very beautiful," I said, gesturing toward the multi-colored array of nets in front of him.

"Yes, aren't they, Daniel," squealed Marie, always bordering on a nervous shrillness which she masked with her enthusiasm. I wondered briefly if she and Daniel were having marital problems of some sort.

The deep blue, violet, and sea-green nets swirled in heaps upon heaps around the aged mariner.

"And so tedious to repair, *señorita*," he answered. He was pleased to have his work appreciated.

I looked from the swirl of nets out to the infinite horizon of the sea. My emotions for Sebastian resembled those nets, dizzying swirls of knots to untangle.

The water sparkled like maple sugar candy in the sunshine. I wanted to turn to Sebastian and tell him how much I loved him, yet how impossible it was to love him. I turned to him again, blinking hard under his steady gaze and the proximity of such a physically beautiful person. I touched his bare arm and ran my hand lightly up to his shoulder. He put his hand on my arm.

"I haven't been this happy since," I faltered, "I don't think I've ever been this happy, Sebastian."

"I wish we could always be like this, *ma cousinne*," he murmured, looking into my eyes, melting into them, melting me.

"You are a nice-looking young couple," interjected the old fisherman with a faint smile. Perhaps our light embrace had reminded of a time when he, too, had been a passionate young man.

His remark startled me back to my senses, and I took my customary step backwards. I felt stripped of all modesty standing in front of everyone in a near-embrace with Sebastian. Besides, Marie and Daniel were nudging one another. But they didn't laugh or make teasing remarks this time.

I was relieved when Sebastian turned his head to the ancient fisherman and let his fingers slide imperceptibly from my arm, saying, "Did you know my great-uncle Antonio Valdez? He once fished here."

The old fisherman squinted in the sun and said that perhaps he had, but that he couldn't remember clearly as there had been so many more fishermen in the old days.

Daniel interrupted our conversation, abruptly stating that he was hungry and that he wanted to go fix dinner.

Sebastian and I said a fond goodbye to the old fisherman, then headed back to the beach house with Daniel and Marie.

✹ TIME RUNS OUT

DANIEL PREPARED a gourmet shrimp dinner, which he served with the elegance of a true Frenchman on the terrace overlooking the Mediterranean and Alicante. A quiet appreciation of the beautiful view of the coastline suppressed any need for conversation that evening. The serenity of the starry sky, the calm sea, and Alicante, which sparkled like a jewel in the distance, created an unparalleled sense of peace. Suddenly a brighter light etched its path across the sky. Fireworks!

"It looks like the show has begun," Daniel remarked lazily.

We got up from the dinner table to sit on the edge of the terrace and watch the spectacle. The fireworks flared brightly against the dark sky and dazzled us, but the cold tiles I was sitting on eventually overcame my desire to watch the display.

"My *derrière* is half frozen," I announced, standing up and shaking myself. "I'm going to bed."

Sebastian laughed as if I had said something clever. He constantly surprised me with his keen pleasure in my offhand remarks. Aspects of myself I had never noticed became worthy of comment and appreciation. Sebastian's friendship expanded my self-confidence. I took full advantage of the phenomenon, saying whatever came into my head, things I would have suppressed if Pierre had been there. I felt happier and more loved than I could ever remember.

As I entered my bedroom, the kerosene lamp cast myriad shadows. Fantastic shapes played on the walls and lent an aura of magic and mystery to the night. I slipped out of my light dress, letting the warm night air fondle my body. I fantasized Sebastian coming in to ask me for something. Then I

211

put on my semi-sheer nightgown.

When I went into the kitchen to brush my teeth, as it was easier there than in the bathroom, where no water had been pumped for the tap, Sebastian was standing next to the water pump. I sucked in my breath and then quickly started hauling a bucket of water up from the well, afraid of my uncousinly desires. Sebastian helped me haul it onto the edge of the tiled sink. Our arms brushed together, ever so lightly. The magnetism of that casual touch made me acutely aware of the night's potential. The veil of shyness disintegrated into the magic of the evening. Sebastian took my hand and kissed it. I swooned. He put his arm around my waist to steady me and our lips brushed.

As he guided me toward my bedroom, I realized with mounting fear that neither of us knew what we were getting into. It was one thing to cavort about like children in the safety of Marie and Daniel's presence, to exchange passionate looks and near embraces, but Sebastian was my husband's second cousin. Guilt and doubt eclipsed my passion. I looked up at Sebastian. All he did was smile and stand in front of me without uttering a word. He had never looked so seductive.

"Sebastian, I just wanted to tell you goodnight," I said hastily.

"Good night, *ma cousinne*," he responded slowly.

We turned and walked to our separate bedrooms.

The next morning I was awakened by a car horn beeping wildly. I didn't want to wake up, but the insistent horn kept on beeping. I ran to the front door and flung it open. A road-weary but exuberant husband stood before me.

"I'm back!" declared an exhilarated Pierre. "What a trip! We drove night and day without stopping. Alain drove while I slept in the back seat of the car and vice-versa. We drove 1,300 kilometers in two and one half days. It was fantastic, Geeny!"

I nodded dumbly at my husband. He may as well just have returned from Mars for all the sense he was making to me. I saw Sebastian step out of his bedroom, rubbing his eyes. He saw Pierre and smiled. They clapped each other on the back.

"That's great, just great...wonderful, fantastic, *formidable*...superhuman. You are Prometheus," I said to Pierre. Then I started laughing uncontrollably.

"What's the matter, Geeny? Aren't you glad to see me?" asked a dubious Pierre. His wife had never acted like this before.

"Nothing's the matter. It's perfect. Perfect. Just perfect. I just need some sleep. I was dreaming and you interrupted my dream. I want to finish it." I looked at Sebastian and then fled to the bedroom, leaving them to sort things out.

When Pierre came into the bedroom later on, I pretended to be asleep. When he tried to awaken me I mumbled incoherently. Then I pushed him away from me. No sex! Pierre walked quietly out of the bedroom.

I got dressed and went out into the bright sunlight of mid-morning. Pierre and Alain had all the gadgets they had bought in Andorra—a new stereo, some water skis, an extra grip Ping-Pong paddle—on display and were playing with them. Sebastian stood in the background and laughed at their antics.

When Pierre saw me, he grinned and went to the car. He took out a 45 r.p.m. record, a record with the single song on it I had requested. He gave it to me and I thanked him. Then I went into the kitchen. Sebastian followed me.

"Alors," he said, "your record, do you like your record?"

I smiled weakly at him.

"You wanted an album, and he got you a single," laughed Sebastian.

"An album would have been nicer," I agreed. "Sebastian, let's take Marie and Daniel to Alicante tonight. Let's show them the town like we said we would."

"And what about Pierre and Alain?"

"They'll be too tired to come with us. They've been up all night driving."

"I love to visit Alicante at night," said Sebastian.

I implored Pierre to come with us, making a show of being a dutiful wife, but he was too tired, and he went to bed before we left. In contrast, Marie, Daniel, Sebastian and I were animated. Thrilled at the prospect of walking through the ancient streets of Alicante at night with Sebastian, I laughed gaily through dinner and my quick preparations to see Alicante by night.

A gentle mist descended over the ancient town that night, a rarity in the month of August, even though this was the end of the month, the end of our vacation. The streets were deserted because of a soccer match in a nearby town.

As we wandered through the ancient, narrow, cobbled streets of Alicante, the night took on almost supernatural proportions. Marie and Daniel walked discreetly behind us. I admired a dress in a shop window. "Do you think it would look good on me?" I asked Sebastian.

"*Tout te va bien.* Everything looks good on you. Of course it would look great on you. Everything suits you, you can't wear anything without looking beautiful...you're...."

"Stop, stop it, Sebastian!" I cried out. I couldn't bear his delirious flattery in front of the two others, who looked at us curiously now.

We kept on walking, walking without any destination in mind. Soon we came upon an elevator at the entrance of a large stone building that loomed high above us.

"Do you want to go in?" asked Sebastian.

I read the plaque above the entrance. "The Cartagena Castle...I've never been here."

"Hasn't Pierre ever taken you?" asked Sebastian. "I go at least every summer. It's a fantastic castle."

"I didn't even know there was a castle in Alicante," I said, amazed at my own ignorance.

Marie and Daniel had faded into the background, following us at a discreet distance.

We wandered through the streets some more until we came to a curious sort of shrine. It was an ancient, turn-of-the-century fire engine in perfect condition.

"And what's this behind it?" I asked, indicating a pool of water in a niche in the wall.

"Don't profane it! That's holy water," Sebastian dipped his fingers into the water, crossed himself slowly across his chest, then kissed the tips of his fingers and blew me a kiss.

I smiled at him, smiled until it felt like my face would crack from so much smiling. Sebastian and I could not stop smiling at one another. We were entranced.

The next evening, Sebastian wanted to see a film by Polanski, a director he admired. We convinced Marie and Daniel to chaperon us. Then I made a show of imploring Pierre to join us, too. I didn't think he would as he was still very tired from his trip, but he consented to go.

As we walked into the only movie theater in Alicante, I reveled in the attention Sebastian and Pierre gave me, both jockeying for position to sit next to me during the film. I sat down between them, but my shoulder stayed firmly glued to Sebastian's as schizophrenia and scenes of a demented Catherine Deneuve murdering men evolved before our eyes.

Sebastian and I made love with our shoulders that night during the movies, rubbing them ever so gently together, then parting only to return like breathless lovers for another kiss.

The next day was Sebastian's last in Alicante this summer. We made the most of it, walking through the narrow streets together, sipping horchata on the esplanade, and talking as intimately as we dared. Sebastian sympathized with my ennui in Morocco, and I with his aversion to Paris.

"We both should have been born in Alicante, where we are so happy together," I confided. He smiled warmly, so warmly that I always returned his smile with equal delight.

In a more serious tone, I added, "Pierre wants me to have a baby now. I'll never get out of Morocco if I have a baby."

"Don't have Pierre's baby." Sebastian looked at me, dead serious.

I smiled happily at him, thinking how much I would love to have his child and live in the beach house with him forever.

When we got back into the car with Marie and Daniel, I started speaking English to him, hoping he would understand what I had said. Daniel snorted at our latest form of intimacy.

"Why haven't we done more things together, Sebastian? You're leaving tomorrow, and we've just gotten to know one another." He smiled and looked into my eyes. I thought my heart was going to explode with love and excitement. We held hands all the way back to the beach house. Daniel drove without saying a word, not even a wisecrack.

That night at the beach house I went to Sebastian's bedroom after he had gone to bed. He sat up in bed and smiled at me.

"I want you to know that...that these days with you have been the best in my life," I said.

He smiled at me, took my hand and kissed it. We looked at each other for a long time, then we said goodnight, and I turned and left.

An overcast sky greeted us the next morning, the result of a storm at sea. I felt terribly tired from the night before. I had been ill in the night, but my fatigue was as emotional as it was physical. I felt that I couldn't bear to be separated from Sebastian.

We had time to exchange only a quick look and a contrite smile of complicity when Pierre and Alain whisked him away to help secure the boat. Marie and Daniel took me to the farm, after which we would go to Benidorm to spend a few days. The possibility of not being able to say goodbye to Sebastian appalled me. What if we left before he and Pierre got back from Santa Paula? Crazed thoughts ran through my mind. I felt as if I would never see him again, or at least not for an incredibly long time, during which so much could happen to change our feelings. Love requires such a delicate balance between people.

An eternity seemed to pass before Pierre's car drove up. Sebastian was in it, to my immense relief. He didn't look at me right away, but talked with the others. Marie wanted some figs from a nearby tree, so we went to pick some for her. Again, it was as if Sebastian and I were alone together. Our gaiety returned.

Sebastian put a particularly fat fig in the basket we were carrying and remarked, "This should be enough to give them all a good case of colic." We both started to laugh.

"We used to have a farm in our family...." I laughed. "But my grandfather sold it...just like that."

Sebastian chortled at my choice of words, the way I picked figs, every move I made seemed to give him pleasure. I basked in his adoration.

At last we had enough figs, and we walked slowly, silently back to the farmhouse. I broke the heavy silence with a gesture toward the heavily overcast sky. "How gloomy it is today. It's like the end of summer." Sebastian nodded sadly.

Pierre, Marie, and Daniel waited for us in front of the farmhouse.

"Which car do you want to ride in?" he asked. "You can ride with Alain and me or Marie and Daniel." I numbly chose the latter. I didn't want to say goodbye to Sebastian at my husband's side.

We couldn't even exchange the customary embrace as I had to get in the car. A brief handshake, and then Daniel started the engine. I looked back and waved at Sebastian's retreating figure. He waved back and then started making a furious gesture with his hands. For a minute I didn't know what he was trying to tell me, then I understood. I smiled at him like a lifeline had been tossed to me. He was scribbling in the air, telling me to write to him. A contact through a card or a letter was inconsistent, but it was better than nothing.

The following days spent in Benidorm flew agreeably by, mainly because of the joviality of Daniel and Marie. It was only when Pierre and I were left alone that I began to feel the emptiness, the richness that had gone out of my life, the impoverishment that was left. I could no longer bear the presence of Pierre. His minor defects were magnified by the perfection of Sebastian. The contrast was too sharp. I thought of when Amina's husband had come back from his brother's wedding and she had asked me for tranquilizers. Now I understood my maid.

Our vacation waned. It was time to return to North

Africa, to Rabat. Once again, we discovered that my passport was missing. Pierre had hidden it so carefully that he could not unearth it. We searched the beach house thoroughly, reported the loss to the local police, and left anyway. Pierre hoped to arrange things with the Moroccan authorities. They were easy enough to bribe, as a rule.

We arrived in Algeciras at sunset the next evening. Pierre tried everything to get me on the ferry that would take us to Morocco, but in vain. I had to have my passport.

Hurriedly, we decided that he would go on without me and arrange things through the American consul in Tangier. I prepared to spend up to a week in the small, port town of Algeciras. The prospect didn't thrill me. Worse still, the next day was my twenty-seventh birthday.

I awakened the next morning in the room overlooking the ocean Pierre had rented for me. I looked out onto a shimmering Atlantic ocean just this side of Morocco, with Gibraltar in between. I resolved to buy enough books to last me a week. Luckily, I could read and speak Spanish.

As I ambled through the narrow, twisting streets behind the port, I was increasingly surprised. To my delight, it was not at all like the filthy port, but a typically charming, quaint Spanish town. Children played happily in the streets, and the people were bright and happy. Soon I felt as happy as my surroundings.

I came upon a local marketplace where everything from tomatoes to horse saddles was sold. I spotted an old gypsy woman with some pretty gold and black-lace mantillas. I fingered them and smiled into her wizened, weatherbeaten face. I only had about six dollars with me.

"How much?" I asked her.

She squinted up at me and grinned, her mouth revealing two teeth. "One thousand pesetas," she announced, firmly.

Lousy bargainer that I was, I knew a pretty mantilla when I saw one, and today was my birthday. I had to have it.

"My husband lost my passport and had to leave me here for a week while he tries to get me into Morocco," I said, plaintively. "And today is my birthday. I want to buy something nice for myself."

She smiled in commiseration, probably thinking I had been abandoned by my husband, and I got the mantilla for the price I offered.

Elated by my victory, I thanked her profusely and walked back to the hotel, my heart high.

Back in my hotel room, I felt like sharing my luck with someone. I started writing letters and ended up writing a heartfelt letter to Sebastian in Paris. I kept the tone light and humorous.

"Come visit us at Christmas!" was my illogical suggestion, because I knew he didn't even have a car. But I couldn't bear the idea of a long separation. Even Christmas was too far away. I wanted to see him here and now. I wanted to see his smile and hear him laugh warmly, to reach out and touch his shoulder. His absence was like a physical pain that I couldn't ward off.

Finally I dropped off to sleep, only to be awakened by someone knocking at my door. It was Pierre. He had managed to obtain a "*laissez passer*" from the consul in Tangier. We arrived in Rabat the next day in the pouring rain, which matched my mood perfectly.

Slowly but surely Pierre and I reinstated our relationship. Only a few cryptic letters came from Sebastian, although the first postcard announced, "I cover you with kisses, my cousin," enough to make my heart stop beating for a full minute. The very thought of him covering my body with kisses furnished me with fantasies for months to come.

Sebastian couldn't visit us at Christmas, but he and his best friend hitchhiked to Rabat for Easter break. I stared at his opened suitcase in our guest bedroom in disbelief, and touched some of his clothing reverently. I couldn't believe he was really here. We had a wonderful time water skiing with Pierre, smoking pot for the first time in our living room with me sprawled out on the Empire sofa, just staring into each other's eyes, but nothing happened. Sebastian got sick and had to throw up in the bathroom. He left in a few days. We continued to write sweet, innocent letters full of infatuation and puppy love. Pierre took it all in good humor, seeming not to have noticed that Sebastian couldn't take his eyes off of me and vice versa.

Soon it was June again. And now the king really was having a lavish birthday party. We were invited. But all I could think about was the month of August, when I would see Sebastian again.

☼ COUP D'ETAT

PIERRE AND I drove in silence to the king's birthday party at his summer palace in Skhirat. The long rows of palm trees that lined the central avenue of Rabat stood stiff as military sentinels. I looked up at them and prayed for respite. Since last summer and Easter vacation, when he had hitchhiked to Rabat to spend Easter break with us, I thought of Sebastian incessantly. To have fallen in love with my husband's twenty-year-old second cousin, who still went to the Sorbonne, lived with his parents in Paris, who was far from being able to support himself and make his way in the world—was insane. But I knew it was over between Pierre and me. I contemplated a separation while looking at the serene, stately palm trees that lined the street. I knew I would have precious little time to sit back and enjoy the view once I entered the working world in the United States. I had no idea what I would do there.

For the time being, it felt good to lean back and admire the scenery as Pierre drove us to the king's summer palace, the majestic palms and the centuries-old walls that surrounded Rabat. The time-worn walls that had protected the city from the ravages of ancient armies and pirate merchants had crumbled in spots, but their sheer height and width, their solidity through the ages, instilled a sense of wonder in me. They had endured, and at this point I admired anything that had lasted.

I hope I can withstand the ravages of time with such dignity, I thought, glancing in the rear-view mirror to make sure there were still no lines around my eyes. If Rabat could withstand the onslaught of the Roman legions, Phoenician pirates, Portuguese marauders, and French colonists, I guess I can handle a few lines in my face, I thought, although the idea of aging evaded me. At age twenty-seven I couldn't even imagine turning thirty.

"They say it gives one character," I mumbled, half to Pierre, half to the walls.

"What?" shouted Pierre into the wind.

"Nothing!" I shouted back as my hair whipped into my face with the wind. I pushed it out of my eyes. "Nothing important."

I turned my head toward the ancient ramparts and watched the parapets where Mouley Ismael's guards had stood two centuries ago. My thoughts turned to the history of Morocco, fascinating as it was gory, as one of the gateways in the venerable walls loomed ahead. It was immense, a full twenty feet in width. I thought of the fierce old sheiks who used to behead their enemies and place their heads on the spikes along the walls. The Moroccan Jews had to salt the heads, a grisly job, I mused. I looked toward the section of town known as the *mellah*, where the Jews lived. According to Pierre and his friends, many had been sent to Israel. Rumors were always rife in Rabat.

Now only a slight odor of urine wafted into my nostrils as we passed beneath the ancient gateway where many a young man paused to relieve himself under the cover of night. I thought of Paris, where you could see only the feet of the men in the outdoor urinals as they contributed the remains of last night's wine to Paris's sewer system. But, of course, even these circular urinals did not shock the eye or have an odor, for in Paris aesthetics hold sway over all else. The French do have an earthy sense of humor, of life, I mused. I looked over at Pierre, hell-bent on getting to the king's birthday party in less than an hour. He did have a good sense of humor, I realized. Nothing seemed to daunt him.

Generally, I hated formalities, but the king of Morocco's birthday party would be an event to remember, I told myself. So I wore my best gold-trimmed caftan for the occasion. "Fit for a king," I thought, smiling.

Hoards of invaders no longer threatened Rabat as they had in the past. No, the Romans, Phoenicians, Portuguese, and many others had come and gone, leaving only traces of their civilizations behind in the form of ruins, as was the case with the Romans, who had occupied Morocco for over three centuries and had built two small cities, one in Rabat and one near Fez, the ancient capital of Morocco. The French had left factories and chic boutiques which quickly went out of business when the Moroccans regained their independence in 1956, putting Mohammed V back on the throne. He was considered the rightful heir as a descendent of the Alouites, or Mohammed, the prophet of Allah, or God in the Muslim religion. When he died of heart failure at the age of fifty-six during a routine dental procedure, his dashing young son, Hassan II, was catapulted onto his father's throne when he was in his early thirties. Overnight Hassan went from being one of the most eligible playboy princes in Europe to the position of potentate of Morocco. At first his rule had been favorably viewed as one of liberality and tranquility, until the old tribal feuds began to resurface in his parliament, once called the most advanced and democratically structured governing body in the modern world. He wanted to eradicate the squalor so often created by proud, vengeful warlords, respected only for their capacity to instill fear.

Moulay Ismael, his predecessor two centuries ago, sired 888 children, approximately half of whom were sons, and half of those had plotted his assassination at one time or another. He had them tortured in the public squares of Marrakesh and left to die in a cage for all to see. When his appetite faltered, he ordered a slave beheaded in his presence. He has been called the Louis XIV of Morocco, for he ruled during the eighteenth century and had almost as much power. Both rulers died peacefully of old age.

Hassan II was idealistic when he inherited his father's throne over twelve years ago. He tried to implement a more evolved form of government than had previously existed in Morocco. But traditions cannot be effaced overnight. Reluctantly, Hassan became more and more a total monarch. His model of parliamentary procedure had turned into a mockery as the members haggled endlessly over legislation, unable to agree. The king, despairing of the shambles his parliament had become, abolished it. According to royal lineage, he was descended directly from the Alouites and Mohammed. He had divine as well as sovereign rights, and he made himself the sole ruler of the country.

I turned and looked at Pierre. His eyes were on the road, creased from too much sun, but he remained boyish-looking and charming. Maybe he isn't that bad, I thought. Marriage, like any other kind of job, had its pros and cons. Lately I read and kept to myself unless there was a dinner party or dance that Pierre insisted I go to. I loved the company of genius—Proust, Camus, Gide, Flaubert, the literary giants of France. I read them greedily, fascinated by their characters, descriptions, and, above all, their philosophy.

Pierre loved the company of his old high school chums and spent most of the day either in his antique shop or playing tennis, golf, or Ping-Pong with them. That suited me, because I wanted to read and write an occasional impression of this almost medieval land I lived in. My only problem was that I was a bit insolent, and this translated poorly on the printed page. But then, in Morocco it didn't really matter because no one read what I wrote.

The sun beat down on us relentlessly as we drove along the beach to Hassan's summer palace in Skhirat. The horizon blurred agreeably into a mirage-like wave of heat. I listened to the waves crashing on the beach and sighed deeply. Life was not that bad here. Pierre drove into the palace courtyard and parked next to a Mercedes Benz. We smiled at Monsieur and Madame Hasnoui, the minister of education and his wife, as they got out of their car. Pierre walked gracefully to my door and opened it. His agile elegance lent a charm to his small frame that other women adored. They always told me how lucky I was to be married to such a delightful man, one who could talk about antique furniture and other subjects of feminine interest. I smiled up into his crinkled eyes. He offered me his arm, and I slid out of the front seat of the convertible to take it.

An overdressed couple walked in front of us and we

looked at each other and laughed. It was fun to laugh at other people's pretensions. Pierre was really not bad, I continued to muse. Our relationship was pleasant and relaxing. We read together every night before going to sleep. I could picture us lying in our huge Louis XIV canopy bed, reading for an hour before going to sleep at ten.

Occasionally I looked over his shoulder and read what he was reading, making comments on the Man with the Iron Mask (Louis XIV's supposed twin brother) or whatever he delved into that evening. But there was no real intellectual meeting ground. He had never read the classics. He used to say, "Geeny, I was the donkey of my high school class because I have such a bad memory." He hadn't been able to pass the rigorous French high school baccalaureate, and he, like Sebastian, still depended on his parents for an income.

Well, the perfect man doesn't exist, I thought to myself as he escorted me into the summer palace.

Built centuries ago, the palace's archways were made of alabaster, intricately carved with designs that represented the words written in the Koran. The palace sparkled like a brilliant diamond on the edge of the cobalt-blue Atlantic ocean.

Pierre and I walked past a bubbling fountain into the throne room to greet the king. It too was made of intricately laid mosaic tile, each tile placed to honor Allah and his prophet, Mohammed. The throne, made of carved alabaster, stood imposingly in the back of the room. King Hassan II sat imposingly on it, looking every inch a king. His appearance embellished by a military uniform and medals, dignity emanated from his intelligent, flashing eyes. He nodded his dark, closely cropped head in our direction. Pierre bowed and I curtsied, a brief dip with the front of my caftan held up in my hands.

I remembered the day when his royal tax collectors came to our antique shop. They looked at our furniture with big smiles wreathing their faces, then took several bolts of silk brocade and velvet to "try out at the palace." We never saw them again. Pierre told me that was how they collected taxes in Morocco.

Hassan beamed majestically from his throne. I looked at him and wondered if he would rule until his death. This was only his forty-sixth birthday. Only strong kings ruled very long in a country where humility was considered a sign of weakness. In the world of sheiks and pashas, servants were meek; rulers were descendants of Mohammed and did as they pleased. Out of the corner of my eye I spotted Pierre's uncle Marc with the mayor of Ouezzane. They began to chat with some friends, so we waved and then sauntered toward the royal golf course to wait for them.

Before we got far, I saw Doctor Duval sipping some champagne, all alone.

"Pierre, there's Dr. Duval!"

We laughed and joined him, our good friend and customer.

"It's the perfect day for a royal affair, don't you agree?" I asked the doctor.

Doctor Duval and Pierre laughed with me. "The king deserves a royal spanking for his royal affairs!" The doctor looked up at me with twinkling eyes, a small man full of pithy humor.

Pierre looked into the distance as we chatted and suddenly saw someone he knew. He nodded to excuse himself while the doctor and I continued to talk.

"Well, Doctor, he was very young when his father died and he became king. He still had some wild oats to sow." I inserted a naive tone into my voice.

"He still has wild oats to sow. The man must be a direct descendent of Moulay Ismael, and he would have as many children if it weren't for...."

"That's just gossip," I laughed.

We looked out over the view of the golf course and the ocean just beyond. It was a magnificent day, perfect for the king's birthday party! Then I looked down into the doctor's wizened but still handsome face. "You would think two wives could keep a man, even a king, satisfied. But then maybe he is trying to live up to his father's reputation. He had twelve."

"What about Moulay Ismael? He had over a hundred after he inherited his brother's harem. Imagine trying to satisfy one hundred women!" The doctor chuckled wryly.

"A tough act to follow," I commented, trying to discern what the doctor was really thinking. Dr. Duval was gay and kept a young Moroccan lover to whom I gave English lessons. I narrowed my eyes and smiled at him while thinking that he shouldn't talk. I couldn't imagine him trying to satisfy even one woman. I could never understand how such a handsome man could be homosexual, unless, of course, women hurt him more than men, or less.

His lover sold the exquisite furniture he bought at our shop in the local *medina* every year when the doctor went on vacation in Greece. Then Dr. Duval came and cried on our shoulders about what his friend had done to him. But he continued the relationship nevertheless. I have never heard of women selling their lovers' furniture when they went on a vacation. But, then again, anything is possible.

Dr. Duval nibbled on his hors d'oeuvres and fumed about the king some more. "It's not his wives I object to, it's his ridiculous golf courses!" He drank some champagne and ate some more caviar. "He spent over a billion dollars on one," he eyed me testily, "given in foreign aid by the United States, *carte blanche*…and then called it the People's Golf Course!"

I turned and looked behind us to make sure no one was listening to our conversation.

"We should watch what we say here, Doctor," I admonished while tippling my own champagne glass. "After all, there are royal ears all over the place, or should I say palace?" I laughed at my witticism, and then took the doctor's arm and steered him toward the swimming pool that sparkled in the distance.

"Why don't you put on a bathing suit and go for a dip with me? I haven't gotten my exercise yet today. Besides, these high heels are killing my feet." I smiled down into his face. "You know I have to get in shape for our summer vacation in Alicante!" I gave him a conspiratorial wink.

A glint of mischief came into the doctor's eyes. "Spending the month of August there again, eh, Virginie?"

"Shhhh! We can't talk about it here!" I admonished him. He should know better than to refer to my most delicious moments, those that I spent with Sebastian—even if they were platonic.

"Ahhh, those marvelous vacations in Alicante..."

"Doctor, I said not to talk about it here!"

"But I haven't said anything, Virginie!" He frowned at me for acting so paranoid. "Besides, Pierre is nowhere in sight."

We all have our weaknesses, I thought absently. "Where is Pierre off to now?" I asked, a trifle annoyed. Pierre was always darting all over the place. His *joie de vivre* had turned into an excess of nervous energy as far as I was concerned, and at this point I could have used some peace and quiet, especially in bed. Other than that, he was a good husband, or maybe I was a good wife.

"Virginie, I really think you ought to..."

Loud, popping noises interrupted the doctor.

"Fireworks!" I exclaimed, propelling Dr. Duval toward the noise, my arm linked through his.

Just then the King's *aide de camp* ran out of the main room of the palace and pitched forward with blood gushing from his stomach.

"Oh, my God!" I shrieked.

Several of the guests staggered in from the pool area, blood pouring from their naked wounds.

The doctor pushed me to the ornate mosaic floor of the throne room we had just entered. "Get down!" he shouted.

Screams of anguish and surprise erupted from all quarters as the "fireworks" continued. The king's guests, the social and military elite of Morocco, dashed frantically in all directions, some dressed in tuxedos, some in long velvet caftans, some in elegant party dresses, all panic stricken.

Those who ran through the front door of the palace were instantly mowed down by machine gun fire. Ra-ta-ta-ta-tat! Others jumped out of the palace windows and ran toward the royal golf course to meet the same fate. The shooting seemed indiscriminate; even foreign diplomats died in the line of fire. King Hassan didn't budge, but stood erect with his commander-in-chief, General Alaoui, his boyhood friend and co-hort, by his side. They confronted the troops from the King's own army who walked into the throne room ready to execute them.

I peered up from where I lay, prostrate on the marble floor.

"Don't move!" hissed Dr. Duval.

Tadatadadatadatadatat! Bullets filled Dr. Duval's leg, and I screamed.

Oh, my God, this is a nightmare, I thought in blind despair. I heard more machine gunfire in the distance. I felt tears roll down my cheeks as I fought to calm myself, to beat down the fear that struck like a huge, thunderous wave pounding me down. I moved with infinite caution to tear off a piece of my caftan. Slowly, with the help of Dr. Duval, we cautiously made a tourniquet for his bloody wounds. I couldn't bear to look at them for long, but it looked like his left leg had been nearly shot off. My fingers trembled as I tried to knot the material, and I thought I would faint. The doctor worked more nimbly, and together we somehow applied the makeshift tourniquet and slowed the blood flow. My stomach turned many times, but I didn't vomit.

"Control yourselves!" shouted the king. "Stop shooting instantly and explain yourselves!" He glared furiously at the young soldiers. Hassan was livid with rage. He stood and addressed them furiously. His courage stopped them dead in their tracks.

"We have orders to shoot...Your Majesty," a timorous voice spilled out, no more than a whisper, from the rear of the group. They looked very young; probably cadets, I thought, regaining some of my wits.

Hassan II scowled at them. "If you kill me, you'll go straight to hell. I am the Imam al Moumineen, and if you shoot me, you will never go to paradise, but to the eternal tortures of hell. I am the divine representative of the prophet Mohammed. You know that!" He stood very straight, seemingly fearless. General Alaoui never flinched at his side. I couldn't believe their courage in the face of death.

The cadets began to exchange nervous glances. The king clearly had impressed them with his bravery. Also, what he said was true according to the Koran. They would go to hell if they killed him.

"Who are you to insult Allah by shooting his divine representative here on earth? Who? Which one of you would be so foolish?" The king continued talking, softening his voice to infuse some royal charm. "You have obviously been misled. You are too young to know what you are doing. And you look as if you might have been drugged. You stagger, falter, your eyes are glazed. I can see that you are innocent Muslims trapped into an insidious plot to overthrow the divine descendant of the Alouites, the earthly representative of the prophet Mahomet."

I turned my head ever so slightly to peek at them. The cadets did look a bit dazed, either from drugs, the hot summer sun, or the incredibly courageous words just spoken by their king. They hesitated, unsure of what to do. They looked at each other, and then back at Hassan II. Perhaps he was right. Perhaps Allah was watching them.

"Bow down upon the floor!" commanded Hassan, in full control now. "You must always prostrate yourself on the floor in the presence of an Alouite. Otherwise you insult Mohammed, Allah, and all that is sacred to Islam!"

The cadets looked as if someone had pushed their off buttons. They no longer had wills of their own. One by one they bowed low and flattened themselves on the floor in front of their sovereign.

Suddenly the door burst open again, and a Moroccan dignitary staggered in brandishing a dagger. "I am here to save you, Majesty! I am here...." He pitched forward, blood pouring profusely from a stomach wound.

The doctor writhed in pain next to me, and I grabbed his arm and held it tightly. I stared in transfixed horror at the dignitary who had just died. Another volley of machine gun fire from the pool area grazed us again, and Dr. Duval moaned. I felt a bullet graze my left shoulder. It felt like a branding iron, but it missed me. The odor of burnt velvet wafted to my nostrils from my caftan. I cautiously looked down to see a black path where it had singed my caftan. I shivered on the cold marble floor.

"Enough!" shouted the king. "These are my guests! Tend to their wounds!"

One of the cadets ran to bolt the door and another ran to assist the doctor, who tightened the tourniquet made from the hem of my caftan; but blood flowed freely from his multiple wounds.

"To hell with your goddamn prophets and royal bullshit, I'm bleeding to death!" roared the doctor, seized by an untimely fit of temper.

As Dr. Duval struggled frantically to tighten his tourniquet, I looked into the cadets' eyes beseechingly. "He doesn't know what he's saying! He's delirious!"

They looked at each other, then picked both of us up and helped us to the banquet room, where we had been eating caviar and drinking champagne a scant hour or so ago.

Pools of blood splattered the room, and dignitaries littered the floor, sprawled in the pathetic positions only the dead assume. The ambassador from Belgium lay inert in his own blood. I shuddered. This man, so aristocratic and distinguished when alive, looked like a sad rag doll tossed to the ground by a careless child. His head lay at a grotesque angle, and an eye stared toward the royal fountain still bubbling gaily in the midst of this massacre.

Where is Pierre, I wondered. I turned my head a fraction of an inch to look for him. What if he was dead? A million thoughts ran through my mind. They ceased instantly as some new cadets ran into the room and pointed machine guns at us. I quickly dropped to the ornate mosaic floor and prayed. As an imaginary bullet entered my spine, my muscles tightened. I prepared for the worst. The doctor lay beside me, groaning.

"I am Red Chinese!" I heard someone shout. "I am for the people! Spare me!" A spurt of machine gun fire silenced the voice.

I began to breathe spasmodically. Cadets ran feverishly

about, shooting at random. I dared not move a muscle. The doctor's warm, viscous blood flowed onto my own legs as we lay side by side like lovers seeking one another's comfort. Too bad he's gay, ran incongruously through my mind.

I put my face down and hoped the soldiers would think we were dead. When the doctor moved slightly to tighten his tourniquet, they instantly sprayed him with more bullets. I closed my eyes and prayed to God. Fear and exhaustion began to take their toll, and I began to shiver spasmodically after I lay for a long time on the floor while more people were shot.

In the next room, one of the generals leading the insurrection stood at the head of a banquet table laden with caviar, exotic fruits, champagne glasses, and spilled blood. The guests stared at him in horror as he, polite as a pope, read off the names of those marked for execution.

"Ahmed Cherkaoui!" he barked.

"Tadatadatadata!" The bullets mowed down Ahmed Cherkaoui, whose eyes bulged in terror before he doubled over and slumped forward onto the table, his blood mixing hideously with the contents of a plate of hors d'oeuvres he had earlier eaten with avidity. "I see Ahmed, traitor to Islam, had a good appetite," mocked the general, whose voice I recognized. It was General Znaidi, and Pierre and I had an invitation to *his* birthday party tomorrow.

He paused, then called out the next name on his list.

"Mohammed Haffid!" That was a common name in Morocco, and it belonged to two men at the banquet table. Both stood up. The general saw that one of the men was a friend and yelled, "No, no, don't shoot!" Too late. A shot rang out as the general lunged in front of his friend to protect him, which, effectively, he did. He caught the bullet intended for his friend. And with the bullet, the general took his misfortune.

"*Mon genèrale!*" shouted the soldier who had just shot him by accident. General Znaidi clutched his stomach. Blood flowed freely from it. His soldiers rushed to him to try to save him, but the general had multiple health problems to begin with and could not last. With him went all semblance of order.

The soldiers panicked and began firing both inside and outside the palace. They killed servants, cooks, caddies, and several golfers on the royal golf course. They fired at people on the beach as far off as two miles. The remaining guests pleaded and prayed. Some ripped off watches and precious jewels to bargain for their lives to no avail.

My own life flashed before my eyes many times that long afternoon, the longest in my life. Finally I thought I heard a faint firing in the distance. I prayed it came from troops loyal to the king. The thought of getting out of the king's summer palace alive made my head swim. Was it too much to ask? The doctor gasped for air next to me. I feared he might be dying. And where was Pierre?

Before I could summon up answers to these questions, the loyalists took the palace by storm, strafing it again and again with machine gun fire. This time only soldiers were hit, as everyone else had long ago either died or clung to the cold mosaic marble floor as if it were their mothers' warm breast.

Heavy boots ran helter-skelter, and the firing continued for a short while. I continued to play dead and hoped that the doctor wasn't. Shots echoed in the throne room, and the thought of rescue cheered me. I just hoped we would be liberated before the doctor bled to death.

Voices emanated from the throne room. They were coming toward us. I recognized Hassan's voice. He emerged from his throne room praising Allah and his loyal troops. I lifted my head and saw General Alaoui walking by his side. Soldiers fell to their knees before the king and prostrated themselves on the floor the minute they saw him. The soldiers who had been instructed to execute the King clapped their hands and cheered him. They proclaimed their loyalty to their sovereign and to Allah.

King Hassan II looked around the gory scene of death and mayhem that was to have been his birthday banquet. He recognized valued members of his royal cabinet among the dead, his minister of health, education, and the ambassador from Belgium. He shook his head in disgust and contrition. They he straightened and announced, "All who remained loyal to me before they died are in paradise." A visible wave of contempt swept over his face. "The rest are in the eternal fires of Hell. It is the will of Allah."

"It is the will of Allah, *inchallah*," murmured the cadets and Muslims nearby. I knew they believed this devoutly.

Suddenly Dr. Duval groaned miserably.

"Your Majesty, he is dying!" I pleaded. I looked at the king with tears in my eyes.

Hassan looked at us, covered with blood and pathetic. "Take these people to the hospital!" he said in a loud voice.

I bowed my head and let out the biggest sigh of relief in my life.

"Take all the wounded to the Avicenne Hospital, where they will be treated. And rout out the rest of the disloyal troops and deal with them as the Alouites have always dealt with traitors!" His voice grew loud and angry.

He turned to General Alaoui. "I am sure Colonel Kaddafi is behind this, the Marxist slave! I don't give a royal damn about him or Libya, but those who betrayed me and my people will pay with their lives!"

"The doctor needs immediate attention, Majesty!" I implored, struggling to stand up and bow before him in my ragged, bloody caftan.

Half a dozen similar cries rang out from the rest of the wounded.

"Take them to l'Avicenne!" barked the king as stretcher bearers scurried as fast as they could to retrieve the wounded.

L'Avicenne is the only hospital in Rabat...and that's twenty-five miles from Skhirat, ran through my head. I couldn't imagine the bleeding doctor surviving a trip in an outdated ambulance to the hospital.

"I'll take him in my car!" I announced. Then I realized I didn't have the keys. Pierre had them. Where was he, damn it all!

The stretcher bearers came and placed the doctor carefully on an old-fashioned stretcher made of sturdy canvas material.

"Please be careful with him!" I implored the ambulance helpers. "He needs a new tourniquet! He might bleed to death!"

They nodded at me and tightened the doctor's tourniquet. Then they ran pell mell with his inert form on the stretcher to the nearest ambulance, which sped away, sirens blaring, to Rabat, to the hospital.

Suddenly, Pierre appeared, looking sheepish.

"Where have you been?" I demanded, stepping over a pile of broken champagne glasses dropped when the servant who carried them was downed by a bullet.

"In the bathroom," answered Pierre with his usual jaunty grin.

"In the bathroom! What were you doing there?" I exclaimed in amazement.

"Do you really want to know?" was Pierre's unflappable reply.

I scowled irately at him for a moment, but his grin was infectious, and we both burst out laughing. "You mean to tell me that while the rest of us were getting shot at, you were safe and sound in the royal head?"

"I didn't plan it that way, Geeny." Pierre grinned a bit guiltily as he surveyed the bloody scene around us. Then the tension of the day welled up in us and we fell into one another's arms. "Thank God you're safe!" we both said. It had been a hideous afternoon, a vile moment in history. I felt Pierre's warm body next to mine and felt safe, secure, and immensely relieved. I sighed a deep sigh of relief. I was alive!

Then a Moroccan woman ran by wailing hideously and tearing her hair in inconsolable grief.

"Madame Hasnoui!" I ran to her, but she pushed me away and continued to wail. She fell to the ground and emitted an eerie, high-pitched howl.

Pierre came and stood next to me. "That is the Moroccan

way of grieving, Geeny. Leave her alone. Her family will help her."

I looked into Pierre's warm brown eyes. An indefinable emptiness over the atrocities I had just witnessed welled up in me, and I began to sob. My body was racked by torment. I could only feel a horrible void in the face of what I had just seen. Pierre held me and tried to console me. "Geeny, life is hard here. People are not always nice to each other."

"But this is too much." His body felt so warm, so sturdy, so reassuring, but I could not get enough reassurance. The sight of all that bloodshed had pressed itself indelibly into my brain. I felt...different. My thoughts spun out of control.

Pierre shook me. "Geeny, Geeny, it's no good to let yourself go like that! You are safe! It's okay!"

I stopped crying and looked at him through my bleary eyes.

I knew that he was right. Pierre had more common sense than anyone I had ever known. I straightened up and put my arm though his. We started to pick our way through the splintered glass and pools of blood to the palace doorway.

The kitchen door had been ripped off violently at its hinges, and I caught a glimpse of more dead bodies as we walked by. I tried not to look at them, but there was something wrong,...even for a dead body.

"Pierre! What's in their mouths?" I couldn't believe my eyes.

"It's called 'smoking the cigar', Geeny," he explained patiently. I began to feel like a tourist in hell. These men had their penises stuffed in their mouths.

Pierre felt me go limp and continued talking. "It's so they won't be able to experience sexual pleasure in heaven."

I put my hands over my eyes and stopped. This was the limit. I couldn't take anymore.

"I'm sorry, Geeny. It's not my fault!" Pierre started to tug at my arm, to propel me toward the beautiful horseshoe-shaped archway we had passed through to enter the king's birthday party.

"But you brought me to this country. I can't take all the

pain and suffering and death." I felt my will giving way. I began to sob. "The ambassador from Belgium, Monsieur Hasnoui, the doctor's legs filled with bullets. I don't even know if he's alive!"

Pierre held me again. I was so exhausted, so spiritually emptied, so sad; yet underneath it all I realized that I was alive, and that I was lucky.

"Life is hard here," Pierre murmured again. "People cannot afford the luxury of thinking life is just or painless, like you Americans. Right now they are ransacking the homes of all of the generals who plotted this coup against the king. Their possessions will be plundered, their wives raped, their children taken." Pierre looked at me. "That's how they punish revolts in this country."

"Then I want to leave this country!" I glared at him through my teary eyes.

He sighed heavily. "We may have no choice."

"No choice?" I echoed, numbly.

He put his arm around me and guided me toward the car, which gleamed in the sun. It looked just the same, as if nothing had ever happened.

"The Moroccans are making it harder for us to stay."

"Yes, I know. That's why we're moving to Spain."

"They're trying to take the farm in Ouezzane."

I looked up at him, shocked. "Not Marc and Sifia's farm! I thought they were safe. I mean, she's Moroccan!"

"No one is safe anymore."

Just then shots rang out as we passed through the ancient archway that marked the entrance to Rabat.

"There must be some more rebel holdouts," said Pierre grimly.

I looked at him. He raised his eyebrows inquisitively, almost comically. In the midst of a *coup d'état*, Pierre looked very stable, very appealing.

"Let's drive to the beach!" I said impulsively. "Away from all of this horror...these atrocities!"

Pierre smiled at me, then continued to drive toward the center of town. "Geeny," he raised his eyebrows as if to implore me to have more common sense, "I have to make sure the shop is okay. I have to put the jewels in the vault."

I realized he was right, of course. There could be rioting or vandalism. So we drove to Avenue Allah ben Abdullah to make sure the antique Berber jewels in our shop were safe. "And what about us?" I blurted out, feeling hurt and angry. After all, I could have been shot to death an hour earlier.

"Geeny, we have to be practical," he answered, resolutely.

I looked at him. He seemed different. No, it was probably just the tension that made me see him through different eyes, the ordeal at the palace. Pierre was always the same, I reflected, always responsible, taking care of business, taking care of me, always loyal. How could I sell him short? Yet in my heart of hearts, I knew I could and probably would.

My battered psyche shifted to Sebastian, to our summer vacation in Spain, to the beach house by the sea. That is what counts in life, I thought. Peace, tranquility, good friends and family. No, everything counts. The thought of the beach house reassured me. It was a bright oasis amid a tide of horror, and my mind focused briefly on it. I tried to smile, but somehow my mouth wouldn't move. Smiling would never be as easy as it had been before.

Pierre pulled up next to our shop, Art et Style, and hurried in to put the ancient Berber jewels out of harm's way.

I ran in and picked up the phone. "*Halo, oui, l'hôpital Avicenne*, Avicenne Hospital?" There was no answer. Another gunshot rang out somewhere in the city.

✷ THE UNIMAGINABLE

PIERRE LIFTED AN amber Berber wedding necklace from its tray to put away. I walked over and gently touched his shoulder. He jumped and the jewels flew in all directions.

"Don't touch me when I'm putting the jewels away, Geeny!"

I quickly withdrew my hand and helped him pick up the jewels.

"Pierre, what about your uncle Marc? And Sifia and your cousins? Are they all right?" I asked while retrieving an antique Moroccan bride's necklace made of heavy silver coins from the glass display case.

"I'm sure they are, Geeny," Pierre replied plaintively.

"I want to go to the farm and see for myself." I steadied myself against a mahogany desk as I stood up. Suddenly, cold fear poured into my veins. "Let's leave! Let's get out of Rabat!"

"Now? Look at you!"

I glanced down at my torn and bloodied caftan.

"I'll change clothes at the apartment!" I bolted out of the store like a scared deer, only to find the car door locked.

"Please be reasonable, Geeny," Pierre shouted after me, hastily jamming the last of the jewels into the vault behind the Louis XIV armoire. "It is dangerous to drive in the country right now!"

"I have a bad feeling." A bullet zinged over our heads and ricocheted off the adjacent building.

"Let's get out of here, Pierre!"

Pierre locked the store, jerked open the car door, and I threw myself in, huddling down in the passenger's seat. Pierre jumped into the driver's seat and gunned the engine.

239

He peeled out of there like a bat out of hell.

"We can't go home," he said, staring nervously at the road. "We live across the street from the military headquarters. There may be some holdouts there."

"So let's go straight to Ouezzane!"

"Geeny, it isn't safe to drive on the open road like that when...."

"Where is it safe?!"

Pierre sighed and drove back out of the city, the ancient wall with the palm trees still standing guard. Only this time, their presence did not reassure me.

Pierre drove at breakneck speed along the narrow road to Ouezzane. It must have been midnight by the time we got there. As we drove up the dirt road to the farmhouse, I heard Sifia wailing in Arabic. Suddenly some soldiers appeared in front of our car and announced, "You can't enter."

Pierre said something in Arabic. Before I could scream, which is what I wanted to do, Sifia, Lassan, and Marguerite ran toward our car. Sifia's lovely diaphanous caftan billowed in the breeze, almost carrying her down the hillside. Lassan caught up with her and steadied her, while his sister grabbed one of the peacocks and put it in the car with us. I almost laughed at the sight of the peacock flapping around our car, except that a Moroccan soldier pointed his gun directly at us. Sifia, Lassan, and Marguerite jumped in the back seat of the car while Pierre gunned the motor. I heard a single shot ring out as we left in a cloud of moonlit dust.

I looked back for the last time at the farmhouse on the knoll surrounded by willow trees.

"Is Marc all right?" I looked at Sifia, distraught and moaning, clinging to Lassan's shoulder for comfort.

"We don't know yet," answered Lassan, firmly. "We have to go to Rabat to find him. We heard that the *caid* of Ouezzane was killed in the coup.

"And why were those soldiers at your farm?"

"Eh, *en brief,* they said we hadn't paid taxes on it and they were taking it back. *Les salos!* The bastards!" Lassan's face remained controlled, but Marguerite kept talking about everything they had left behind.

"They came and chased us out with no warning! Every-thing we own is there—everything!"

"Something must be wrong," said Lassan in a soft, con-trolled voice. "The *caid* would never let this happen to us. He was with my father today."

I turned around and looked sympathetically into his deep-set brown eyes. His thick eyelashes fringed his eyes, which were full of the pain and fear that his voice concealed. I realized he was scared to death. Sifia clung to him. "Mama, mama, don't worry. Everything will be all right," he mur-mured to her as she began to make a low moaning sound. "Papa is safe, don't worry!"

Lassan's youthful manliness and concern for others in this terrible moment was poignant. He was prepared to be the man of the house, if necessary.

When we arrived at Rabat it was almost morning. The sun streaked the sky and silhouetted the ancient ramparts with soft hues of pink and blue.

Pierre sped to the hospital. Outdated ambulances parked at careless angles blocked the entrance to the hospital built by the French many years ago. I knew that the medical equipment was as old as the ambulances and that the treat-ment patients received at l'Avicenne Hospital was not the most modern. Pierre parked as close to the entrance as he could.

"Where is my husband?" demanded Sifia, throwing open the car door and dashing out into the night. Lassan and Mar-guerite followed her, looking desperately for a way into the hospital. Pierre and I joined them just as they clambered over the hood of an ambulance into the courtyard of the hospital. Lassan held his arms out for his mother and she slid down and screamed. I scrambled up on the ambulance to see her slump into Lassan's arms. She had landed in the middle of a pool of blood. Marguerite and Lassan shook her gently.

"Mama, Mama, it's going to be all right. Papa will be all right. If he isn't here, he's with the *caid,* or friends!" Lassan's voice remained calm and reassuring. My heart skipped a beat as the moonlight etched his profile against the archway that marked the entrance to the hospital.

I gave him a furtive look and ran into the hospital. Moans and horrible screams, like none I had ever heard in real life, the shrieks of agony, of the dying, echoed down the hallways.

"Geeny, be careful!" shouted Pierre as I nearly fell over a dead man lying prone on the stretcher the porters had carried him on. I gasped and staggered forward. Lassan put his arm around me to steady me. His strong, firm body against mine made me feel even more faint, but I managed to smile slowly up at him and steady my nerves. He reminded me of Sebastian with his resolute innocence. Youth is irreplaceable, ran through my dislocated thoughts.

"*Merci,* Lassan," I said.

He looked at me with reverence. "*De rien,* Virginie."

The stench of blood and death made me feel faint. I steeled my nerves and headed toward the nearest door. The others followed me, and inside we found a doctor operating on a patient without anesthetic. I looked again and again felt weak. It looked like Dr. Duval.

"Dr. Duval!" I gasped.

This time Pierre put his arm around me and steered me away.

Then I went down. I fainted.

The next thing I remember is being lifted from the floor and moving slowly through this hospital turned hell, past dismembered and bandaged bodies, nurses and doctors frantically operating and calling out for what little anesthetic was available. One hundred people had died during the coup at the palace in Skhirat, and many more were seriously wounded. I wandered through this phantasmagoric atmosphere like a zombie. Pierre, Lassan, Marguerite, and Sifia took me by the arm from time to time. We walked for what seemed like hours until I heard Lassan ask a military guard if he knew where his father might be.

"The hospital is full. They had to take some of the bodies to the pound," replied the guard.

Sifia began to sob again as we wove our way through the debris of blood, stretchers, and bodies back to the entrance, over the ambulance blocking the door, and into our car. Pierre drove silently to the dog pound. No one said a word. It was too horrible to imagine. We stared straight ahead into the first glimmers of dawn, numb with dread.

At the dog pound, we found the same disorder: ambulances everywhere, people running frantically around; only this time there were no doctors, just family members searching for their loved ones. The pound attendants and a few of the king's loyal soldiers tried to keep a semblance of order. The unearthly sound of dogs barking, wailing like the dogs of Hades, sent shivers down my spine.

As we walked into the pound, the stench of blood and putrefaction was overwhelming. Sifia began to tear her hair out. "No, Mama, no! We can't give in to despair!" cried Lassan, again taking the situation into control as tears streamed down his handsome face. Marguerite embraced her and cried. Lassan embraced both of them and tried to console them. I felt tears well up in my eyes. I began to cry inconsolably. The loss of so many lives was too sudden, too inexplicable, too horrible; and to end up in a dog pound.... No, this was not fair.

But Marc was not there. We decided to drive back to the farm. Pierre was past exhaustion, but he drove the long, four-hour drive back to Ouezzane, only stopping to get gas.

When we arrived they had already confiscated the farmhouse. Lassan jumped out and declared bravely, "You can't do this to us! We're Moroccans!"

"We have orders from the *caid*," answered the soldiers solemnly.

"Orders from the *caid*? Is he alive? Is my father alive?"

"Yes," they answered again, shifting their bayonetted rifles slightly. "He's at the *caid*'s house."

"He's alive!" Sifia threw herself into her son's arms and sobbed with relief.

Lassan put his hand on her head and soothed her. "Not now, Mama, not now. It's going to be all right.

"I want to see my father!" he demanded.

Gaunt and worn out, Pierre drove us to the *caid*'s house.

We could hear the furious argument as we drove up to his home on the outskirts of Ouezzane.

Sifia, Lassan, and Marguerite jumped out of the car to help Marc. Pierre and I looked at one another. We could barely recognize each other through the heavy weight of fatigue, shock, and tears.

A weary Marc emerged from the *caid*'s house. "They say we can pitch a tent on the corner of the land and stay there," he announced, shaking his head with angry disbelief. "I never thought it would come to this."

That night we all slept together in a large tent, Marc, Sifia, Lassan, Marguerite, Pierre and I. I could hear Sifia sobbing, telling Marguerite she could go to France with her French fiancé. They, at least, could get married and have a normal life. Pierre and I slept huddled together on a Moroccan rug with some blankets thrown over us.

I slept fitfully. Toward dawn I had a dream about the king of Morocco. He came toward us from his throne and smiled grandly. He said something to the effect that the Alouites would help us. Then he reached forward and took a bright red rose from a shattered vase and gave it to me. I smiled at him gratefully. Suddenly I was in America, a teenager running gleefully after an ice cream truck with my little sister, happy and free.

☼ TAKING CONTROL

I LEANED OVER THE RAILING of the terrace and looked out onto the garden below. The vines wound a hoary pathway up the trellis, the bougainvillea shimmered, the scent of honeysuckle wafted warm and pungent into my nostrils. The contours of my in-laws' home were visible from where I stood. I could see the terrace where Pierre and I had danced an impromptu swing so gaily while the rest of the family applauded from the terrace of the farm. Worn out from a sleepless night talking to Marie Hélène, I began to regret writing that letter to Sebastian. Too melodramatic.

Why hadn't I just talked to him? I wished I could just get it over with. The more I thought about our relationship, the more I realized marriage would never work for Sebastian and me. Out of respect for Pierre, he would neither bed nor wed me. I imagined him married to another. It was time to go back to the States.

What really bothered me was what would I do there? All I had was a bachelor's degree in psychology, which meant I could be somebody's secretary or analyze urine in a laboratory. I had always refused to learn how to type. Didn't want to be a secretary or a lab worker. These thoughts batted incongruously around in my head as I stared into the timeless setting of the farm. I inhaled the fresh early morning air. It was refreshing.

I looked up at the rising sun for advice, whatever advice the sun had to give to me on an isolated farm in the south of Spain in 1971.

Pierre knew I was going back to the United States. We had edged around the subject like an open wound, afraid of hurting one another too much. We had been inseparable for so long that to think of divorce was unbearable. Neither of us even broached the subject. I was ostensibly returning to California to recover from a seemingly incurable case of dysentery.

He didn't want me to go to the United States, just as he hadn't wanted me to go to Paris without him to see some doctors about my health. He had cancelled my trip three times before he reluctantly agreed to let me go alone. He knew I would see Sebastian. Our platonic romance had flourished to the point that I was leaving Pierre, getting a divorce because I was so unhappy. Yet Pierre and I had been perfectly happy when Sebastian and I fell in love.

Pierre and I had decided we wanted children that summer as we strode confidently through the streets of Madrid on vacation. We radiated happiness. Perhaps that is why Sebastian, depressed from his long exile from North Africa in Paris, "a place that is inhospitable to the soul," needed both Pierre and me so much. For his friendship with Pierre never flagged once I returned home. I had become obsessed with Sebastian and couldn't stand being married to someone I no longer loved, at least where love had failed so miserably in the conjugal bedroom. But I didn't hate Pierre either; on the contrary, we still cared deeply about one another. I have never met a warmer, genuinely kinder soul. But to have such foresight as to realize that I was leaving a whole family that loved me as well…was too much to ask of a girl raised on "go-getter, bottom-line" values.

In America women brandished bras like banners, while I languished on the Bonmari family farm in Alicante. I had so much to learn, so much to catch up on. The hippie movement just looked like so many bare bottoms running into the surf at San Gregorio Beach in *Time* magazine. While visiting my family the summer of 1970 I had gotten a whiff of the changes. The Bank of America next to the University of California at Santa Barbara had just been burned to the ground in protest of the war in Vietnam. Donning my sister's torn jeans and tie-dyed shirts with gusto, I had joined her in her classes at the University of California, where rag-tag students appeared barefoot with their dogs, and the professors held their tongues in fear of more student unrest. What a welcome change from the daily monotony of Rabat.

Then I flew back to rejoin Pierre and his family in Madrid. He had been on Ibiza, like now, and Jaime Salinas and another of his cousins had picked me up at the airport. Our faces glowed with happiness as we strode through the sunlit streets of Madrid. Pierre's family was like a huge net of people always ready to pick you up, take you to a great restaurant, show you points of interest, exchange the latest political gossip and sallies. Why should I leave?

Why does anyone leave her husband? For a better life, like a new continent; for the unknown, but it would become my life. Perhaps I could find someone to love as much as I loved Sebastian. I didn't know. I didn't care. It was time to start afresh. Too many coups, too much Ping-Pong, too many crazy trips to Andorra, too many cousins. Yes, one cousin too many and too beautiful to forget.

Perhaps I was stupid, I thought as I packed my suitcases with the many dresses my seamstress in Spain had made for me, with the shoes Pierre and I had bought for next to nothing during the August sales because my size was 5 and 1/2, one of the smallest, a Cinderella size. Did I have a Cinderella complex? No. I planned to get a job, not alimony. Pierre didn't want to give me any, and I didn't have any children to worry about, so I would fend for myself. At age twenty-nine, I had plenty of time to carve out a new life.

Pierre paced back and forth in the bedroom nervously, talking of this and that, of how he would try to send me some money. Finally, he kissed me and tucked two hundred American dollars under the belt of my leather tunic. I thanked him, and he shouldered my suitcases, just as he had when we moved in together in his apartment at Felipe II in Madrid.

"I'll write you every day, Geeny," he promised as he drove me to the Rabat international airport.

"And I'll write you, Pierre," I responded. I knew I would.

I was a faithful correspondent. Pierre was my best friend in the world.

The jet taxied into the nearly empty airport, and I showed my ticket. Pierre kissed me goodbye. As I looked out of my window as the plane taxied down the runway he ran along the terrace of the airport café, frantically waving good-bye, his huge smile wishing me all the luck in the world. My heart ached. This was one of the hardest decisions I had ever made. I felt a twinge of regret. Too late. My new course was set.